PRAISE FOR

SANDRA BLOCK

"A psychological suspense story smartly narrated…Zoe has a quick wit that emerges in wickedly unexpected ways."
—*New York Times Book Review* on *Little Black Lies*

"Sandra Block's heroine is smart, heartbreakingly vulnerable, and laugh-out-loud funny. I am a forever-fan of the Zoe Goldman series and will read anything Sandra Block writes. You should too."
—Lisa Scottoline, *New York Times* bestselling author

"The suspense keeps building throughout until the shocking ending. This is a riveting debut from a promising new author."
—*Booklist* on *Little Black Lies*

"*Little Black Lies* is a darkly intriguing mystery with a feisty young doctor as its protagonist. Sandra Block pulls you in deep and doesn't let go."
—Meg Gardiner, Edgar Award–winning author

"In Zoe, Block has created a character who is complicated, smart, and sympathetic. I can't wait to see what Block has in store for Zoe next."
—Heather Gudenkauf, *New York Times* bestselling author

"Sandra Block's compelling debut is the epitome of the psychological thriller, as the author delves deep into the inner makeup and subconscious of her heroine while maintaining an exciting plot. [It] also works as a heartfelt story about families and how secrets can both pull people apart or keep them safe." —*Sun-Sentinel* on *Little Black Lies*

"Block is a clever writer with an inventive plot." —*Toronto Star* on *Little Black Lies*

"*Little Black Lies* is a real treat for fans of intricate suspense novels with plenty of twists." —Mysteriousbookreviews.com

THE SECRET ROOM

THE SECRET ROOM

Sandra Block

GRAND CENTRAL
PUBLISHING

NEW YORK   BOSTON

Copyright © 2017 by Sandra Block
Teaser from *The Girl Without a Name* © 2015 by Sandra Block
Reading group guide copyright © 2017 by Sandra Block and Hachette Book Group, Inc.

Cover design by Elizabeth Connor
Photograph of door © Barnaby Hall/Getty Images
Photograph of woman © Annie Tsukanova
Cover copyright © 2017 by Hachette Book Group, Inc.

Grand Central Publishing
Hachette Book Group
1290 Avenue of the Americas, New York, NY 10104
grandcentralpublishing.com
twitter.com/grandcentralpub

First Edition: April 2017

Grand Central Publishing is a division of Hachette Book Group, Inc. The Grand Central Publishing name and logo is a trademark of Hachette Book Group, Inc.

The publisher is not responsible for websites (or their content) that are not owned by the publisher.

The Hachette Speakers Bureau provides a wide range of authors for speaking events. To find out more, go to www.hachettespeakersbureau.com or call (866) 376-6591.

Library of Congress Cataloging-in-Publication Data

Names: Block, Sandra, author.
Title: The secret room / Sandra Block.
Description: First edition. | New York : Grand Central Publishing, 2017.
Identifiers: LCCN 2016054254 | ISBN 9781455570201 (trade paperback) | ISBN 9781478916253 (audio download) | ISBN 9781455570218 (ebook)
Subjects: LCSH: Women psychiatrists—Fiction. | Psychological fiction. | BISAC: FICTION / Suspense. | GSAFD: Suspense fiction.
Classification: LCC PS3602.L64285 S43 2017 | DDC 813/.6—dc23 LC record available at https://lccn.loc.gov/2016054254

ISBN: 978-1-4555-7020-1 (trade paperback), 978-1-4555-7021-8 (ebook)

Printed in the United States of America

LSC-C

10 9 8 7 6 5 4 3 2 1

For Charlotte and Owen
My sun, moon, and stars

Chapter One

Hey, baby."

The prisoner is fondling himself. I quicken my pace, and a load of spit hits the wall, followed by a round of laughter. "Almost got her that time," another inmate says with a throaty chuckle.

"When you gonna suck me off, baby?"

"You so tall, girl. Come on over here and talk to Big Daddy."

Two more long strides, and I am finally through. I take a deep breath as I spy our office ahead, with Jason at a computer already. As I reach home base at last, my hunched-up shoulders relax.

"Ah," Jason says, "another lovely day at the Buffalo Correctional Facility."

"Jesus." I sit down next to him. "Why don't they ever bother you?"

He shrugs. "They just ignore me or call me *faggot*. Business

1

as usual." He takes a sip from his Tim Hortons coffee. "Doesn't stop the spitting, though."

"Yeah," I say. "I heard they're putting up plexiglass at some point."

He clicks on his computer. "Anyway, it's better than the neo-Nazis."

"That's true." And he's right about that. The white-pride folks routinely call me *kikebitch* (as if it's a compound word) and Jason *chink, gook, slanty-eyes,* and some others he told me he "actually had to Urban Dictionary." Sitting at the computer, I put in my password wrong twice before I remember that I had to change it from Arthur0 to Arthur1.

Jason straightens the cuffs of his tweedy zip-collar sweater. It's a change from our psychiatry residency, when he favored matching pastel ties and button-downs in every conceivable shade. But on the first day of our forensic psychiatry fellowship, he astutely observed that "wearing a tie in this place is just asking for strangulation."

"You feeling okay?" he asks. "You look a little pale or something."

"I'm fine. Just up all night."

"Larissa?" he inquires.

"You guessed it." Larissa is our not-so-favorite nurse. The one who calls at three a.m. for an order placed at five p.m. the day before. "But I'm heading home after this. Anyone I need to see?"

Jason checks his computer. "Andre Green. I already saw Jimenez for you."

"What's up with Jimenez?"

"Stuck a paper clip in his penis."

"Ooh. That doesn't sound pleasant."

"Not impressed," Jason says, not batting an eye. "Your basic attention seeking."

"Yeah, but I'd pick a different orifice, at least."

"Now me, I would stay away from all my orifices."

"Good point," I say. "Okay, how about Andre Green?"

"Stabbed his father. Thought he was the devil."

"Hmm . . . sounds like schizophrenia," I muse, opening his chart on the computer. "Wonder what he's doing here. I would have thought he'd be NGRI." In other words, not guilty by reason of insanity.

"Bad lawyer, I guess," Jason says. The overhead speaker interrupts our conversation.

Code 523. Northeast wing alert. Code 523.

My ears perk up. *Code 523* means a prisoner's been found. Dead.

But at least it isn't a 327. Which means suicide.

Jason's text message alert goes off. "It's Dr. Nowhere," he says. His real name is Dr. Novaire, but everyone calls him that, because he's generally nowhere to be found. At seventy-five years old, Dr. Novaire is the head of the forensic psychiatry fellowship, and though he's lost interest in training fellows, he maintains a strong interest in his coin collection, his bridge club, and swimming at the Y, all while still drawing in a nice university salary.

"What does he want?" I ask.

"Meeting with the warden about the 523. Three p.m. in his office."

I check my watch. "That's only ten minutes," I say, trying to keep the panic out of my voice. I openly dread any and all meetings with the warden. He still blames me for what happened this summer and doesn't even to try to hide his antipathy toward me. The man can barely even stand to look at me.

Jason stands up with a yawn. "I have to talk to one of the COs. Meet you there?"

The hallway outside the warden's office is freezing, and I blow on my hands, standing against the wall. Minutes later Jason joins me. "No one's here yet?" he asks.

I shake my head. "Did you hear who the 523 was, by the way?"

"Oh yeah, Maloney told me," Jason says. "OD. Carrie Cooke."

I feel suddenly ill. "Oh no."

He uncaps a tube of pale-green hand sanitizer and offers me a squirt, which I accept, the harsh smell of alcohol shooting through the room. "She yours?"

"Yeah." I am picturing her hopeful, round, freckled face, her penciled-in eyebrows. *I'm gonna do it this time, Dr. Goldman. I'm gonna get clean for Taylor.* Her son. Who doesn't have a mommy anymore. Ironically, getting clean isn't always so easy in prison.

Jason chucks my shoulder. "Can't save them all, Zoe."

"Yeah," I mutter. "I know." It sounds heartless, but you have to develop elephant skin in this place. I'm learning that. "But she told me she wasn't using anymore. She was on her second step, even."

"What was her drug of choice?"

"Heroin."

Jason shakes his head. "That shit's deadly." Neither of us comments further on the obvious, and now fully fulfilled, statement.

The warden walks by us then, and we hush. He is a tall African American man with a bit of a swagger. We rarely see Cam Gardner, though I pass by his smiling photo every day in the prison lobby. He is not, however, smiling right now.

Dr. Novaire trails right behind, his gait stooped. He is pale to the point of translucent, with light gray hair that blends in to render him almost indistinct. As we sit on the little couch, Cam Gardner takes a seat in his huge, imposing office chair and waits for Dr. Novaire to bumble into a seat beside us. It's as if we're practicing blocking for a scene without a director.

The warden fixes his gaze on all of us.

"We've got a problem here, folks." Silence follows, as no one contests this. "Two deaths in the last six months. One suicide and now an OD." He pushes his chair out, squeaking the wheels on the carpet. "And I want some answers." There is more silence, as no one offers the requested answers. "Dr. Novaire," he says, in a commanding voice.

"Yes, Warden," Dr. Novaire answers with a faint trace of his residual German accent. His tone is as hesitant as Cam Gardner's is brazen.

"What do you have to say?"

Dr. Novaire coughs. "I understand the concern. More than understand," he says, his head nodding with a fine tremor. "But when you look at the trend in the last five years, this is likely an outlier."

"You call it an outlier. I call it unacceptable. And it needs to be corrected. Who was caring for Mrs. Cooke?"

Jason side-eyes me nervously.

"I'm ultimately in charge of all the patients," Dr. Novaire says.

"Me," I say. "She was my patient."

The warden turns to me. "And what was her status?"

I rub my hands, which are mottled purple now from the chill. "Improved. She was going to meetings, had an inmate sponsor...We had actually just changed her to every-six-month follow-ups because she was doing so well."

"Or so you thought," the warden says.

"Right," I admit. "It's always a judgment call, but—"

"Yes, and that's exactly what's lacking here. Judgment." He raps his large fingers in a rhythm on his desk. "I would think after what happened this summer, you might try to use more of it."

Heat pricks my face.

"These are totally different cases, though," Dr. Novaire argues. "You can hardly blame Dr. Goldman for a patient overdosing on heroin."

Warden Gardner stares at him for a moment, then replies with unnerving calm. "I'm only going to say this once, Dr. Novaire, so you might want to pay attention." Gardner waits a beat to ensure that we are all doing so. "Get your house in order. Right now. Or I will do it for you."

⟵

I stare at the walls, at the fresh coat of sage paint. The walls have always been a neutral shade of oatmeal, matching the carpet. I must admit the green is more soothing.

"Dr. Novaire is right," Sam, my psychiatrist, says, pushing his glasses up on his nose. "The warden shouldn't blame you for that."

"I feel bad about it. Terrible, obviously. But, it's not the same as…"

I don't say his name, because I don't need to. We both know what happened with Dennis Johnson this summer. But Sam said that could have happened to anyone. It was only my first week, and Dr. Novaire should have been around to help me. After the initial brouhaha, people finally stopped talking about it, at least. But obviously the warden hasn't forgotten.

Sam shakes his head, looking befuddled. "The warden seems to lack a certain…subtlety…when it comes to these things."

"Yeah, he is kind of a blunt object," I agree.

Sam smiles. "Anyway, how has everything else been going? How has your focus been?"

"Good. Surprisingly." Last year we added Strattera to my drug mix for ADHD, depression, and anxiety with a hint of OCD. I'm a walking *DSM-5*.

"And the fellowship overall?" he asks.

"Overall, things were going well until today."

Sam moves his mug to the top of a stack of papers. The mug has a faded picture of him and his wife in raincoats, holding an impressively long fish. I've decided you can tell a lot about people by their mugs. "How's Mike?" Sam asks.

"Good. I think I'm finally getting used to the cohabitating thing." Meaning Mike moved into my place and I'm still trying to remind myself it's "our place" now. Arthur loves him unconditionally, however. They say dogs are supposed to be loyal, but Arthur quickly determined that Mike was the more competent parent. "And Scotty's still driving me crazy with those rings."

He smiles. "Did he ask her yet?"

"No, not yet." My brother, the former Lothario, has been going on about asking Kristy to marry him for a solid six months now. He sends daily texts with different engagement ring options, and I finally told him that if I heard one more word about the five C's of diamond rings, I would physically hurt him. "Mike wondered about my attitude, though. He said it was almost like I was against marriage."

Sam looks up from his pad. "What did you say?"

"I said I wasn't against marriage, just annoying little brothers." I pick up Sam's newest desk toy, some liquid motion thing. The pink oil blobs join the royal blue oil blobs to form a black-purple mess. "I'm not sure I'll ever be really good wife material, though."

When I admitted this to Mike, he barely hid an injured look. Barely hiding an injured look is big for Mike, who once

8

told me he doesn't like to "dwell on my emotions too much." (And yes, we both got the irony of his dating a psychiatrist.) He glossed it over with some joke, but the damage was done. We haven't discussed rings since.

"One thing at a time," Sam says.

"I suppose." I fight off a yawn, stealing a look at my watch with dry, heavy eyes. I need these visits with Sam to keep myself sane, literally. But I've been up since three in the morning, and right now what I really need is some sleep.

Kicking off my boots, I stumble into bed. As if I'm completely drunk or just ran a marathon, neither of which applies. In seconds my eyes are closing when I feel warm breath on my face.

"Arthur," I moan. "Come on. That's just gross." I turn my body the opposite way and hear footsteps patter to the other side of the bed. "Ugh. Come on, Arthur." My hand reaches out of the covers to pet his stiff, fluffy labradoodle head, and he sits back a moment, appreciating the caress. "Okay, Arthur. That's all for now. Mommy's really tired." I am practically slurring my words. "I'll walk you after my little nap."

This elicits an unhappy whine.

"I promise."

He whines again, then licks my chin, and I pull the covers up. With that he realizes the battle is lost, and I feel his familiar form bounce up on the bed and settle in beside me. Immediately he is snoring, and I'm considering the possibility of a patent on canine CPAP machines when sleep hits, hard.

Hours are lost in a dreamless, heavy sleep, and then I wake up to the heady smell of garlic. It is dark outside, the lit-up reindeer across the street mechanically lowering and lifting their heads, perpetually eating snow. They must have diabetes insipidus by now. "Hon?" I call out. Arthur is gone. I pad down the stairs, still bone-tired despite my nap. More tired, if possible. "What are you making?"

"Pasta alla carbonara." He says it with a put-on Italian accent.

"Oh. Sounds complicated."

"Or 'Thanks for cooking dinner'—that's the other thing people might say."

I laugh, leaning on him. "Thanks for cooking dinner."

He tosses Arthur a piece of cheese, which the dog gobbles up. Mike stirs the sizzling pan. "Had a slow shift anyway." The ER is always slow in December. No one wants to get sick until right after Christmas. "How was work for you?"

"Crappy." I crumple into a kitchen chair, and Arthur runs over to assess my likelihood of having food, then quickly returns to the more certain spot by the stove and is rewarded with more cheese. I tell him about Carrie Cooke, and how the warden was blaming me for her death.

"That's bullshit," Mike says. "You can't be responsible for an overdose. That's like every other code in the ER these days."

"Yeah, well," I grumble. "The warden's acting like I shot her up myself." My phone chimes with a text. It's a picture—a selfie of my brother Scotty and his girlfriend with her holding out her hand, showing off a rather lovely diamond ring. Underneath it he has written, SHE SAID YES!

"Whoa." I show Mike the picture.

"Good for him," he says.

I text back congratulations, promising to call him later. "I can't believe he actually did it." I turn the phone sideways. "I gotta say, he did a good job with that ring. It's beautiful."

Mike doesn't answer, the sound of stirring and sizzling filling the room. In the ensuing quiet, I can't help but think back to that injured look and walk my heavy body over to the stove and lean into him, kissing his cheek right by his ear. The way that drives him crazy, good crazy. "I love you."

"I love you, too," he says. "Now go make the salad. I'm hungry."

Scrunching up some iceberg, I hear a text alert go off again, but when I look over, it's Mike's phone.

FYI, you were so right! Total tibial fracture! Smarty pants. See you tomorrow, Adonis (hahaha) XO Serena

We both see the message, and I grab the phone. "Who the fuck is Serena?"

"Just a doctor I work with," he says, flustered. "It's nothing."

"'XO'? 'Adonis'? Doesn't sound like nothing to me." He doesn't answer. "And who the hell follows up on a tibial fracture?" I stare at him, but he still doesn't respond. The noise

11

of the pot of water bubbling beside us sounds suddenly explosive.

"Okay," he says, finally. "There's nothing going on between us, I promise. But..." He scratches his stubbly chin.

"But?"

Mike sighs. "She might have a little crush on me."

Chapter Two

This was my life before I met you.

Wake up.

Eat breakfast. Kill time. Eat lunch. Kill time. Eat dinner. Kill time.

Lights out. And repeat.

An existence, I can't even call it a life.

I don't know how these girls do it. Day after day after day. I met some lifers in here, and they're like a different breed. Most of them are older and pretty much stick to themselves, acting like no one else understands them. And you know what? They're right. No one understands them. Their eyes are blank, dull, the lights gone out. Like they've already died. I was like that, too. Just biding my time, getting through the minutes, the hours, the days.

Until I met you.

I still remember the very first day. We called you the Professor. It was kind of a joke at first, but the nickname fit, so it stuck. You sat at the scratched-up circular table in the library and announced that you were here to teach us to write. We were all going to start keeping a diary. An outlet, *you said,* for the real you.

I don't even know who the real me is, *I said. And I wasn't lying.*

That's why you're writing a journal, *you said.*

With a sly smile. A smile that said you knew everything about me. So I took a closer look at you, the Professor. Your plump lips, curly hair, and green-brown eyes. The color of a forest. And tattoos poking out of your buttoned-up sleeves.

I decided right then that I wanted you.

This is different than loving you. That came later. This was just a pure, animalistic desire. I wanted to unbutton your shirt and catalog every tattoo, trace my fingers over every edge and kiss every color.

I wasn't original, though—all the girls wanted you. It was painfully obvious.

Fawning over you, giggling when you walked by, tossing their hair back, batting their eyelashes, and sticking out their tits. Like bitches in heat.

But I'm not like them, and even then, you knew that.

Scary to think, I almost didn't even take the class. But one of my friends said it would help me get time off. And I figured it would be a welcome distraction, at least. Turns out I was right, more than right.

I didn't realize what would happen.

I didn't know this class would become everything to me. This hour would be the only thing keeping me whole, would become my life. The only time I am truly me. The real me, like you said, who's been gone for so long.

Wake up. Eat breakfast. Kill time. Eat lunch. Kill time. Eat dinner. Kill time. Lights out. Repeat. That was my life. That would be my life, for years, too many years to come. Until I met you, Professor, and everything changed.

And I knew that I could never go back to my life before you, that half a life, that living death. Never.

And I would do anything it took to keep you. Anything.

Even kill for you.

Chapter Three

The first thing I notice is his bright-red gloves.

Andre Green sits on an unmade bed. The room is tiny and claustrophobic and smells of urine. He is the first patient of the day, the one I didn't get to see yesterday after the warden's meeting.

I just finished reading through his chart, which tells me Andre is a sixteen-year-old African American male in prison for the attempted murder of his father. Andre is saddled with the unfortunate delusion that his father, Abraham Green, a soft-spoken, widowed accountant, is the devil.

At first blush it looks like your typical schizophrenia. Andre was a straight-A student, first clarinet, and chess team champion when something happened. Something always happens. Usually it's voices, whispering evil secrets or a malicious running commentary on the day. Or sometimes patients get delusions, like our Andre, and the devil one isn't uncommon.

But this case is more complex.

Andre's mother died just a year ago. Soon after, Abraham was teaching his son how to change a tire when Andre grabbed the wrench out of his hands and swung it at his face. His father managed to back off quickly enough to end up with just a broken nose. Andre admitted that he thought his father was the devil and was trying to kill him, and was soon after admitted to the children's psych floor with a working diagnosis of psychotic depression. After release he was doing reasonably well until, one day, Andre took a kitchen knife from the butcher's block and stabbed his father in the chest. Abraham recovered, but he pressed charges.

And Andre wasn't fifteen anymore. He was sixteen now. So he went to prison.

Which brings me back to the teeny room, the unmade bed, and the red gloves. I sit down in a chair next to him, while a guard watches right outside the bars.

"I'm not taking them off," Andre threatens, by way of hello.

"No problem." I lean back in the chair, doing my best to look relaxed. "Why are you wearing the gloves anyway?" I try for a curious, rather than confrontational, tone.

"The devil. He's trying to plant seeds in my fingers," he says, quite matter-of-factly. Andre lifts his wrinkled comic book up to his face. "And I'm keeping them on."

"Yeah, I got that. I'm not here for that."

"Okay." He shrugs. "Why are you here, then?"

"Just to talk."

"To find out if I'm crazy, you mean."

I smile at his deft assessment. "And are you?"

"No," he shoots back with disdain. But as he peers over his comic, his expression is less certain.

"Let's talk about your father," I say.

He pulls the comic book farther up, covering his face. "What about him?"

"Can you explain why you stabbed him?"

He rubs his elbow, which is dry and scaly. "I don't know. Not exactly. I was confused, I guess."

"Something about the devil?" I ask. Andre glances up at me, then back at his comic. It's a look I recognize. The microsecond debate. *Do I trust her?*

"I don't know if you're crazy, Andre." I lean my elbows against the cold, white-painted wall. "But I can at least try to help you figure that out. And I can help you get better."

He flips a page. "How?"

"By treating you."

"Crazy meds?" Andre shakes his head. "I don't think so."

"Okay, then." I decide to change tack. "Let's talk about the devil planting those seeds."

"Why?" He runs his hands through his hair, a modified cone Afro. Some coils sprinkle onto his white T-shirt. "You won't believe me. Nobody does."

"Try me."

He exhales with impatience, putting his comic on his lap. "Sometimes I see them, sometimes I don't."

"Okay. How about this, can you tell me what the devils look like?"

He glances down at the splayed-open page. "Like us, sort

of. But with fur. And that devil tongue, you know…" He grasps for the word.

"Forked?"

"No, not forked. More like a double tongue. And they slither, separately, you know? One half of the tongue goes up, and the other half goes down. But both ends are reaching out, trying to get me."

"And you see this devil?" I shiver, as if someone just walked on my grave. "Not just imagine it, but actually see him?"

He nods, his caramel-brown eyes fearful. "He looks real. Realer than you or me. And I hear him. All spooky-like. Whispering. Like that dude in…" He scratches his head, brushing out some more strands. "Did you read that book with the wizard dude?" I'm shaking my head, and he thinks a minute, then comes up with the name. "*Lord of the Rings.* Gollum." His voice is animated, and now I know how to connect with Andre Green. Fantasy. Comics. "Do you remember him?"

"Sort of," I say.

"He's hissy. Scary sounding." His voice drops to a whisper. "I hear him a lot."

I scoot my chair closer. "What does he say to you?"

"Stuff. Different stuff."

"What kind of stuff?" I push him.

"Mean, crazy stuff."

Again, schizophrenia. Unfortunately, the voices aren't usually very nice. They're more likely to tell you to rot in hell than that you should have a nice day. His gaze falls back to his comic book. A big-chested hero with kick-ass purple boots. "What does this have to do with your father, do you think?"

A knock on the door breaks up our discussion. It's Simon, the kindly social worker. I've met him more than a few times by now. "Ready for school?"

"Oh yeah. Sure." He leaves his comic on the bed.

Andre is enrolled in high school in here, his junior year. Hopefully, he can keep up with that until we can get him stabilized in the hospital, then back home where he belongs.

Because he sure as hell doesn't belong here in prison.

Later in the day, I'm at the clinic with another new patient: Aubrey Kane.

Her arms are a strange tapestry of scars. Linear, jagged, and squiggly, in shades of magenta, pink, and white.

"Tell me about the cutting," I say.

Aubrey stares at the floor without answering. The noises of prison are muffled in our little white box of a clinic room, with the big red button on the wall right next to me for an emergency. I haven't had to push it yet, and I doubt Aubrey will bring my first opportunity. Shoes clap down the hallway, along with scattered cussing and yelling, and the piercing squeaks of cells opening and closing.

"I don't know," she says, finally, tucking strawberry-blond hair behind her ear. "I just do it." Aubrey just turned twenty but looks younger. Bony thin, five foot one, she is petite, delicate. As if she might have been a ballerina, or a figure skater, a model even, if she hadn't ended up here. If she hadn't robbed a convenience store with her boyfriend's gun to pay for heroin. She traces one of the newer, fluffier scars with some detachment. "It helps."

"Helps with?"

"Everything, I guess." She picks at another scar, not fully healed. The scar from when her razor went too deep and nicked a vein that bled under the door and into the hallway, alerting the guards that Aubrey Kane might not be playing this time. That Aubrey Kane might be dying in there. The scar that got her in to see me.

"When do you get out of here?" I ask.

The abrupt change in questioning obviously surprises her, and she looks up at me, her eyes a soft green. "Fifteen. But they say it's usually more like seven. With good behavior."

"And do you think this qualifies as good behavior?"

This gives her pause, but she shrugs it off. "Doesn't matter. I'd be back in here soon enough anyway."

"Why do you say that?"

"Because I'm an idiot."

"You have a problem with drug addiction, Aubrey," I correct her. "That doesn't mean you're an idiot."

She shrugs again, raising up her collarbones. "Idiot. Addict. Same thing."

"Have you been to the drug rehab program yet?" I ask. "That would qualify as good behavior."

She drops her eyes to the floor again. "I signed up. Just

Sandra Block

haven't gotten to a meeting yet." She rubs her knees, bony in her orange pants. "You might not believe me, Dr. Goldman, but I'm trying. I really am."

"I do believe you." I lean toward her to make my point. "But the cutting isn't helping."

She doesn't answer.

"They'll put you in solitary again, Aubrey."

A visible shiver runs through her. "I don't want that."

"I don't want that either. But it's a two-way street. They need to keep you safe." A long pause follows this statement, broken up by hooting and hollering outside the room.

"I made a friend," Aubrey says, like an offering. "In the cell, next door." She blushes right down to her strawberry-blond roots, which makes me wonder what kind of friend.

"Friends are good to have."

She nods with verve, as if my trite statement were utter truth. "Todd never wanted me to have friends."

"Todd?"

"My boyfriend. He just—" She shakes her head. "He said they weren't good for me. A bad influence."

I have a feeling this Todd has a lot to do with her cutting. "He sounds like an asshole."

She smiles at me then, fully, her green eyes glowing. As if we're sidekicks, plotting some mischievous childhood prank, bonded together in our bad behavior. "How?" she asks, pausing uncomfortably and reaching up to her own neck. "How did you get yours?"

Involuntarily I reach up, too, touching the faded gash. She hasn't asked about the scars on my hands yet, even more

22

ancient vestiges of my history. I debate telling her the truth, then decide this may be the only moment I'm given. If I lie to her now, the door she just opened up an inch for me might slam shut forever.

"Someone stabbed me," I say.

"Thanks for coming in, Zoe," Dr. Novaire says.

"Oh, sure, no problem." I almost slip up and call him Nowhere.

"I wanted to talk to you about something, but..." Something catches his eye. "You want to see something?"

Here we go. "Sure." I say this with zero enthusiasm, but, despite being a psychiatrist, he has yet to acknowledge any of my nonverbal cues that I have literally no interest in his coins. (Though I *would* appreciate some guidance in treating my criminally insane patients.) He opens a little wooden case with some majesty, revealing a gold coin atop blue velvet, then breaks into a smile. "I finally got it." He holds it up high. "The master of all masters."

"Oh, wow."

"The 1986 Silver Eagle dollar." The silver catches a glint off the sunlight as he twists it between his fingers like a magician. "A beauty, ain't she?"

"She sure is," I say, wondering if a coin is, in fact, a "she." There are rules about this. Ships are always female, for instance. But then again, so were hurricanes until someone decided this was downright sexist, and all those godly hissy fits were just as likely to be testosterone- as estrogen-derived.

He puts the coin back. "Now, where were we?"

"You had wanted to see me?" I remind him.

"Oh yes, yes." He pauses, and I feel jitters in my stomach, hoping nothing else has gone wrong since the OD. I've been on high alert ever since the Dennis Johnson fiasco. "Why don't we just go over the patients?"

"Sure." I release my breath in relief, pulling out my iPad. "I've just got a couple right now."

Pushing the coin box to the side with some rue, he catches himself staring at it again and shuts the box. I understand the temptation, having issues with bright, shiny objects myself. "Go ahead."

"Aubrey Kane," I start. "Twenty-year-old with cutting and questionable suicidality."

"Meds?" he asks.

"Nothing yet. And no other past medical history."

"Axis two?" he asks, meaning personality disorders.

"Dependent, maybe. But I don't think so." Unfortunately, there is no axis for *fell in love with the wrong guy, got hooked on drugs, robbed a store.*

"Anyone else?"

"Andre Green. Sixteen-year-old African American with delusions and visual and auditory hallucinations."

"Schizophrenia."

I nod my assent. "Probably. Refusing meds right now."

"Do we need a medication over objection?"

"Working on it."

"Okay, next up—"

"About Andre…" I interrupt. "He really doesn't belong in jail. I don't see how he wasn't NGRI."

Dr. Novaire lifts off his glasses, rubbing the indented skin on the bridge of his nose. "Did they try for it?"

I shake my head. "His lawyer pled out."

"Then there's not much we can do."

"He got five years."

"Five? That's nothing," he says in a jolly tone. "Two years with good behavior."

"But he's only sixteen. This is—"

"Oh, I know what I wanted to meet with you about!" Dr. Novaire bursts out, making me jump with surprise. "I have a research project for you."

"Okay," I say. Research is a necessary evil, as I see it, something smart people should do for the common good. But me, I would rather chat with patients. Still, I do need to complete a project for the fellowship.

"Cognitive behavioral therapy for sociopathy," he says with great enthusiasm. "CBT."

This loosely translates into teaching sociopaths not to be sociopaths by thinking good thoughts. The premise does not sound promising. "Should I start with a literature search, maybe?"

"Oh no. I want to get down to brass tacks here. We don't have a lot of time, so I was thinking a small pilot, maybe ten patients."

"Uh-huh." Ten patients I can handle.

"Initial evaluation, run the Hare scale, CBT, then run it

again. Actually, I already have the first one picked out for you. She agreed right away."

"Oh, all right." I pull out my phone. "Do you have the medical record number?"

"Just the name," he says. "Sofia Vallano."

My mouth goes starchy.

"Listen, I know you have a certain…relationship with her." He shifts uncomfortably in his chair. "Which is why I've been taking care of her up until now. With Jason's help, of course," he adds. (Or, to put it another way, Jason has been treating her while Dr. Novaire is off shining his coins.) "Now, I know this might seem a tad unconventional, but…" He claps his liver-spotted hands together. "I truly believe she's the perfect candidate."

I swallow. "Sofia?"

"Yes."

I pause a moment and realize he is quite serious. "I'm not sure that would be such a good idea."

"See, now, I think it could be a fine idea, for a couple reasons." He must read my face. "Hear me out, okay? Number one, she's become quite religious—"

At that I start giggling, shocking both him and myself. Dr. Novaire raises a thin gray eyebrow. "Dr. Goldman?"

"I'm sorry. It's not funny." I giggle again and then cough, refocusing myself, trying to think about unfunny things, like starvation and avalanches. "It's not funny in the least, obviously." Then I start laughing again and cover my mouth. Jesus, what is wrong with me? I shoot my memory back to the morning and definitely recall taking my Adderall. So that can't be it. Dr. Novaire is staring at me in obvious displeasure. "I'm sorry. I laugh when I'm nervous sometimes."

"I don't see what there is to be nervous about," he says. "Ms. Vallano has made a lot of progress thus far. I think her focus on religion is a big part of that. She has expressed interest in being part of the project. And she was thrilled with the idea of meeting with you as well."

I'll bet she was. I pull at my turtleneck sweater, which is suddenly stuffy and tight. "It's not that I'm against the pilot. But maybe we should start with a different patient."

"Zoe," he says, "I understand your trepidation. But this is more than just about the project. I think this could be perfect. Not only are we helping a patient, but it might also help provide some closure."

"Closure." I chew on my lip. "For which one of us?"

"For both of you, of course."

"Of course, of course," I say. I chew on my lip some more, pausing, stalling, while he waits for my answer. Sofia has found religion, right. It appears our narcissistic, sociopathic Sofia is back at it. A vision of her comes to me then, her shiny black hair, her deep-blue eyes, that furtive smile.

"I'll think about it," I say.

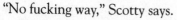

"No fucking way," Scotty says.

"I haven't said yes." I take a burning sip of cappuccino.

"You haven't said no either."

I shrug, licking some foam off my lips. "I'm not exactly Dr. Novaire's favorite fellow. I have to be diplomatic, at least."

Scotty snorts. Which is an entirely appropriate response to the idea of my being diplomatic. "The woman is a fucking sociopath, Zoe."

"I know. Which, I guess, is unfortunately the point." I take another sip. "They're saying she's grown quite religious."

Scotty rolls his eyes. "That's a joke."

"Probably." I put my mug down with a clink. "I don't want to think about her right now. Let's hear about you! Tell me all about it. What happened, every detail."

"There's not much to tell," he says, blushing. Scotty never blushes.

"How did you do it?"

"Nothing too crazy. Took her out to Oliver's. Booked a violin group to play her favorite song."

"Aw, that's romantic. What's her favorite song?"

"'Moondance.'"

"A classic." I drink the remaining foam. "I always thought that song was kinda boring, though."

"Yeah, me too." He stands up, grinning as if he's just won the lottery. And he did win the lottery. My little brother, who flunked out of college and has worked at the Coffee Spot for the last five years, somehow snagged Kristy, a knockout who just got promoted at the top local venture capital firm. I asked her over too many glasses of wine one night what she ever saw in my little brother.

"Po-ten-tial," she slurred. "And nice eyebrows."

Which I found an odd answer at the time, but by the next morning it made sense. He's a start-up, and she's providing just the right amount of capital. Plus he does have nice eyebrows.

"Do you have a date picked yet?" I ask.

"Kristy's looking into it."

"Uh-huh." Knowing Kristy, she has a spreadsheet prepared already. "You having it at temple or no?"

"I doubt it. She wants it at Westminster." Scotty straightens up in his chair. "Don't talk to Sofia. There's a reason Dr. Nowhere is taking care of her and not you."

"Yes, yes," I say without a fight.

"Seriously, she stabbed you in the fucking neck. Remember?"

"Yes," I grumble. "I remember."

"And I don't care if she's your…" Scotty pauses, but doesn't say the word. "Just don't see her, okay?"

Chapter Four

One week you were sick and we had to miss class.

That's when I realized it beyond all doubt.

The guard, that asshole Maloney, told us the news like it was no big deal. No college today, sweethearts. You'll just have to think big thoughts in your cell.

The other girls were disappointed, I could tell. But I was hollowed out, gutted. Of all the things that have happened since I got here, this was the worst. Worse than the mushy breakfast that ushers in every morning. Worse than the female guard thrusting her hips against my ass when I was about to take a shower. Worse than the hours staring at the ceiling, thinking about my sister, who won't even speak to me.

But the next week you came back. And it was like someone turned on all the colors again. I could feel the numbness fading, like novocaine wearing off, and the messy, stinging, gorgeous sensation of life surging back into me. We all sat around the beautiful circular scratched-up desk, and you asked us to write *about one of our earliest memories. One of your exercises, as you call them.*

I remember exactly what I wrote that day. I described the gold chain my mom wore.

I loved that chain. It was thick and heavy, like a snake. Easy to grab on to without breaking it. I remember doing that, when I was a child. The warmth of her neck, the comfort of hanging on to her. And she let me play with it sometimes. Twirling it in looping circles with my hand. Watching it dance and glow until I felt dizzy.

I read my memory exercise out loud. All the other girls were jealous, I could tell. They had been clowning around.

Oh no, I don't wanna read mine, Prof.

Okay, Mr. Teacher, why don't you make me?

So I raised my hand. I volunteered, and I read mine. My voice sounded stupid, reedy, little-girl-ish. But I just kept reading. I saw you watching me. And the girls were watching me, too.

I think of the necklace now and all I feel is sickness, guilt. Thinking about what I did to her. But I didn't tell them that part. I just told them about the weight of it in my palm, that gorgeous, glittery chain. Then I came to the last line, when I told them where I saw the necklace for the very last time.

On my mother's neck, when they buried her.

When I looked up, the room was silent. You didn't say anything at first. But you looked at me with pure appreciation. Not horror, not sadness, just understanding. Like you knew me and accepted me. Like we were one and the same.

I think maybe that's when you started loving me, too.

Chapter Five

Y our boy lost it," Jason says.

"Who?"

"Mr. Red Gloves," he answers.

"What happened?" I ask, opening Andre's chart in the computer.

"No idea," Jason says. "I was dealing with some tweaked-up-on-bath-salts guy."

"Got in a fight," says Harry, the guard with salt-and-pepper hair and a beaked nose.

"That's not like him. I wonder what set him off." I start reading though his chart. "Looks like his father just visited. Maybe that was it?"

"Doubt it," Harry says. "They seemed to be having a good time in there. You know, drinking pop, joking, and all that."

I log off the computer. "He's in his cell?"

"For now," he says. "Wanna see him?"

So we walk over to the C wing, where Andre is pacing the shoebox of a room, rubbing his red-gloved hands together.

"What's going on, Andre?" I ask.

"Some kid tried to take them off me," he complains. "I told him not to touch me."

"Your gloves?"

"Yeah. And now he's getting inside me. I know it."

"Who's getting inside you?"

"My father."

I pause. "I thought it was the devil."

"He *is* the devil. Head devil. He's got a whole army. They're trying to seed me." Andre starts madly waving his hands in my face, which bizarrely reminds me of an angry mime. "Seed me. Don't you get it?"

"Whoa there, fella," Harry says, closing in on us.

"He wants to convert me," he says, but steps away again, pacing. "But I won't do it. I told him I won't do it. He can't get in me, though. He can't get through. I told him that. It's impossible. I got Techno Glove."

"Techno Glove?" I ask.

Harry busts out laughing. "He's talking about Doom Patrol."

I stare at both of them as if they're speaking a foreign language.

"Comics," Harry says. "But a pretty obscure one."

"Doom Patrol is not at all obscure," Andre argues, sounding at once oddly normal. "Anyway, that's not the point. He can't get through them. I made sure. They're antidevil."

"Uh-huh," Harry says.

Suddenly Andre leaps to the side, banging into the bars and surprising us both. He looks up at me in panic. "Did you see that?"

"See what?"

He motions to the corner of his cell with his chin, just an inch, so as not to draw attention. "In the corner," he whispers. And despite our better sense, Harry and I both look. "Did you see him?"

"I'm not sure," I answer.

Andre looks disappointed now and points, forgetting all decorum. "Over there!" he whispers, his face pale. Harry steps closer to him again. "The Gollum." His breathing is rough. "You don't see him?"

I shake my head.

"He's got a hundred ribs going up and down under his fur," he whispers. "And his tongue is moving." He points to the corner again. "Clear as day. You don't see him?"

"I'm going to give you something," I say. "Something to fight the devil."

Andre scratches at his scalp, viciously. "He's planting the seeds in my head, too—"

"Medication, Andre. It will help."

"No pills," he argues.

"Not just any pills," I counter. "Magic pills." This gets his attention. "Pills that will ward off the devil. They've been blessed." Harry is looking at me now as if I might be the crazy one.

"Magic pills," Andre says, his voice wavering with a tendril of hope. "Like Nuke has?"

"Right," I say, though I have no idea what he's talking about. "With an antidemonic coating," I add, for good measure. He stares at me a long moment, debating, then nods. The coating seems to seal the deal. "At noon. The nurse will hand them out. Blue ones," I say. "Make sure."

He nods again, looking hopeful for the first time. As if I just gave him the secret code—access to a superpower. It's all I can do until I can get him out of prison and into a hospital, where he belongs. And I'm not lying to him. Antipsychotics *do* fight the devil.

Sometimes.

~

Later in the day, I'm walking down the hallway of the women's wing when a bright light stops me. One flash, then another, like a strobe light, leaving a fuzzy afterimage of the bars burned into my retina.

A gaggle of prisoners run up to check it out and are waved off by the guards. "Don't worry, sweethearts. You'll all get your turns," Officer Maloney says. He's your standard-issue officer, buzz cut and beefy arms.

"What's going on?" I ask him.

"I don't know." He sounds annoyed. "Some kind of crap for the *Buffalo News*." Another flash goes off. "I have no idea why the warden would agree to this shit. Just gonna make us look like a bunch of turds."

I wonder if he realizes that he has used three different

words for feces in the last twenty seconds. "Maybe it won't be a bad thing," I say.

"Jee-yeah," he scoffs, something between *Jesus* and *yeah*. "We'll see. These bleeding-heart libtards sure aren't gonna write about how great a job the COs are doing."

I debate schooling him on the offensiveness of adding *tard* to any word, but decide not to waste my time. Which means the extra Strattera dose is working. A flash lights up a cell, turning it ghostly white. "Who's writing it?"

"I am," says a young man, coming over from his spot beside the photographer. "Logan," he says. I shake his hand, and Maloney offers only a terse nod. Logan is pure hipster. Eyebrow ring, nose ring, and earring. The circle kind that stretches out your earlobe. Puppy dog–brown eyes, and longish sideburns that will probably be in style in two weeks. "Just doing a feature, nothing heavy hitting. It's my first year at the *News*."

"I'm Zoe Goldman," I say. "It's my first year at the prison."

He smiles. "You're a—"

"Psychiatrist," I fill in. "In the forensic psychiatry fellowship."

"Cool." He looks impressed. "I always thought psychiatry would be so fascinating."

"It can be." Depending which side of the couch you're on.

The photographer jogs over. He's wearing a beret. He actually is. "I think we've wrapped up. I was just going to get some outside shots."

"Sounds good." The photographer nods and heads back to the cell to start packing up. "We're going to do some staff interviews, too," Logan says. "You want to contribute? I'm sure your viewpoint would be enlightening to a lot of folks."

"No thanks," I answer. Too quickly to be polite, I realize, as Logan laughs.

"So I take it you don't want to think about it, then?"

"It's just...not a good idea. Clinically," I add, which makes no sense, but sounds more official. "So, what got you interested in prison life anyway?" I ask, changing the subject.

"Actually, my brother was in prison," he says with some pride. "Briefly," he amends, so as not to boast. "So I try to help prisoners, send care packages, do some volunteering and that."

"Oh, that's nice," I say with a smile. He's a do-good hipster.

"And we're working closely with the warden on this one." He lowers his voice, as if this is in confidence. "It's no secret. You guys have had your share of bad press lately."

"That's true," I admit.

"Every month it's something," he goes on. "The one lady who got murdered in the shower, the d.t.'s guy. Then that kid who hanged himself over the summer."

My smile stiffens.

"The warden wants to highlight the new programs in place. Reformation," he says with grandeur. "That's the theme, anyway," he says, toning it down a notch, "for both the inmates and the officers." He looks back at his photographer, who is zipping a bag. "Plus I'm trying to get my way out of the wedding beat. If you know what I mean."

I don't, really. But I would imagine it's similar to digging myself out of my own hole. The photographer emerges at our sides then, beret and all. "You all set?"

"Sure." Logan turns to me. "Hey, Zoe, if you change your mind about that interview." He hands me his official *Buffalo News* card.

"Thanks." I pocket it, politely. Until I can find the nearest garbage can, that is.

That night I decide to visit Mike in the ER, ostensibly to surprise him with dinner, and less ostensibly to do reconnaissance on Serena, the woman who's been XO-texting him about tibial fractures.

"Do you know anything about comics?" I ask.

"Comics?" Mike asks, through a yawn. "I think I have a *Calvin and Hobbes* book somewhere."

"No, I mean real comics. Like action heroes and stuff."

"Oh no. I was never really into that." He signs off on an order from the computer. "My brother Anthony was. Why do you ask?"

"Nothing really." I yawn, too. It's contagious. "Just trying to figure out one of my patients. He's built this complex delusion around various comics characters."

"Huh," Mike says. "Interesting world you live in."

A patient is whisked by us then, only moving the right side of his body. His expression is shocked, though on the right side of his face only. The left side remains slack. "Looks like a stroke," I observe.

"Ooh!" Sean, his asshole PA-in-training, says. "Nothing gets by the ultraclever psychiatrist, huh?"

Mike gives him a death stare, and Sean vacates the area with an obnoxious chuckle. Sean is fairly detestable. He's the type of person who calls everyone *bro* or *dude*. "One more month," Mike says.

"'Til what?"

"Sean goes to Derm. The entire ER is counting the days. Felicity is even throwing a last-Sean-day party." Felicity is the head nurse in the ER. She is fair, and smart, but not particularly felicitous. You really do not want to fuck with her. Mike motions to my white plastic bag. "Did you bring something for me?"

"Oh yeah, I almost forgot." I start laying out little trays, wrappers of soy sauce and duck sauce. A veritable picnic in the central ER station.

"Sweet." Mike gives me such an earnest, happy look that I feel like a cad for not doing this more often.

"Yours is the lo mein. And I've got soup."

He reaches over for an egg roll. "You got three?"

"Yeah," I say, guarding the remaining two. "I was hungry."

"Hey, Mike?" a mellifluous voice calls out.

"Yeah?" He stands up. A woman with cheerleader-blond hair and cornflower-blue eyes emerges from behind the curtain of room four. She sashays over. "Oh, hi! I'm Serena," she says, shaking my hand.

"Hi, I'm Zoe." I grip hers, extra hard. I feel like King Kong, and she's the blonde in the white dress.

"So," she says, turning her body and attention to Mike, "Room four needs an LP." She puts her delicate pink hand on his shoulder and leans in. She might as well just give him a lap dance. "Can you witness it for me?"

"I'm sure you could find a nurse to do that," I say without thinking. As if my Adderall just took a vacation. Mike scratches his neck uncomfortably while Serena looks at me askance. *Who invited her to the party?*

"No, it's fine. I can do it. Back in a sec, Zoe," he says, and tags along. Morosely I take a bite of my egg roll, then rub the nubby end into the duck sauce. So this is XO Serena.

Indubitably a worthy adversary.

Chapter Six

Dr. Chen (the PhD kind) opens the door and offers me the chair across from her desk. Trying to get a better grasp on Andre's case, I decided to call his high school principal, who was kind enough to meet with me.

"Thanks for seeing me," I say.

"I'm so happy you called," she returns, her voice soft and genuine. "Andre was always one of my favorites. I've been wondering how he was doing." On her desk stands a silver-framed picture of two young kids with bulky snow suits and red-tinged cheeks. Her mug is in the shape of a big red apple and says "Straight-A Principal."

After the bitter cold outside, her office is a sauna. I shrug off my coat. "He's still quite sick."

"Oh," she intones, "that's a shame." She plays with the stem of her apple mug. "The delusions still?"

"Yes, mainly about his father and the devil." I shake my head. "He really doesn't belong in prison." Neither of us

41

speak for a moment, both of us struck by the pitiful situation.

"So what can I do to help?" she asks.

"I really just wanted to get some more background." I reflexively take out my phone and pull a new note up. "The only Andre I know is the boy who stabbed his father and is constantly hallucinating, you know? Andre the patient."

"Right."

"I was hoping you might have some insight on what he was like before all this."

"He was wonderful," she breaks in without hesitation. Her eyes are beaming. "Honestly, he was. Anything you could ask of a student, that's what he was. Kind to the other kids, respectful to teachers, hardworking, smart. Brilliant, even." She looks down at her desk with a sad smile. "I've been at this almost fifteen years now, Dr. Goldman, and Andre was the real thing."

I write "real thing" in my note. "But you noticed a change?"

Dr. Chen folds her hands. "Yes. I did. After his mother died, Charmayne. Well…" She hesitates. "Not *right* after." She thinks back. "At first he was quieter, more sedate. Which is to be expected. Mourning."

"Of course."

"He missed some school, but not an alarming amount. Again, to be expected." She regards her hands, which are shiny with lotion or perhaps just good skin. "But then about six months or so later, he started acting differently. More on edge, belligerent even. He got written up." She points to her computer. "I have all the records."

I nod at the computer and the referenced records in there.

"Which we still assumed was mourning, or maybe depression." A blaring announcement comes through the overhead, about a clothing drive for Christmas. The words crackle, then fade away. "Sorry about that. They need to fix that."

"That's okay."

"Where was I?"

I consult my note. "Getting written up."

"Right, yes. And he was missing more class. One day it was a headache, another stomachache. Like the anxious kids."

"School avoiders," I say, having treated my share of those in my pediatric rotation.

"Exactly. And again, we thought this was still in keeping with the change in his situation, depression, et cetera. And he looked a bit ill. Pale, tired. Like he wasn't sleeping well. But then he said something very upsetting, very…disturbing to Ms. Clark, our social worker. Which you're well aware of. That he thought his father was the devil. And then it was all mixed up in the comic books stuff."

"Right."

"And he was afraid his father was trying to replace him. That his father was part of a coven, he said. I remember thinking the word was quite advanced." She nods with admiration at the memory. "And that he was replacing his mother and putting in a double for Andre, too."

I write this down. "Coven. Andre double." It doesn't change anything, though. If anything, it further supports the schizophrenia diagnosis. Delusions can be quite ornate.

"And poor Mr. Green just couldn't deal with it."

43

"He had a lot on his plate," I say.

"Yes, he did. And he didn't want to believe there was a change. I met with him about it, and he said Andre had a strong imagination. He blamed the comic books."

"Denial."

"Without a doubt," she agrees. "But I should have pushed the issue. He wasn't equipped to deal with it right then, clearly." Her jaw clenches, her eyes troubled. "I was going to call CPS, but it was already late in the day. So I put it off to the next day."

"What did CPS say?"

She sighs. "I never got a chance to call them. The next day Abraham Green was in the hospital, and Andre had been arrested."

Aubrey is strapped into a chair.

She struggles against the black bindings, screaming and sobbing. Sweat runs down her neck with the effort. I was just getting to the clinic when they called me in stat.

"What happened?"

Her shrieking echoes through the hallway, as if she's being sliced open. "We don't know. But we're hoping you can calm her down," Officer Maloney says. He is out of breath from wrestling with her, though he outweighs her by over a hundred pounds. At six four, he's just a bit taller than I. "She said she'll only talk to you."

I can barely hear him above her sobbing. "Aubrey," I say, my voice calm, but forceful. "Let's relax here. This isn't helping." The hoarse shrieking continues. Her forehead is swelling up, an ugly purple egg. "What set her off?"

"Beats me," Maloney says. "One second she's fine, then she's slamming her head against the wall."

"It was a letter," says the female CO, a largish African American woman. Her name tag says "Destiny."

"What letter?"

"Her cellie said she got a letter. From some guy on the outside."

"Todd?" I ask.

The screaming stops. Her eyes search me with desperation as her breath turns hiccupy. She struggles against the straps again, more halfheartedly, then stops. As if her engine has run out. Tears run down her red, heated cheeks. "Todd," she says, in a whisper. "He said..." She struggles, still crying. "He said...he broke..."

"He broke something?" I ask. "What did he break?"

"Broke up?" Destiny queries.

Aubrey is silent then and finally answers with an embarrassed nod. Maloney snickers, and Destiny pats her arm. "You want to rest in the quiet room for a little bit?" she asks. Aubrey nods again, her nose runny. She looks like a little girl, crying over a lost snowball fight.

Destiny gives her another pat. "It'll be okay. You'll see."

"Please don't put me in solitary," Aubrey begs.

"Don't you worry about that right now," Destiny says, cooing.

"I can't go in there."

"If you would cut this crap, we wouldn't have to send you there," Maloney says. I'm thinking much the same, but it's not the time or place to discuss more effective coping skills.

"I can't go back there. The room." Aubrey is talking to herself now. "He kept me in a room."

"Who kept you in a room?" I ask, but she doesn't answer.

"We're all set here now," Maloney says. "Right?"

Aubrey mournfully nods.

"Which means I have a fucking mountain of paperwork," Maloney gripes. Destiny starts to undo the straps. And I grip Aubrey's sweaty shoulder in support, then step away to return to the clinic.

Turning around, I nearly bump right into another inmate. An inmate walking down the hall with a certain sway. I would recognize that sway anywhere. She stops and looks at me. Standing right there, my nemesis. Orange doesn't become her. But her black hair still has that sheen, and her eyes are still a deep, deep ocean blue. Sofia looks right at me and smiles that mocking *Mona Lisa* smile.

And I turn around and head to my office, pretending I didn't see her.

When it's almost quitting time, I get called for a consult at the men's wing.

On my way there, I find myself quite ravenous and make

a pit stop at the vending machine for my usual nutritional supplement of M&M's. When I reach the clinic, Jason's still there. I pour myself a palmful of candy then tilt the package toward him.

"I'm on a diet," he says with a tinge of disgust.

"You're always on a diet," I answer, my mouth full of chocolate.

"I don't know how you don't get fat." He sizes me up. "You're always eating such crap."

I sit down at a computer. "Timothy Gordon, huh?"

"Yeah, self-harm."

"Another one? It seems like we have a sale on that lately."

"And the other guy's Fohrman," Jason says. "He's on a hunger strike, so we're supposed to make sure he's not suicidal. I would see him, but I gotta get out of here. Got a date."

I close out a chart. "I thought you said you were 'sworn to celibacy' after Dominic."

Dominic was his last asshole boyfriend. "I was," he says. "For a couple weeks." He clicks off his computer. "Ciao, babe."

"Ciao," I say, already reading through my new patient's chart. Timothy Gordon dropped a thirty-pound weight on his left arm *to see if the bones were real.* Turns out they were, and he broke several of them.

After a bit the guard brings a ginger-headed Timothy Gordon into the clinic room. Timothy shuffles with his shackles on, then sits down heavily, and the guard exits the room. Timothy's left arm is in a metal cast with screws in place, like some kind of ancient torture device.

47

I point to it. "Do you want to talk to me about that?"

He shrugs. "It's nothing."

I tap my finger on my lips. "I wouldn't say that really. It's multiple compound fractures requiring screws, and who knows what other hardware in there."

He examines it. "Pretty, huh?"

"Yeah. You'll be setting off metal detectors for miles."

This gets a smile, at least. "It's getting better."

"Which is good. And thank God for Ortho. But do you know why they called a psych consult?"

He shakes his head. "I can't say as I do."

"Because we're kind of wondering, why did you do it?"

His foot is tapping, clinking the ankle cuffs in a rhythm. I wait him out, checking him over. He's your typical male prisoner, muscles defined from hours of working out to defeat boredom. But no cutting scars. He's never been in for self-harm before. He hasn't been in the hole for over five years, so he's not a troublemaker. And this certainly isn't a typical suicide attempt either.

"I had to find out..." He lifts his arm and examines it as if it were a piece of artwork. "If it was real."

"If what was real, your arm?"

He nods. "The bones."

"Hmm," I say with interest. This is not your typical self-harm. This is something different. "Did you think the bones were something else?"

"Chicken bones, maybe. Or rubber."

"Uh-huh." I tap my pencil. "Do you think someone implanted bones in you?"

"No." He scoffs. "I'm not crazy or something. It's just my arm. Didn't feel like it was mine."

Depersonalization, I think, with enthusiasm that's probably inappropriate. It's been a while since I've had a good case of depersonalization. When patients think they're not real somehow, like fake humans in this world. "Usually it wouldn't just be a limb, though," I comment without meaning to.

"Huh?"

"Nothing, sorry, just thinking out loud." My phone rings then, and I shut the ringer off, seeing it's Newsboy. The phone vibrates on the table. "So, how do you feel about that now? Your arm?"

He thinks about it. "Not sure. I never did get to see the bones."

This isn't the answer I was hoping for. The guard yawns outside the room. "What if I could get hold of the X-ray, to show you?"

He stares again at the arm, which may or may not be his. "Sure," he says, as if humoring me. "Might be worth a shot."

Arthur licks peanut butter off his nose until he's cross-eyed.

I slather some onto my bread, a bubble breaking through the sheen of the top coat. After perfecting the next slice, I lay them together and take a heavenly bite. My stomach unclenches. My appetite is soaring lately, which makes me wonder if my meds are off. Mike is bringing home Thai food tonight, so this is my predinner snack.

I finish the sandwich in approximately 3.7 seconds, faster than Arthur would have, then light the fireplace and put on some Buffalo Philharmonic Orchestra Christmas music.

The music soothes me. It's already dark out, snow falling in lazy flakes in the porch light. Mike won't be home for a couple hours yet, so I decide to wrap some Chanukah gifts, fully aware of the incongruity of the music.

Humming to myself, I measure out some blue-and-silver paper. A bulky navy sweater for Mike, as his current bulky navy sweater has gotten thin at the elbows. I got Scotty the same sweater in gray and still have no idea what to get Kristy. Gift number two is a solid rectangle. Mike's favorite cologne, which adds a pleasant pine scent to the wrapping and has easy angles to boot. Next is Arthur's huge rawhide, which is neither pleasant smelling nor easy to wrap. I settle on a roll-and-scrunch method. Because he is, after all, a dog.

Surveying the mess of tape, uneven wrapping remains, and scissors, I feel as if I'm missing someone, and with an unexpected pang of sadness realize that it's my mom. I probably would have wrapped up a muslin pouch of lavender bath beads, or maybe a black cardigan. I try not to think of our last Chanukah, lighting an ugly menorah in the industrially cheerful great room of the nursing home. Mom blew them all out, thinking they were birthday candles, and Scotty tried to wipe away a tear before I could see it.

A rousing rendition of "A Holly Jolly Christmas" sweeps away the memory, and I have moved on to a bag of sponge candy for Mike (which I might partake in as well) tucked into a Buffalo Sabres coffee mug when the phone rings. I peek over at the screen, and the call seems to be coming from the *Buffalo News*. Seems too coincidental to be anybody but Newsboy. After it goes to voice mail, I tap the speaker icon to hear the message.

"Hi. This is Logan, the annoying guy from the *Buffalo News*." I shear through the paper with my scissors. "I hope you don't mind me calling your cell again..."

"Actually, I do," I say with a piece of tape in my mouth. "I think it takes some major brass, to be honest with you."

"But I couldn't reach you at work..." he goes on.

"Because I ignored your call."

"But if you'd have time for a quick talk, I'd really appreciate it. Let me give you my..." And he drones on, but I tune him out.

Talk to the *Buffalo News* about my patients? Even I'm not *that* stupid.

Chapter Seven

I dreamed about you last night, Professor.

We were in the library. And you had me cornered in between the shelves and you were kissing me. I was biting your neck, and you shoved your thigh between my legs, and I was grinding on you. Like an animal.

Then you stopped, and I started whimpering, but you led me over to a bed. (In the library, weird, I know.) And you threw me on it, pushing me into the mattress, and I could smell your sweat, feel your weight on top of me.

You were yanking off my panties. I was touching your soft chest, circling my fingers over all your tattoos, and you were lying on me. I was moaning, guttural moans, moans I couldn't even control, and the bed was creaking so loud, and I thought we might get in trouble but I didn't care.

The girls in the class were leaning over us, surrounding us like we were in a show. They were tittering and pointing, but I didn't *care. I liked it even. Let them watch. Let them be jealous. Let them yearn for you. The rhythm kept building and you were pushing so hard that I could feel myself arching my back.*

And when I woke up, my hand was between my legs, and I was coming.

Chapter Eight

"Andre's in solitary," Jason says, as soon as I walk into the clinic.

I throw my heavy black coat over the chair. "What happened?"

"I don't know. He was going on about the devil and some Nuke guy, and then he tried to bust out the window."

I stamp clumps of snow off the heel of my boot. "So the magic blue pills aren't working, I take it."

"I'd say not."

"Maybe I could talk him into the higher dose. Magic orange ones."

The phone rings on his desk, and Jason answers it. After a brief conversation, he puts his hand over the receiver. "Any idea where Novaire is?"

I log into my computer. "Is that a rhetorical question?"

"Pretty much."

"Why, what's up?"

"Tariq the guard is on the phone. Andre's father is here. He came to visit, but obviously that's not going to happen. So he's demanding to see the *attending*." He says the word with false esteem. "I don't know what the hell to tell the guy."

I think for a second. "Tell him the attending is deeply involved in a case of numismatics, but I can see him if he'd like."

Jason stares at me. "Numis-whats?"

"Numismatics." I write the word down for him, and he grabs the paper.

"Okay. I don't know what that even means, but I will tell him." Jason faithfully relays the message, and I make my way down through hell hall, complete with "ooh-baby-come-fuck-me, show-me-your-pussy-girl, I-can't-wait-to-titty-fuck-you" et cetera, but finally I get to the visiting room, and Tariq leads me over to a table.

I've never been in the visiting room, and it's pretty nice. New paint, fresh carpeting. Mr. Green sits with his legs crossed, reading the *Wall Street Journal*. His double-breasted gray suit strains against his broad chest. Former football player, maybe. Looking up at me, he smiles, revealing a gold eyetooth, and stands up. "Dr. Goldman?" He offers a vise grip of a handshake.

"Hi, Mr. Green."

"Abraham," he says. "Friends call me Abe."

"Zoe," I return, taking a seat next to him. "What can I do for you?"

"Well, not for me, so much as my son."

"Of course."

"I'm just..." He squeezes his hands together, his fingers rubbing against his large knuckles. "Trying to understand this all."

"Yes, I know. It's hard."

"And I would like to know what's being done for Andre. When he's going to get better."

I nod, wishing it were that simple. "Just so you know, I talked with Dr. Chen."

"Oh." He squints, as if the name rings a bell. "His old principal?"

"Yes, that's right, to get some more history. And she said this started after his mother died?"

"That's right, my wife, Charmayne. She passed about a year ago now." His voice is hushed.

"I'm sorry."

"Thank you." There is the uncomfortable pause that always follows such exchanges.

"No inklings of anything before that?" I ask.

"No. He was fine, just fine. But after she died, he...he just..." His voice is gravelly as he searches for the right word. "Changed. That's all. He changed." The story of schizophrenia, when a promising young brain turns cruelly upon itself.

"Go on."

"He was convinced the devil got her. Just kept saying that. And that he should have saved her." A man walks by our table for a hug from his family, sending the scent of cologne wafting up. "And then, over time, somehow it became *me*. I was the devil who killed her." Abraham slumps a bit, as if sickened by the words. "The first time he just took a swing, and that was one thing. But then he came at me." He makes a stabbing motion toward his chest. "Luckily he's not very athletic or I wouldn't be here to talk about it."

It seems an oddly uncomplimentary thing to say about your son, though maybe he's just being honest. And Andre *did* try to stab him and beat him with a wrench.

The heat turns on, crackling his newspaper. "Maybe it would help to think of it this way: It isn't actually your son doing these things."

His eyebrows invert, puzzled. "How's that?"

"It's his brain. The chemicals misfiring. Not him."

Abe looks at me as if he's not buying it. "That's just words, don't you think, Dr. Goldman?"

"No, not really." I ponder the best way to put this. "Do you think Andre *wants* to see the devil? Or hurt you? Or wear red gloves?"

He shakes his head. "Not the Andre I used to know."

"Exactly."

Tears jump into his eyes. "He was a fine boy. A good boy."

"And he still is," I tell him, "underneath all this. That's what I'm saying. I'm just trying to reach that boy again. Get his brain chemicals right."

"It did seem like he got better after the first time in the hospital," he says, almost as if convincing himself. "When we got him on those meds."

"And that's a good sign. We can get him there again."

57

He exhales. "I'm just afraid to get my hopes up, I guess. After last time." He puts in elbow on the table, and a gold cuff link shines in the sun. "And he said he was *taking* all those medicines. He swore it up and down."

"The thing is," I say, "he is still a kid, who doesn't always want to do what he's told, or what he should. But unfortunately, he's also got a bad disease."

Mr. Green scratches at a bushy eyebrow. "And I didn't even want to put him in jail. I just wanted him safe. They said that was the only option."

"I don't know what happened there," I say, thinking of Jason's assessment: *bad lawyer*. "But we'll get him better again, and he'll go home. He's got his whole life ahead of him."

Abraham folds up the newspaper, stiffly. "You really think you can help him? I'm putting my faith in you now."

"I know I can."

He grabs my hand then, which is unexpected. "Thank you." His eyes are desperate and fierce. "I just want my boy back."

Her forehead bruise is eggplant purple now. "I think those pills might actually be working," Aubrey says with obvious surprise.

"Good," I say. But I'm thinking placebo effect. It's only been a few days.

She twists a lavender friendship bracelet on her wrist. I

don't remember seeing it last visit. "It wasn't just the letter, though, that got me going. Just so you know."

"No? What else was going on?"

She tucks her hair behind her ear, three empty holes dotting the cartilage. "It sounds stupid."

"Try me."

She pauses, then looks at me. "You remember that girl I was telling you about, Portia?" Aubrey twirls her hair. "Supposedly she told Stacy that she wasn't that into me, and then Jasmine told me she was dating Brianna on the side."

"Oh," I say, at this preposterous soap opera that also happens to be her life.

"Dumb, right?"

"Well, I understand if you were upset. It's only natural."

"Yeah, I guess." She looks relieved at this cheap bit of validation. "Anyway, it wasn't even true. Stacy admitted she and Jasmine were just fucking with me."

The cuffs of her pants are rolled and dusty. She suddenly seems too young to be in prison wear. "Sounds kind of high-school-ish," I say.

"Totally," she agrees.

I pause. "Hurting yourself, maybe that's a little high-school-ish, too?"

She shrugs her birdlike shoulders. "I guess." Her cheeks flush, and I wonder if I've gone too far. I don't mean to shame her, just help her make the connection. "Maybe," she admits. She plays with the ends of her friendship bracelet.

"We need to talk about other coping mechanisms. More

healthy coping mechanisms. That won't land you in solitary."

She flicks the frayed bracelet ends. "I used to steal my mom's pain pills."

I pause. "Your mom was on pain pills?"

"Yeah. She had gobs of pills, from like ten different doctors." She gets a faraway look. "She was so out of it half the time, she didn't even notice."

"Addiction's a tough one," I say. "And it does run in families."

"Yeah, I heard that before."

I give her a gentle smile. "Still not a very good coping mechanism."

"It worked pretty well for a while, though." She drops her head, her hair falling over her face. "Until it stopped working."

"And then you started cutting?"

"No. Then I met Todd. And he showed me that pills were kid stuff. He showed me the real thing." Her expression morphs into a dreamy, magical look, speaking of the man who adorned the left side of her chest with a calligraphy tattoo heart, before he broke it.

"You mentioned a room."

"What?"

"A room," I say, to change the subject from heroin and the suddenly exalted Todd. "When you were being restrained, you said something about that."

"A room?" The dreamy look vanishes, and her lip twitches. "I don't remember that."

"Okay," I say, to her obvious lie. "If you do remember, Aubrey, and you want to talk about it, I'm here."

⌒

Destiny (the guard, not the manifest kind) brings in my next patient: Barbara Donalds, a forty-three-year-old white female. Under the "Appearance" heading of the mental status exam, I could write, "Rode hard and put away wet." We shake hands, and she sits down as Destiny leaves. I barely had time to look over her chart, but the chief complaint was: Patient is sad. Which could describe most people in this place.

"How can I help you?" I ask.

Her eyes fill up, and I offer a tissue. "My daughter," she says, her voice strained.

"Yes?"

"She just died."

"Oh, I'm so sorry, Mrs. Donalds."

"Barbara," she says. "And thank you." She rubs her nose, which is red and swollen from crying already. "Ran into a tree. She was drunk." I shake my head, because I can't think of any words to offer. "It was my fault."

"Your fault?" This gives me pause. "What do you mean by that?"

"She was just following in her mother's footsteps." She lets out a laugh that is also a sob. "I was a rotten drunk for her whole childhood. Then I came here and got clean so I could miss her adulthood." She shakes her head. "Want to guess what got me in?"

"I don't know."

"Very ironic," she says, bitterly. "Manslaughter. Driving without a license after my third DWI." She dabs at her eyes. "Ended up killing a woman on her way to get married." She sighs, her eyes filling again. "I knew God would punish me somehow. Take something away from me. I just didn't think it would be her."

"I'm sorry," I say again. I could say it's not her fault. I could say her daughter's in a better place. But the words won't help her. So I reach over and put my hand on her arm, and she grasps my hand, as if it's a lifeboat. Her grip is strong and warm, her skin scratchy-dry.

We talk then for a while. Mostly she talks, and I listen. I set her up with a grief support group in the prison and some Prozac. And I am sure to ask the question. Ever since that first week, I always ask the question. "Barbara, are you thinking about killing yourself?"

"No." Her answer is immediate. "Never. I was taught you go to hell for that, and I believe in that completely."

"Okay. Then I've made an appointment for next week. Let me know if you have any problem on the medication. And promise me, if you even think about harming yourself, you'll tell someone. You can call me anytime, or tell anyone."

"I'm not going to. As I said, I'm a strong Catholic, and I believe it's a sin. But I promise, if I ever changed my mind, I would tell you."

"Good."

It's a natural end to the meeting, but she is still looking around the bare room, as if there's something more she wants to say.

"Is there something else I can help you with?"

She bites her lip, looking uncomfortable. "There is just one more thing." She hands me a torn-off piece of paper, shoves it at me really. "Someone wanted me to give you this. She said it would help you. But please don't get me in trouble, okay?"

"In trouble? Who said—"

Destiny is back to collect Mrs. Donalds before she can respond, and I close my hand over the paper. As soon as they leave, I open my hand up again and read the message.

Meet me, Tanya. Or I'll tell the news reporter everything.

Tanya was my old name, before my parents adopted me. And there's only one person who calls me that.

My ex-patient. Sofia Vallano.

After seeing two more patients, I'm finishing up my notes when Jason comes out of a room and sits down at the computer next to me. He lifts a tea bag out of his mug, filling the air with a spicy scent.

"Tea," I remark. "How civilized."

"It's echinacea, okay?" he grumbles. "I'm getting a cold." His voice does sound a bit raspy. His phone rings then, and he looks down, then turns off the ringer. "Jesus, that newspaper guy won't stop calling me."

"Who, Logan? You met him, too?"

"Yeah. He wants to 'interview' me." Jason uses dramatic air quotes.

"So what? He wants to 'interview' me, too," I say with air quotes of equal gravitas.

"Oh, please, Zoe. That guy is so gay it isn't even funny."

"You think?" I consider it. "Maybe. I didn't get a vibe one way or the other."

"He so is. He was two seconds away from asking me out."

"Maybe," I say, considering it. "Either way, I'm just trying to avoid him."

"You and me both," he says.

We sit in silence for a bit while I watch him typing in his computer chart, debating the best way to broach the topic of Sofia.

"What?" he asks, looking up from his screen.

"What what?"

"You're watching me type a note. That is not normal."

"I'm allowed to watch you type a note," I argue.

"Whatever."

He keeps typing, and I keep watching. "Okay, fine," I say, relenting. "It's about Sofia."

"Okay." He keeps typing, hunt-and-peck style. "What about Sofia?"

"How is she doing?"

He turns from the screen, giving me a questioning look. "She is doing fine."

"What do you mean by fine, exactly?"

"Zoe, what are you trying to ask me?"

I take a deep breath. "Did Dr. Novaire tell you he thought we should meet?"

"Yes, he mentioned that."

"That he wants to do some meshuga project on CBT for sociopaths?"

"Yes, he mentioned that, too."

I find myself chewing on my eraser, a nervous habit that hasn't emerged since grade school. "So, what do you think of the idea?"

"Honest opinion? Completely moronic."

"So you don't think she's reformable, then?"

He guffaws. "You seriously need an answer for that?"

"I don't know," I mutter. "Novaire said she's found religion."

"Yeah. Her and everyone else in this place."

"That's true." I turn back to my notes. "I will probably meet with her, though. Just to get Novaire off my back," I say, trying to sound nonchalant. I don't mention the fact that Sofia is blackmailing me. Though any reporter worth his salt could dig up the information on his own. But it would take time. And he'd probably be done with the feature before I'd even have to worry about it.

Or Sofia could hand him the irresistible scoop on a silver platter. "Yeah, I think I will."

"Up to you," Jason says, sipping his tea again. "She's *your* sister."

I feel it as an actual blow, as Jason explodes the land mine that I've been tiptoeing around. That everyone's been tiptoeing around, ever since I found out. "*Biological* sister," I stress.

He doesn't answer. And the truth is, the distinction is inconsequential. It doesn't matter if I didn't grow up with her or even know she existed until she tracked me down. Until she became my patient and I finally learned the whole truth about my birth mother's death. That the reason my birth mother died, the reason I was adopted in the first place, is that, on one dark night, when I was only three years old and Sofia only fourteen, she killed our mother. It was a night I'd completely blocked from my memory. And my adoptive mom (may she rest in peace) tried to hide the ugly truth from me for as long as she could.

And I can pretend Sofia doesn't exist, but she does. And for better or worse, the bald fact remains. She's not just an ex-patient who stabbed me in the neck. She's also my sister.

"Yeah, I'll talk to her," I say, to myself as much as anyone. And Jason sips his tea and doesn't answer.

Chapter Nine

Maybe it was the dream that called you forth, conjured you to me.

Maybe it was all those nights staring up at the ceiling and picturing you. Luring you with my thoughts, with the pure need, the pure desire in my head.

After class, the girls had left. You were looking at someone's journal and it was like déjà vu, my dream of you in the corner, your presence drawing me in like a net. I walked toward you, my heart pounding so hard it hurt, and you looked up.

I was about to say something, but you grabbed the V neck of my shirt, pulled me toward you, and kissed me. Hard.

I remember every second.

The warmth of your lips. Your open mouth as soft as the inside of a grape. Your hand gripping the back of my neck like a vise until the room was tilting and I could hardly breathe. It was like the romance novels the girls in here are always going on about. Bullshit, I always thought. But that was before I met you.

You'll think I'm foolish. Maybe I am. It's not like I've never been kissed before. I've been with plenty of men. Too many men. I've slept my way through my share of rough spots, like every other girl in this place. And sure, it's been a long time since I've been with someone. Other than stolen, sloppy kisses from some of these bull dykes trying to act like men.

But it was more than that, I'm telling you. This was different. Different than I've ever felt before. When you pulled away, I nearly fell over. I had to catch my breath. And you looked me up and down with a smirk. That same sly smile as the very first day I met you. Like you were measuring me, checking out a new purchase. Like you owned me, and I didn't even mind.

Then you looked around to make sure no one was there and leaned in again and whispered, I heard you know someone. Someone important to me.

I asked who it was, and you told me. I nodded, and you said you wanted me to do something for you. You said you needed names. Patient names. You said you already took care of one of them. I didn't understand what you meant, and you told me it was a girl who had been in our class, but not anymore. She died, overdosed, and you helped her get the drugs. I thought for a moment, and it came to me. The woman with the penciled-in eyebrows.

Carrie Cooke? *I asked.*

You looked puzzled but said yes, you thought that was her. Like you barely remembered. But she was nice to me. I did remember her.

You said, I need more names.

Looking back, I wonder what would have happened if I had just said no. No, I can't do that, you sick fuck. I can't get you more names of patients to mess with. If I had just said no, I won't do that, it would have changed everything that came after. I wouldn't be here right now, trembling in my cell, praying to a God that I don't believe in.

But that's not what happened. Because I said yes. Of course I said yes.

I could never say no to you.

Chapter Ten

Andre is back at his comic books. He scans the page with a red-gloved finger, more maroon than red right now with dust and dirt. He concentrates on each page as if he's studying for a test. Hearing the keys clang, he looks up at me and the guard.

"How are you doing, Andre?" I ask.

He shrugs. "A little better, I guess." Andre looks longingly at the comic book page again. "The devils are quieter."

"And why do you think that is?"

"Dunno." He scratches the back of his neck, which is dry and patched with scales. He looks pale and sickly after his time in solitary. "The pills, I guess. But..." His voice drops off.

"But what?"

"It also could be because he hasn't come."

"Your dad?" I ask. Andre nods in response, and I move in closer, smelling the mustiness of the bed. "He tried to come, Andre. But you were in solitary."

"Really?"

"Really. It might be hard for you to believe, but he really does love you. He cares about you, so much."

He plucks at the tip of each finger of one glove. "I just wish I could tell for sure."

"If he loves you? I can tell you. I'm certain of it."

"No, no. Not that." Andre puts aside his comic. "The devil thing."

"Tell me."

He inhales sharply. "I saw him at the funeral, my dad. He was in the bathroom. I walked in, and he was looking at the mirror, fixing his tie." Laughter erupts in the cells down the hall, along with the laugh track of the sitcom playing on the flat-screen television mounted to the wall. "And when I looked in the mirror, I saw it wasn't him in the reflection. It wasn't my father." Andre looks right at me then, his eyes intense. "He was still standing there, but the face in the mirror wasn't his. It was just a flash, but I saw it. I'm not lying."

"Okay."

"He looked like...a monster. His skin melted down to the bones, like wax, and it turned a stretched-out pink color. Bubble-gum pink." He grips the cotton sheet. "And his tongue turned into that double snake, and it rolled out, like a long belt or something. And it touched the mirror." His hand relaxes on the sheet now. "Then he turned to me, and it was him again. But not him. He never looked like himself again."

"You suffered a great loss, Andre, when your mom died. And you know, your mind can play tricks on you. When it's hurting enough. They call it psychosis. Reactive psychosis."

"No."

"Grief can be a very powerful thing," I counter.

"No," he repeats, firmly. He takes a breath then. "I'll take the medication, Dr. Goldman. Because you need strong magic to fight bad magic. And I think you're right. The pills are helping."

"Good."

"But it wasn't just me being sad. It was more than that. I don't know how, but the devil latched on to him. And he killed my mom. Took her soul."

Sitcom laughter pours out again. "How did your mom die? If you don't mind my asking."

"Heart attack." He shrugs. "That's what the coroner said, at least."

"You don't think so?"

"No. I don't think so. She was too young for that."

"All right," I say, reminding myself to talk to Dr. Koneru, the pathologist, about Charmayne Green. But the conversation would likely be fruitless. Heart attack is common, more common than the devil latching on to a person's soul. But Andre clearly isn't ready to have this delusion challenged right now. "See you next week, okay? And keep taking the medication."

"Yeah," he says.

As I stand up, he calls me. "Hey, Doc."

"Yes?" I turn back to him, as does the guard.

"If I don't see you," he says, opening his magazine again, "merry Christmas."

I have five whole minutes to kill in my little box of a clinic room before the next patient.

So I decide to scope out more information on Charmayne Green. First stop, of course, is Facebook. Her page comes up, essentially a memorial at this point. Pictures of her with her family, a smiling Abraham Green and a beaming Andre. He looks so young and innocent, vibrant. A far cry from the shell of a boy I've been counseling lately. Pictures of them with a Disney castle looming in the background, at the beach in bathing suits with a sunset behind them, Andre holding up a comic book with a blissful smile in front of a Christmas tree. Then the comments.

RIP Charmayne.

See you in heaven, honey.

Jesus took you too soon.

A knock interrupts my reading, and Harry (Andre's fellow comics aficionado) lets my next patient into the room and then walks out. I am expecting to see Tyler Evans, a newly scheduled sociopath for my pointless Novaire project, but it's not. I check my schedule and see there's been an add-on. Barb Donalds, the one whose daughter died in a car crash.

As the guard leaves, she looks nervous.

"Is everything okay? Any issues with the Prozac?"

"No, no, that's just fine, thanks." She rubs her arms, as if she's caught a chill. "It might even be doing something, I think."

"Oh, good, good." She does seem less desperately sad today. No quick tears or reddened nose. No flat voice or affect. But I'm not naive enough to think a week of pills will cure all her ills. And she has come back unexpectedly. So I ask the question again. "Are you feeling suicidal at all?"

"No," she says, barks almost. "I already told you that. Definitely not. Never."

"Okay, then. So, then, what brings you in?"

Her gaze flits around the room. "There was another issue from the last visit."

"Yes, there was."

She picks at a fingernail, looking embarrassed. "Look, I'm sorry. I didn't really want to get involved. But this woman seems to have pull. And I'm afraid she might make trouble for you—"

"Tell Sofia I'll get in touch with her. She doesn't have to go through you anymore. I'll let her know when I'm ready."

Barb nods, looking relieved. "Okay, I'll tell her."

"Good." I walk over to the door to open it fully and call to Harry, the guard.

"Thanks," she says with some chagrin, as Harry leads her back to her cell. A few minutes later, he returns with Tyler Evans, my sociopath. He would look like a clean-cut young man with a cheerful smile and a buzz cut if it weren't for the tiny swastika etched under his eye, matching the larger one that spans his chest. Harry doesn't stray far from the door this time. And I definitely have my eye on the big red button. Just in case I can't talk Tyler Evans out of hating Jews and anyone else who doesn't share his ghost-white skin. "Don't know what I'm here for," he says. "I ain't got no business with you." Not an auspicious start.

"Did Dr. Novaire speak with you?" I ask, hating the quiver in my voice.

The name brings a light of recognition to his eyes. "Oh yeah, German dude. My brother." He reflexively makes a heil-Hitler sign, which might be comical were it not so chilling. "Said he got a project for me." He looks me up and down. "Didn't say there'd be a Gold-Jew involved, though."

"No, I'm sure he left that part out."

"So what's up?" He leans back, looking as if he would put his legs up on my desk if he could. If they weren't shackled, that is. "Am I getting time off for this?"

"That's doubtful," I admit, though I'm sure it would help my results if I told him he was. "Here's the deal. We're going to have a few visits, give you some homework on anger management and a couple other things, then carry out a scale on you."

"Sounds like bullshit," he says, pleasantly enough. "But whatever. I got plenty of time."

"So that's a yes?"

"Anything for my German brother. Let's get rolling."

I pull out some notes. "Let's start with your childhood, then. Tell me about your parents."

"FTW through and through," he says, as if it's a fight song, and makes a fist, showing off the blue tattooed "FTW" lacing through his knuckles. "Poor as shit. Never got new shoes and all that, but you don't see me crying about it like a fucking baby." He gives me a quizzical look then. "You sure you a Jew?" he asks with doubt, in case I'm pulling one over on him. "You don't look very Jewy to me."

"Yes," I say, quite tired of Novaire's project already. "I'm positive." I don't tell him that my biological parents were not Jewish. Because in my heart and upbringing I am a Jew "through and through." I just don't subscribe to Tyler's notions about bloodlines.

"Huh," he says, staring at me with open curiosity now. "I never actually met a Jew in real life before."

After seeing Tyler, I feel as if I need a shower, but I did get a history and manage to record a Hare scale. It surely won't take long to prove that CBT will not touch this guy. I barely have time to take a breath before Harry has returned with Aubrey, my next patient.

As he wanders away, she takes a seat and immediately launches into the petty misdeeds of all the girls on B wing, expounding on who is fighting with whom, who is romancing whom, who is the *absolute biggest bitch* in the whole clan, and finally I interrupt her.

"How are we doing with the cutting?"

She whips up her orange sweatshirt sleeve with a measure

of pride, revealing an aborted line. Deep, but short. "I started to, but I stopped."

"That's a good step," I encourage her. "What brought it on?"

She stares down at the gray tile. "A nightmare. About Todd."

I nod. "Do you want to go over dream rehearsal again?" Sam taught me this for my nightmares, though it didn't work for me. "You practice your nightmare, remember? But change the ending. Then you control it, and your nightmares can't control you."

"I can't do that." Aubrey twists her bracelet. "I can't go back there. I just can't."

"To the alley?" I ask. "With the needle turning into a viper?"

"No," she cuts me off. "Not that one." Her bracelet is rubbing against her skin now, leaving a fine red mark. "The room. I can't go back there." Her eyes are fixed on the floor.

"Do you want to talk about what happened in there, Aubrey?"

"No," she whispers, shaking her head. "I can't."

I give her time, but she doesn't say any more.

"Okay," I say, and her body relaxes. Her fingers leave her bracelet alone for now. "When you are ready to share, I'm here. I'm not trying to force you, Aubrey, or pry or anything. I'm just here to support you."

"No, I know that."

"Talking about it will lessen its power over you. I can help you with that."

She nods again, smiling, calmer now. I pull up her medication list and start highlighting her medication refills.

"Hey, wait a second! I got something for you." She reaches into her bra and starts scrounging around. "It's in here somewhere."

I watch her with cautious interest.

"I know it's gotta be," she says, flummoxed. "I could swear I had it…"

"It's okay," I reassure her.

"Got it." Her hand emerges in victory. Looped over her fingers is a pale-pink friendship bracelet. She hands it to me, not quite catching my eye. "Made it out of dental floss and pink lemonade dye." She clears her throat. "It's your holiday, right?"

It takes me a second. "Oh right, Chanukah, yes."

"Yeah, so. It's for you," she says, shyly. "A gift."

I hold the light, waxy snake of string in my palm with uncertainty. I'm torn. It's against the rules to accept gifts from prisoners. But she looks so young, hopeful. Like a child holding out her artwork, breathlessly waiting for her mother's approval.

"Thank you," I say. "I love it."

And I slip it over my wrist.

The sounds of sizzling fills the room, along with the heavy scent of oil.

My kitchen will smell for days, but I don't care. Scotty makes exquisite potato latkes; they're worth it. He is putting each one on a paper towel to drain the extra grease now, his lanky body all motion. The windows mirror the primary-color candles of the menorah. I dolled the place up for Chanukah. A jaunty, off-center Happy Chanukah sign spans the mantel, with piles of silver-blue presents on the floor. (Except for Arthur's bone, which is *on* the mantel, or it would be ripped to shreds by now.) Over the kitchen table a dog-eared cardboard dreidel hangs, spinning dizzily every time someone stands up and head-whacks it.

"Do you do sour cream?" Kristy asks as we set the table.

"I'm more into applesauce," I answer, reaching over and hitting my head on the dreidel.

"Either one is just calories upon calories." Kristy has a perfect body, not an ounce of fat. When I asked her about it once, she commented offhandedly, "I have a calorie account every day. When it's done, it's done." Plus Scotty says she works out obsessively. "What about you, Mike?" she asks.

"Huh?" He is stroking under Arthur's chin.

"Sour cream or applesauce?" she inquires.

"Oh, I'm happy with either one. Just as long as I'm fed." He seems a bit off tonight, distant. But that happens to him sometimes after a bad case. After some prodding yesterday, he confided about coding a teenager with a burst appendix.

We dig into the food, my plate overflowing with a chicken leg and five slathered potato latkes. "So, how are things at work?" I ask Kristy, between chews.

She answers with words I don't understand, and I nod along. Something about economies of scale and opportunity costs. "It's a gamble," she finishes, swallowing. "But I think it's a risk we can manage."

"How about you, Scotty?"

He ladles some lima beans onto his plate. Scotty is the only person I know who voluntarily eats lima beans. "Same old same old, you know."

"Did you ask them yet?" Kristy turns to him.

He flushes. "Not yet."

"Scotty is thinking about buying part ownership in the Coffee Spot," she says with pride.

"Interesting," I say. Scotty never mentioned wanting to own the Coffee Spot. We both came into some money, not a ton, but enough, when my mom died. He creates websites as a side business. I always thought his true dream was to do something more with that.

"Gotta start planning for the future, right?" She gives him a side hug, her ring catching sparkles off the dining room table light.

Scotty gives a strained smile back, and an uncomfortable silence follows, until Arthur plays the clown and steals the napkin off Kristy's lap. He dashes behind the couch. "Arthur has a thing about napkins," I explain, grabbing another for her. "I've learned to sit on mine."

Kristy tucks it into her lap. "But how does that function as a napkin, then?" she asks (which is a fair question).

"He can't help it. Napkins are just an urge he can't control."

Scotty guffaws. "Zoe's diagnosed her fucking dog with OCD."

"At least I convinced her not to medicate him," Mike says, half-joking. Well, not joking at all, because I *was* in fact considering it.

"Time to stop feeding," I announce, standing up to stretch as my belly strains my pants. Mike joins me in clearing plates. Warm vanilla scents the kitchen as Scotty starts pouring decaf all around, Coffee Spot brew, of course. I grab Kristy's hand to admire her ring again—he really did an unexpectedly fantastic job with it—and we chat about the wedding plans a bit. Then, for reasons unknown, I decide to ruin the perfectly pleasant evening.

"So I've decided to meet with Sofia," I say, out of nowhere.

A stunned silence follows my pronouncement, which Scotty finally breaks. "Why the hell would you do that?"

"Well, the thing is…" I stammer, "my attending wants me to. Dr. Novaire. For research." I don't mention Sofia's threat to talk to the *Buffalo News*. "He thinks it might be good for me. For us, I guess. For closure."

"Closure?" Scotty looks at me with indignant disbelief. "Zoe, she killed your mother." He throws up his hands. "She tried to kill *you*." This observation leads to more silence, as I don't have an answer for this, nor does anyone else at the table.

Finally Mike stands up, banging his head against the dreidel. He claps his hands together with a forced heartiness. "All righty, then. Who wants to open some presents?"

Chapter Eleven

*T*he first time I saw the room, I hated it.

Do you have a name for me? *you asked. I told you, and you grinned, like I had passed a test, and said you had a surprise for me.*

We walked out of the sanctuary of the library. Then you turned, and I followed you down a long, deserted hallway. Finally we reached a nondescript metal door. You took out a boxy key, opened it, and said, Ta-da.

I forced out a laugh. It was a musty old storage room, dank and windowless, a mound of dust in the corner. You lay down and pulled me next to you. I asked how you found this, and you said you paid off a guard. I said you were smart. And you said, Well, I am a professor, after all, and I laughed, for real this time.

We lay together. My head resting against your chest. The soapy smell of your detergent on your undershirt. The warmth of your body against my cheek. The rise and fall of your every breath.

What's her story? *you asked. I could feel your deep voice vibrating in my ear.*

Who? *I asked.*

The girl, *you said.*

So I explained what I knew. I heard she was depressed because her daughter just died. Car accident. But I didn't know much more than that.

Your eyes smiled. You think you can get her to kill herself?

I lifted my head off your chest, not expecting the question. I thought about it a moment, or pretended to, and told you that I don't think so. That she never said anything about killing herself.

You pursed your lips, those soft lips, thinking. I traced the swell of a vein on your arm, and you shifted away from me. You said you had pills I could give her, medicine you take for headaches. The pharmacist said not to take too many at once or they could stop your heart. You said you Googled it, and it was true. You could give them to her.

I paused. Yeah, but I can't make her take them.

You could mix them in something.

What? *I asked.* She'll know it's in there.

I don't know. Orange juice maybe, *you said, getting annoyed.* I'm sure you can think of something.

I'm not sure. *I was stalling. I could tell you were upset but couldn't bring myself to agree to this. We lay there for a tense moment until finally you stood up in a huff.*

Forget it, *you said, and I could feel our moment slipping away. I grabbed your arm. Because I couldn't let you leave. I just couldn't. So I said I would do it. You looked at me like you weren't sure. I promised you that I would, as soon as you got me the pills.*

Sandra Block

Then I pulled you back down to the floor with me, and you allowed yourself to be led.

I started undoing your belt, and you pushed my hand away, instead yanking down my pants, my underwear falling away with them. You gave me that wicked grin again and moved your head down to start licking me. But then I saw the moldy mop in the corner, felt the rough, dusty cement floor against my elbows, and tried to get up so I could kiss you or touch you, but you held down my thighs, and I couldn't move.

No, you said. Stay still.

I started to say something, but your fingers dug into my skin so I let you keep going. I tried to forget about the cold floor and the rust-colored water stain on the ceiling. I laced my fingers through your curly hair, your beautiful curly hair, and focused on your tongue, soft and insistent. It had been so long, and my nerve endings lit up in seconds, a thrumming that was turning into an ache. You were teasing me, keeping up the lightest touch until I was squirming, bucking against your face, and finally you gripped my thighs and drove your tongue inside me, and with an utter, exquisite relief, I could feel my body shaking as I came.

Chapter Twelve

The next morning I meet Sofia.

She is leaning back in the chair, relaxed and expansive, as if she owns the place. Unaware, perhaps, that the place owns her. Sofia looks older, her perpetually youthful Elizabeth Taylor looks wearing down. Her curves shrunken in her orange suit. The finest of crow's-feet creeping in. Her near-forty years are catching up with her in prison. Prisoners' shoes squeak down the hallway, along with the crackling cacophony of officers' two-way radios.

"So," I say, breaking the fragile silence, "we have a project going on. I assume Dr. Novaire talked to you about that."

"He did. In laborious detail."

"Good." I've decided the best way to play this is purely professional. "Then you know that we start with an initial intake, then I'll give you some homework, also known as CBT. Cognitive behavioral therapy. And then we'll—"

"Let's cut the bullshit, shall we?"

I look up from my computer, taken aback at the interruption. She blinks at me with a hint of a smile, and my professional facade starts to crumble.

"You aren't here to do a project. Though I'm happy to play along with all that rigmarole if we must. You're only here so you don't see your name in the newspaper next to mine. You're here because I played the only card I was dealt."

I shift my seat over, closer to the red button. "Well, in any case, I'm here," I say, adopting her no-nonsense tone. "So what is it that you want?"

She drums her fingers on the table. "It's really quite simple." She waits a beat, then gives me that all-knowing smile again. "I want your forgiveness."

"My forgiveness?" I stare at her in shock. "I wouldn't call that simple, Sofia."

Her fingers are galloping again. "Did Dr. Novaire tell you how I've been working on some things while I've been in here?"

"Yes," I admit. "He said you found religion, supposedly."

"True. Well, partly true. Actually, religion found me."

"Of course it did," I say with plenty of sarcasm at her ham-fisted cliché.

"And as part of my conversion," she continues, "I've been practicing self-reflection."

"Self-reflection," I echo.

"Yes. And you can mock me all you want. But I'll tell you, it's been quite enlightening."

"Oh, I'm sure it has been. Highly." I cross my arms. "And let me ask, did you find yourself...lacking perhaps? In some area?"

She pauses, crossing her arms, too. We stare at each other like children in a schoolyard tiff. "I know you don't like me."

I nod. "That's astute, Sofia. And do you have any idea why that might be?"

She looks down at the table a moment. "I can't change the past, you know. And neither can you. We can only change the future. The here and now." She looks back up at me. "And that is what I plan to do."

"Well, good for you. And I do appreciate all the self-help philosophy you've absorbed in here. But I must tell you, in this case, the past defines the future."

"But you see." She leans forward, her blue eyes sparkling and alive. "It doesn't have to."

"But it does. You killed our mother. You nearly blinded our brother. And lest we forget, you then tried to murder me a *second* time."

She looks down at her nails, which I notice have a decent French manicure despite her lack of a nail file. "Things are different now, though. I'm different."

"The way you got me here, Sofia, doesn't seem like a sea change to me."

She shrugs. "It was the only way you'd come." And I shrug, because she's right. "I'm not saying we'll be best friends. But I'm going to do what I can. You can hold on to your anger. That's your decision."

"Right. Thank you so much."

"And whether you accept it or not, as part of my religion, I need to apologize for my wrongdoings."

"Oh," I say, as it comes to me at last, "I get it. The religion thing. You need my forgiveness to move to the next step in your Jesus workbook."

"My Jesus workbook?" Sofia laughs, a low, guttural sound. "Please. Do you think I want to turn into a sanctimonious prick like Jack?"

A flash of the true Sofia shines through.

Jack, our brother who lost his eye when she stabbed him in it. Our brother who was left to fend for himself in a slew of foster homes until he found heroin, and ultimately, and fortunately, religion. Thus a sanctimonious prick.

"I gotta say, Sis. That doesn't show a hell of a lot of self-awareness right there."

Sofia straightens herself in her chair. "I'm not becoming a Christian. I have no desire to be part of a religion steeped in hypocrisy and false magic."

"What, then, your own religion? Wicca?"

"I'm converting to Judaism," she says, the eerie *Mona Lisa* smile back on her face. "So I can get closer to my sister." I am fully horrified, as she likely intended. "We can all get what we want from this, Tanya. You do your thing with Dr. Novaire, and I can make us a real family again."

"That's..." I croak, backing up in my chair. "That's insane."

"Guilty as charged," she purrs, and just then a noise overhead thankfully breaks up our conversation. We both look up at the ceiling.

Code 327. D wing. Code 327.

Sofia reads the look on my face. "What? What does that mean?"

"Nothing," I tell her. "Don't worry about it." But I am worried about it. Code 327. Suicide. Please God, don't let it be one of my patients. Please, please, don't let it be one of mine. "I have to go."

"We will meet again, though," Sofia says, not as a question.

"Sure," I say, not even thinking. A text dings out on my phone. It's from Dr. Novaire.

EMERGENCY MEETING IN 10 MINUTES. WARDEN'S OFFICE.

⟵

I shiver in the freezing room, sitting uncomfortably close to Jason on the little couch in the room. The windows are rimmed with ice. Warden Gardner is crouched on the corner of his desk, like a predator ready to pounce, and Dr. Novaire is in the chair next to him, silent as a mouse trying to avoid becoming his prey.

"I assume you've all heard the news by now," Gardner says. "Another suicide occurred this morning."

"Yes." Dr. Novaire nods. "Who was it?"

"Strangely enough, it was one of Dr. Goldman's patients again. Barbara Donalds."

My pulse rushes into my ears in waves. "No. No, that's not possible."

"Unfortunately," he returns, "it is. And it was."

"No. She said she wouldn't do that. It's a sin, she told me."
I knock my fists together. "She promised me." I steal a panicked look over at Jason, who is staring at the carpet. "What happened? How did she do it?"

The warden jets off his desk and starts pacing, his shiny black leather shoes creaking. "It appears to be an overdose of some kind. We're still checking on a tox screen."

"How do you know it was a suicide, then?" I ask. "Did she leave a note?"

"We're still looking for that, Dr. Goldman," he says, glaring at me. "But in spite of your fine-tuned diagnostic skills, apparently she told several inmates that she wanted to die."

"But…" I am speechless.

"We need a plan, Novaire," says Warden Gardner. "And we need it now."

The doctor puts his pale, waxy hands together in a prayer position. "I was thinking about a small research study—"

"Not good enough." The warden turns on his heel from his pacing, like a soldier. "That might have been good enough six months ago. But let me tell you, that ain't gonna do it right now."

"How about," Dr. Novaire starts, his pointer finger up to make a point, but then he falters.

"Three deaths. On your watch. Doesn't that bother you, Dr. Novaire? Just a little bit?"

"Yes," Dr. Novaire answers, offended. "Of course it does."

"Good. We are on the same page, then. Now I need to know what you're going to do about it. Let's start with—"

His phone interrupts him, and he pulls it to his ear, while Dr. Novaire plays with a thread on his lab coat, looking as if he would like to blend into the wall. After a brief conversation, the warden writes something on a yellow sticky pad, then puts the phone back in his pocket. "The toxicology report is back." He reads off the pad. Ami-tri-p-" he says, struggling, "ami-try-"

"Amitriptyline," I finish for him. "Or Elavil. QT prolongation, probably."

Jason nods. "Makes sense."

"Yes, well," the warden interrupts us. "That's not very helpful at this point, is it?"

"No, it isn't," I agree. But then, all of a sudden, it hits me. "I never—"

"There will be an inquiry," Gardner announces over me. "Changes will be made." He stops pacing and takes a seat in his office chair, like the captain of a ship. "Meanwhile, all of Dr. Goldman's records will be overseen."

"I do that already," Dr. Novaire says, "for both of the fellows."

"With all due respect," Warden Gardner says with no due respect, "that doesn't appear to be working very well. You will be speaking with Dr. Goldman daily, about every single case."

"We practically do that already," Dr. Novaire mutters, in weak protest.

"And if we have any more incidents," Gardner says, "there will be a change in leadership within the fellowship." Now it's Dr. Novaire's turn to glare at me. "And if it's another one of Dr. Goldman's patients, we will be talking about suspension." The warden stretches out his arms with apparent satisfaction. "Dr. Goldman, do you have anything to say to this?"

I pause a moment. "Yes, I do. I have a concern."

"A concern." His smile is unkind. "By all means, Dr. Goldman. Do tell."

"I'm wondering if someone might have manipulated her. Or tricked her into taking the pills or something."

He crosses his arms. "And do you have any evidence for this pet theory of yours?"

"Yes," I say. "She wasn't on Elavil."

"We all lose patients, Zoe," says Sam, who was kind enough to fit me in for an urgent visit after the warden meeting.

"It seems like it's becoming a habit, though."

His smile is sad. "We can't help everyone. We're only human."

"But it seems like it's only *my* patients. All of Jason's patients are doing just swimmingly," I grumble. "I know it's not a competition, but..."

"It hurts to lose someone. We've all been through it. You feel bad for the patient and their family. You feel guilty."

"Like a failure."

"Yes," he agrees. "Like a failure. Doctors are perfectionists, but we can't be perfect. And this is not grounds for dismissal." He removes his glasses, the red plastic of the temples glossy and fresh. The switch from tortoiseshell to red was striking, but it works somehow. "You'll get through this. The warden has a big bark, but you can't fire someone for losing a patient. Not like this."

"Patients," I correct. "Plural."

He clasps his hands in front of him. "It's easy to remember the bad cases. Those are always the ones that imprint on our minds and stay with us. But too often we forget the good cases, the people we've helped."

"Candy," I say, referring to my case from last year.

"And Janita," he says, referring to her sister.

"The weird thing is," I say, twisting the buttons of his water toy, which sends the oil blobs down like marching soldiers, "they found Elavil in her system."

"Hmm. Not a great choice for suicidal patients," he says carefully.

"Yes, I know that. I always avoid tricyclics in those patients. But that's the thing, I wasn't writing her for it."

He taps his fake Montblanc on his notebook. "Another doctor, maybe? The neurologists use it for headaches."

I shake my head. "Not on her med list anywhere."

His expression turns thoughtful. "How did the warden explain that?"

"He didn't. He blew it off." The wind picks up outside the office, whistling in the window casing. "Obviously she got it from somewhere. Another inmate, I assume."

Sam pauses, then changes the subject. "How is everything else going?" he asks. "Impulse control?"

"Fine." (I didn't try to strangle the warden, for instance.)

"Doing anything for the holidays?"

"Mike's family is coming to town." I yawn. "I'm a little nervous, but it should be okay." I turn the toy upside down to start with an empty canvas. "I met with Sofia today."

He looks up from his desk, his usual poker face revealing surprise.

"Just briefly, for something Dr. Novaire wants me to do. Then I found out about the suicide, so…" The meeting was only a few hours ago but feels like years ago right now.

"How did that go?"

But I don't answer the question. Instead I ask another. "Do you think a sociopath can change?"

His sofa chair creaks as he shifts in it. "Change? As in?"

"Sofia, for instance. Dr. Novaire is having me do this pilot on CBT for sociopathy."

Sam raises a skeptical eyebrow.

"Right. Probably dead on arrival, but…Novaire seems to think we can get a positive study out of it. Which begs the question. Do you think it's possible? That someone with sociopathy can change? That they can get better?"

He purses his lips in thought. "I don't know. I think they can learn to fit in with society, play by the rules, so to speak. But can they actually learn to feel empathy over narcissism? I have my doubts." He leans in toward me. "Why? Do you think Sofia has changed?"

I tinker with the knobs. "She's trying to tell me that she has. Said she wants me to forgive her."

He taps his pen again. "That's a tall order."

"You can say that again." I put the toy down. "And to

make matters worse, she's claiming she wants to convert to Judaism."

"Judaism?" he asks with another skeptical eyebrow raise. "And what are your thoughts on that one?"

"My thoughts?" I snicker. "That it's a master manipulation move. And while I'm all for broadening religion, I'd say she's one person we really don't need in our tribe."

And uncharacteristically, Sam renders his opinion, too. "I couldn't agree more."

I'm lying on the couch, my head in Mike's lap after my third glass of wine. "Maybe I *am* just a terrible psychiatrist."

"You're not a terrible psychiatrist," Mike reassures me. "It's not your fault she got a hold of Elavil. Maybe she was trying to get high or something."

"Maybe." I rub my socked foot against Arthur, who is sitting on my feet. "She said she wouldn't kill herself, though. She promised me. She got angry when I brought it up, even."

"Sometimes these things are spontaneous. You can't control everything." He rubs my arm in consolation. "I don't know what the warden's talking about. People die in prison all the time." He shakes his head. "Gardner's an idiot. You just ran into a string of bad luck."

Grabbing another tissue, I wipe my raw nose. "Maybe."

"Definitely. And Dr. Nowhere just needs to retire already."

I adjust my head on Mike's thigh, feeling a crick in my neck. "I won't argue that one with you."

"You're a wonderful psychiatrist." Mike pushes a stray hair off my forehead. "Don't worry. They're not going to suspend you. This is on Novaire."

I raise my head to finish off my generous glass of Chardonnay (my fourth, but who's counting). As I lay my head back down, the room takes a brief, pleasant spin, as the wine is finally doing the trick. My limbs are feeling mellow and soft, my brain wiped clean.

"You want me to go get the pizza now?" he asks.

I don't answer, as I happily realize at that moment that my face is conveniently planted against Mike's anatomically perfect thigh. I stroke the inside of his leg, feeling him squirm.

"Um, Zoe, what are we doing here?" To make it more obvious, I start kissing his thigh, biting at the fabric just a bit. "Ah, okay." His voice comes out a bit choked. "See now, I thought I was comforting you."

"You were. But I was getting bored of the comforting."

"Bored of the comforting," he repeats.

Without finesse I undo the scrub tie with my teeth. Then I reach underneath his scrubs for the other perfect part of his anatomy. "I have an idea," I say.

His eyes are closed. "What's that?" he murmurs, his warm hand reaching under my sweater.

"Let's skip the pizza," I whisper.

Chapter Thirteen

In the parking lot, I see Newsboy and try not to catch his eye. My head is still pounding from all the wine last night, and I couldn't find any Motrin in my purse. All I want to do is get into work to score some Tylenol off Jason. But unfortunately, the reporter sees me.

"Oh, hey, Zoe!" He says this with forced surprise, which makes me think he was waiting there for me. He lifts a wait-a-minute finger to his cameraman, who is getting out of the car.

"Oh, hi, New—" I almost call him Newsboy.

"Logan," he reminds me. "You have my card, I think."

"Yes, I do. Sorry about that. I'm in kind of a rush, so..."

"Oh, no worries. I'm on my way in, too."

"Okay," I say, because I can't exactly refuse. We walk into the bitter wind, the top of my head stinging because I keep forgetting to buy a hat to replace the one that Arthur snacked on. The wind isn't helping my headache either. As I dig my mittens out of my pockets, snow whirls up in front of us like an apparition.

"Freezing out, huh?"

"Yup." And we walk on, hard snow crunching at our feet. I suspect he does not want to talk about the weather, but I'm also not about to offer an easy opening. The cameraman trails a few feet behind us, like Logan's personal butler.

"Did you think any more about what I said?" His breath comes out in puffs. "About the interview?" He pushes his hair back, revealing the tip of his ear, already turning pink with cold. I'm sure his silver earring is especially frigid right now.

"I'm sorry. I've been really busy, Logan."

"Sure, yeah. It's just that...I've been hearing some rumors."

"Is that so?" I walk faster.

"Yeah, I have," he goes on. "That the warden isn't happy."

"I've never known the man to be especially happy."

He allows a smile. "More unhappy than usual, I should say, then. Another suicide, I heard."

"Off the record, Logan, incarceration isn't exactly the safest lifestyle choice."

"Yeah, I get that." He nods. "But just so you know, your name came up, in some of these rumors."

I don't answer, climbing the stairs to the prison and feeling as if I'm reaching home base.

"Listen, I don't want to be rude here. But the fact is, the *News* wants this story, the warden wants this story. It's going to happen, whether you like it or not. But if you talk to me, then you get to tell your side of things." He combines an impish grin with an eyebrow raise, a look that probably gets him laid a fair amount. He pushes the door open for me. "What do you think?"

"What do I think?" I repeat, rubbing my mittened hands together. For a second I consider telling him about everything. About the Elavil that I didn't write for Barbara Donalds. About the fact that the warden seems to have it out for me. About Dr. Nowhere, who is barely equipped to treat a cold at this point. Maybe Newsboy could be my ally, instead of my enemy. I consider it, but decide not to. As my mom chided me over and over throughout my childhood, *Zoe, you don't have to say every single thing that's in your head.*

"I think," I say, as he scrounges in his satchel for a notebook, "that you shouldn't believe everything you hear."

"Please tell me you have some Motrin."

"You look like crap," Jason says. "And no, I don't have any Motrin. I'm not a pharmacy, you know." He inches away from me. "And don't get me sick."

"I'm not sick. Just hungover."

He scrolls down on his computer. "Hope it was worth it."

"It was," I say, but don't elaborate further. "My clinic is really light today," I say with surprise. "Just Aubrey and one other. Hey, I'm not complaining, but what's up with that?" Jason shifts in his chair, staying suspiciously quiet. He busies himself with his ever-ready hand sanitizer from his pocket. "Is something going on?" I ask him.

He clears his throat. "They're sort of giving me most of the patients right now."

"Oh." I turn back to the computer screen so he can't see my face. "But I still have Andre, right?" I am trying not to sound as crushed as I feel.

"Yeah. But he's on the med floor right now."

"Why?"

"Tried to pull off his thumbnail in shop class."

"Seriously?" I rub my temples. "I don't get it. He was doing better on his Abilify increase."

Jason shrugs. "Made a damn mess of himself, but I don't think he got the nail off." The thought makes my stomach quiver. "And he was saying some freaky shit. About some furry thing with—"

"A hundred ribs going up and down," I say.

"Sounds about right."

I start looking through his chart for the incident note. "Oh, guess who was stalking me this morning?"

"Newsboy," Jason answers. "Don't feel so flattered. He's stalking me, too. *And* he is definitely playing for my team. My friend saw him at Fugazi."

"What's Fugazi?"

"Gay bar." He rips open a snack bag of pretzels from his pocket. He probably has a hat rack and umbrella in there like Mary Poppins. But no damn Motrin. Catching me eying them, he hands me a pretzel. "You never heard of Fugazi? You must not get out much."

"No, you're right. I don't go to gay bars all that often."

"Point taken." He stands up with a stretch, then goes off to see his patient.

Out of the corner of my eye, I see Dr. Novaire's slightly stooped form loping my way. I'm surprised to see him show up in clinic, and smile at him in greeting.

"Ready to go through your patients?" he asks with false cheer.

"Yeah. Sure. Don't have too many, but—"

"Oh, before we get into that. I heard you saw Sofia yesterday," he says, a sunny lilt in his voice. "How did that go?"

"Fine," I say. He waits for further explanation, but I don't know what to say.

"Well, that's good. She thought it went very well, too, and wanted to see you again."

"Uh-huh." I roll my pen on the table.

"So I told her you would come to meet her, later today."

I nod as my pen falls off the table. "See, today's pretty busy, though—"

"You just said you didn't have that many patients."

I open my mouth to speak, but have nothing to say. Because he's absolutely right.

"Okay, then," he says. "Who shall we start with?"

On my way to the women's clinic, I stop by Medical to see Andre.

He looks ashen, lying on the cot with one gloved hand handcuffed to the rail and the other hand, wrapped as if it were in a white gauze boxing glove, resting on his lap. The other red glove is on a shelf on the metal table, stored in a baggie for safekeeping. He stirs as I approach the foot of his bed. "Oh, hi..." he says with an embarrassed yawn.

"How are you doing?"

"Okay." He glances down at his bandaged hand. "I know I shouldn't have done it. But I could feel him burrowing in. The seeds were taking hold."

Going to the head of the bed, I put my hand on his shoulder. "Andre, have you been taking your medication still?"

He doesn't answer right away. "It makes me groggy. I hate feeling that way."

"We can try something else eventually, but let's see if this will work first. Just give it a chance, okay?"

He nods, moving in the bed and clinking his handcuff against the railing. After a few more minutes of stunted questions and answers, it is clear he's not in a talkative mood, so I write a quick note before continuing to the clinic.

After a few minutes, Aubrey is let in. She settles herself in the chair and flashes her red fingernails at me. "What do you think?"

"Nice." But the shade of red on top of the fluorescent light isn't helping my headache.

"Portia did it for me. For Christmas." As she displays them, I can't help but notice three new slash marks along her wrists. When I point to them, she pulls her hand back.

"Solitary, Aubrey," I remind her. "You won't be given a choice next time."

She bites the inside of her lip, then looks up at me, her green eyes oddly luminescent. Her fingers push on the new cutting marks. "Maybe it's time to talk about the nightmare."

I nod. "I'm ready when you are, Aubrey."

She pushes on her cuts again. "I should have listened to my family about him."

"About Todd?"

"Yes. They hated him. And they were right, it turns out." She rubs her hands together. "It's about what happened that night. The nightmare."

"Yes."

"In the room." She takes a deep breath, her chest rising. "Todd said we needed more money. We were staying in a motel. Some fleabag place. Dirty carpet, smelled like piss, you know the kind of place."

"Sure." I didn't but could easily imagine.

"We couldn't be picky, you know. Anywhere cheap, that would let us in. That's where we'd end up." She squeezes her hands together. "He said he was going to score. And I should wait for him. So I did." She appears to be trying to steady her breathing. "He was gone for a while. I was still pretty high, but I could feel it wearing off, you know, by the time he came back." I nod for her to keep going, and she licks her lips. "But when he came back, he..." She pushes on her slash marks again, hard. "He..." She takes another deep breath and lets it go. "I can't do this right now. I'm sorry, Dr. Goldman. I just can't."

Chapter Fourteen

Later that day I go to see Sofia as per Dr. Novaire's "suggestion."

She sits in the clinic room, idly looking out the window. "I love watching the birds."

"Okay, I'll bite," I say, grumpily. "Why do you love watching the birds?"

"Because they remind me there's still a world out there," she says, talking to the window, "where people are free." As if on cue, the black birds scatter across the sky like an ink blot.

"What about your last gig, the mental hospital? Weren't there birds there, too?"

She turns away from the window. "There was a chance of freedom there, at least. There was some hope."

"Yeah, well..." I cross my arms. "Maybe you should remember that next time you stab someone with a nail file."

Sofia laughs, which is unexpected. "You're funny, Tanya."

"Dr. Goldman," I practically growl. "And I have exactly

ten minutes." I tap my watch. "Then I'm done. I have actual patients to help."

Sofia snorts. "I hear that's going real well."

I stand up. "Okay, I'm done. Have a fun twenty years, Sofia. I'll make sure to be there at your parole hearing."

"Wait," she says. "I'm sorry. Look, I don't...I'm trying, okay?" She looks almost guilty. "It's a process." As she puts her head in her hands, I suddenly see her as she is—a pathetic middle-aged woman in orange clothes and leg chains. "I've just been angry with you for so long."

"Angry with *me*?" I put my hand on the back of the chair but don't sit back down. "That's rich."

"I'm not saying it's right," she amends. "In fact, I'm saying it's wrong. But I can't help it...It takes time. The rabbi talked about old patterns and trying to reconfigure our—"

"Sofia," I groan, "you are so full of shit."

"Wait a second. Hear me out." She moves closer to the table, clanking her chains. "You have your own issues with self-control, right?"

I shake my head. "I'd hardly say they're in the same plane, Sofia. The same solar system."

"Okay, but"—she clasps her hands so tight that the web of lines on her knuckles stands out—"I'm just trying to explain." She pauses, then clears her throat, as if she's rehearsed this. "All my life, I listened to a voice. The wrong voice. A bad voice. It told me to do things, and I did them. Bad things."

"Uh-huh."

"Things that kept getting me in trouble. Fucking patients. Fucking doctors." She looks at me to gauge my response.

"Trying to kill doctors," I add.

"I'm trying to listen to the good voice now," she says, ignoring my jab. "Not the bad one. I'm training myself to do that. And it isn't easy." The noise of a prisoner shouting and arguing emerges outside in the hall, and a guard rebuking him then passing by us.

Finally I do sit down. "Why should I even trust you for a minute, Sofia? Why on earth would I do that?"

"You shouldn't. And you don't, I know. But I'm going to change that." She pulls her chair closer to me, her deep-blue eyes drawing me in. "Somehow I will show you that this isn't just another game. This is me, the real me."

"New and improved, huh? The perfect Sofia?"

She shakes her head. "I never said I was perfect. I'm still a bitch, for instance," she says with a wry little smile. "But I am different. And all I'm saying is, we don't have to be mortal enemies."

We sit a moment, appraising each other. I can feel myself fighting against her magnetic pull. Sofia is like this. You have to watch yourself or you end up in her net. This is what Sam warned me about.

I back my chair up, rubbing my temples. My headache is roaring now, and I'm exhausted. "Look, I'm not feeling great, Sofia. Why don't I come back later, another time?"

Her lips turn down in disappointment. I don't know if she's truly trying to change or not. Probably not. But in either case, I figure I can drag this out a bit longer, until Newsboy is done with his article, at least. "I promise," I say. "When I have more time."

"More time." She glances around at the mottled concrete walls of the clinic room. "I sure have plenty of that."

✎

With one hand on the steering wheel, I pop some Motrin in my mouth and chug it down with some fizzy, lukewarm pop from the convenience store. Sofia's mind games have me whirling, and I decide to speak to the only person who really understands my relationship with her, my biological brother, Jack. He lives in Chicago, so I never see him and rarely call, but I figure it's worth a shot.

"She's playing you, Zoe," Jack says, his voice a warning. "I don't understand why you're even talking to her."

"I know I shouldn't, but..." Making a sharp turn, I put down the pop, letting the sentence hang. I don't tell him about the news article, which would certainly bias him, as well it should. "I just wanted to get your opinion. It's probably all an act, I know. But there's something about what she says..."

His laugh booms over the car speaker. "That she found God? Are you honestly falling for this? It's just her latest excuse, Zoe. That's all it is. It's never Sofia's fault. Remember, she claimed she was high on PCP and that's why she did it? Then it was our father abusing her?"

"Yes." I was never sure whether she was lying about that one or not, though.

"Now it's just a mean voice in her head, I guess."

"Yes, I'm sure you're right. But I can't help feeling like..." A horn honks at me, and I proceed through the just-green light. "There was a kernel of truth in there."

"Truth?" he says with scorn. "Sofia is a liar, through and through. You don't ask the devil how to get to heaven, and you don't ask a liar for the truth."

"You're right." I pull into the Galleria mall parking lot. "It's just, I feel like ever since I met her, I've spent so much time hating her that I've never actually gotten to know her."

"I know her well enough," he mutters. "And you took care of her for months last time, right?"

"True. But that's just a little window of time. And I was her doctor, so that's different."

I hear him breathing deeply through the speaker. "Zoe, I don't know how to say this, but I'm just going to say it." There is a long pause as I put the car in park. "You were able to get out, right?"

"I guess."

"No, not *I guess*. You got out. You got adopted, sent to good schools, and ended up with a good job in a good place. You have a different perspective on all this. I was eight when this happened. That's young, but not that young." His breathing sounds almost labored. "I remember every goddamned thing. And I'm sorry, I don't need a minute to think about it. I don't need to consider her side of things. You know just as well as I do. She's a manipulative demon. I'm not afraid to say it. A demon. And I won't believe that she's found God now, or any other piece of crap that comes out of her mouth."

"Okay," I say, in a calming tone, turning off the Bluetooth and grabbing the phone. "I get it, Jack."

His breathing has steadied. "Now, I'm sorry. I didn't mean to get angry with you. You're not the one at fault here."

"No offense taken, really," I assure him, walking in the brisk, cold night. The moon reflects off a row of cars. My head is starting to clear, as if the Motrin is finally taking effect. "I have to get going." I'm meeting Mike, Scotty, and Kristy for a little holiday shopping. "I'm sorry. I really didn't mean to upset you."

"You didn't, Zoe. Just be careful, okay? Sofia is tricky, always has been. She's not a normal human. She's not in God's image, at all. And I appreciate you trying to dig deeper into that. I applaud you for it, even. But you don't have to. I'm telling you right here and now. She's the devil. And you don't need the devil on your side."

Mike rubs the purple rings under his eyes and lets out another yawn. As the low man on the totem pole, he's been covering for everyone else's vacation the last few weeks. "Do you think my mom would like this?" He picks up a prewrapped, glitzy gift bag filled with hot pink tissue paper.

"Yeah, she'd love it." I grab an almond-colored lotion and plunk it in the basket. "Coconut for Jason, and matching hand sanitizer."

Mike picks up the tester lotion and gives it a sniff. "Not bad."

"You want some?"

"Nah, I'd smell like a beach."

"Ooh," Kristy says. "Babe, what do you think of this for my mom?" She holds up the same glitzy hot pink package, calling out to Scotty across the aisle.

"Looks good, babe," he calls back, picking up shaving supplies in the teeny, black-signified men's section, a safe harbor in this touchy-feely-smelly women's space.

"Okay, babe," Kristy calls back, putting it in her basket. I kinda want to vomit when they call each other babe. Scotty wanders over toward us. "Here, can you check out?" Kristy asks, thrusting the basket at him. "I have to hit the Apple Store."

"Sure." He takes the toppling basket from her, gazing longingly across the hall at the Apple Store himself, as Kristy strides off. Then he shuffles back to the men's section.

Looking around at the aisles, I wish I could get Aubrey a little something but know I can't. And anything here would be lost on Andre, if he even wanted anything other than a comic book. Examining some rose-scented bath oil, I feel as if I'm forgetting someone and suddenly realize who it is, my eyes growing moist.

My mom. Not my birth mom, but my real mom. Sarah Goldman, up in heaven with all her faculties now, perhaps taking a lovely rose oil bath this very moment. I wonder if Scotty is thinking about her, too.

"Do we have everyone covered, then?" Mike asks, through another yawn.

"I think so," I say, quickly swallowing back tears. I throw

a freesia lotion into the basket. "Are you getting XO Serena anything?" I ask him, joking.

"You think I should?"

It is not the answer I expected. I stare at him a second. "Why, did she get you something?" He looks at the floor, but doesn't answer. "Wait a second, what did she get you?"

He pauses, looking sheepish. "A pen."

"A pen?" I repeat, stupidly. "Like a Bic pen?"

"No, not like a Bic pen, Zoe," he says, a bit irked. "Who buys someone a Bic pen for Christmas?"

"I don't know. I don't celebrate it, obviously."

"She bought me a nice pen, okay? A Parker, I think."

"Oh well. La-di-da. A Parker pen."

"I'm keeping it at work, Zoe. I knew you'd get upset. That's why I didn't tell you."

We don't say anything for a moment. Maybe it's the sleep deprivation or my hangover or both, because we never fight. I hate fighting with Mike. Even if some girl did give him the biggest phallic symbol there is. "Here," I say with a sigh, "give her some lavender lotion. A little one. It says friends, but just friends."

We wander over to a painfully long line, which wraps around a tower of hand sanitizers, and Scotty heads over to join us. Mike gives me an apologetic smile. "You really think lavender lotion says all that?"

"It's better than a pen," I mutter.

Chapter Fifteen

T he first time we made love was after I killed Barbara Donalds.

Tell me every detail, you said, your forest-green eyes glowing.

So I told you about it. It was too easy, in the end.

You got me the pills, and I ground them up with a spoon. Then, during breakfast, I brought her over some hot chocolate. It was as simple as that. I made it seem like a gift. That I knew she was having a hard time and just wanted to do a little something to help. Barb Donalds was a nice lady, trusting.

She was ever so grateful while I was murdering her.

I could tell she was getting sleepy by the end of breakfast. She was starting to slur her words, so I made sure she got over to her cell. She said she wasn't feeling great and was going to take a nap before her grief counseling group. I put the pill bottle under the sheets, with the paper name torn off.

The 327 was called an hour later.

You were lying down on your stomach with your chin in your hands, listening to me, entranced in the story. And when I was done, you kissed me.

And we made love, in our beautiful, awful, musty storage room.

I don't want to ruin it by describing it in the journal. We made love, and it was everything I thought it would be. Afterward, I cried. I know it's a cliché, but I did. You wiped off my tears, and we lay there on the floor for a while, and we talked.

When I think back on it now, it's pathetic. That's the only time we ever really talked.

How did you end up in this place? you asked me.

No one told you?

I want to hear it from you, you said.

So I told you. I let it out, all the stuff I've been holding back in this place. Like a flood, an uncontrollable torrent, the words rushed out. I told you what I did. I told you about my mother's death, what I did to her. I told you about my sister, how she can barely stand me now. I told you how much I hate it here, every single second except when I'm with you. I told you that you are the only one who makes this place just barely livable.

You told me about how your brother died. You told me you still cry when you think about him. That you miss him. You said you never told anyone about it before. But you could tell me because you trust me. That being with me was like being at home.

I told you that you are my home. And we started kissing again, for the hundredth time. My lips were swollen from all our kissing.

Then, in the middle of a kiss, you said you needed another name. I was disappointed at breaking off the moment, but I understood. I said I'd try, and you praised me then, saying how well

I'd done so far. I couldn't help the smile growing on my face. You said if I kept helping you, you'd keep helping me. And I shushed you because I didn't want to talk about that stuff. I didn't want to think about that stuff. It made me feel too bad. I just wanted to be with you.

You said you had another idea, another way to get to her. You paused, waiting for me to ask you about it, eager to tell me. But I didn't ask. Because I was tired of talking about her. And truthfully, I didn't want to know.

Then you were quiet for a bit, thinking about your new plan, I guess, and finally you climbed on top of me again, for something to do maybe. And this time you plunged inside me, not tenderly, but hard, and I was sore, but I didn't care. Because I loved you.

I still think about that moment, sometimes. Lying there on the cold floor, taking every thrust, gripping the taut sinew of muscle on your arms while you rocked me as hard as you could. You wanted to hurt me, I realize now, because that turns you on, hurting people. But I didn't care about that right then. If I'm honest, I still don't.

Loving you is a fate, not a choice.

Chapter Sixteen

My hangover has somehow morphed into a sort of flu.

And there's no time for that because we have about a million things to do to get ready for the invasion of Mike's family. He has already put my Chanukah decorations to shame. First, we have a sweet-smelling Scotch Pine—and we went over the merits of every species at the tree farm—towering in the corner, complete with silver and bronze globe ornaments, which sent me into a mild OCD fit of making sure they were exactly evenly distributed on the tree. Holly is hung down the railing, a homey Santa is on the front porch getting snow on his bag, and a wreath is on the front door. I feel a bit like a stranger in my own house, but Mike looks so cheerful and chipper that it would have been churlish to object.

I have swept dog hair from the most improbable places imaginable, Windexed the windows though the sharp smell is nauseating, and moved my tower of forensic psychiatry books to our room, and now we are awaiting our company.

Mike has debriefed me on his whole family. Jeff is his older brother, an accountant, and his oldest brother is Anthony (not Tony) who is also an accountant. Erica is Jeff's wife, and they have one child, Nathan, who is three years old and utterly worshipped by Mike's mom, whose name is Margaret, but everyone calls her Peggy, which is apparently commonplace among Catholics.

We are waiting for them to arrive now, Mike nervously tidying the kitchen still. Arthur is lying down, exhausted from all the activity, and I have the strong urge to lie down on the floor right beside him.

"Did you hear from Scotty?" he asks.

"No, why?"

"No reason. I just wondered how it went with Kristy's mom."

"Oh yeah." Mike is caring enough to remember the fact that he was meeting Kristy's family. I had forgotten all about it.

Mike finally sits down on the couch beside me with a happy sigh. "You okay?"

"I'll be fine. Just coming down with something."

He assesses me clinically. "Did you get your flu shot?"

I lean down to pet Arthur, stalling. "I keep meaning to."

He groans. "Zoe, I tell you every year—"

I am saved by the doorbell as the first wave of family arrives, climbing out of a cab, though Mike offered to pick them up more than once. I open the door to a shorter, heavier, slightly older version of Mike. "Hello!" Jeff sings out, merrily. Mike reaches over for a male hug, and Erica trails behind him carting a red-cheeked, cranky-looking Nathan. Mike's mom (Margaret/Peggy) runs over for a hug as well, looking up at me in poorly hidden surprise. My actual height often surprises people upon the first meeting. It's one thing to say you're over six feet and another thing to actually inhabit that space.

"Come on in," Mike says.

Presents are placed around the tree, Nathan is given a snack, small talk is had, and three hours later the whole family is in the warm kitchen, which smells of turkey and thyme. I wander around feeling like an extra thumb, trying to be helpful and failing. Finally we sit around our dining room table though I'm hardly even hungry. I grab for a pair of tongs as everyone closes their eyes and crosses themselves (including Mike), and Nathan stares at me with open disdain, catching me out as the least adult, and certainly the least Catholic, at the table.

"So," Peggy says, "I hear you work with criminals." She makes it sound salacious.

"That's true," I say, scooping out some cheesy potatoes, though my stomach is now churning.

"That must be fascinating." Her brown eyes light up. Mike definitely has her eyes.

"It is," I say agreeably, wondering how much longer I'll be able to do it before the warden kicks me out. "And what do you do?" I ask, turning to Erica.

She is cutting turkey on Nathan's plate. "Oh, I stay at home."

"Great," I answer.

The conversation dies then to the sound of cutlery. "I was doing some interior designing," she says, as if apologizing for her current stay-at-home status, though it's not necessary.

"Yeah," Jeff says, supportively, "she was great."

"And I might get back to it when Nate's in kindergarten."

"No," Nathan says, simply.

"No?" Erica laughs.

"I want Mommy home."

"Well, I'm sure you do, honey, but Mommy will have to do some work eventually." She smiles at us all, a you-know-how-it-is-with-kids smile.

"No." A fork is slammed. "Mommies stay home." Everyone stares at Nathan, who's clearly been watching a lot of *Mad Men* lately.

"Not all mommies," she answers, singsong.

"Mommy stays home!" His voice rises to an eardrum-bursting level, his eyes glistening with tears.

"I'm sure you guys can work that out over the next year," I say pleasantly, as if the three-year-old understands logic.

"Mommy stays home!"

"Here," Erica says, flushed. "Have some turkey, honey."

"Yeah, champ," Jeff says, looking uncomfortable as well. "Eat up. You're probably hungry."

"Not hungry! Not hungry!" Turkey is flung.

"He gets meltdowns sometimes," Erica explains. "This is a lot for him. He's not good with transitions."

He is tilting out of his booster. "Mommy stays home!"

"All right, champ," Jeffrey says, reaching over to him. "Someone's getting a time-out."

"Noooooooo!" he sobs at the injustice of it all as Jeffrey whisks him into the "naughty corner," which is the bottom step of our stairs, where he sits, quite astonishingly. Arthur appears to feel sorry for the similar-sized creature and wanders over to lick his face, while Jeffrey resumes his spot at the table, spooning some gravy.

"Tough age," Peggy says.

"Yup," Erica answers, "some prolonged terrible twos. Are you two thinking about kids?"

"Kids?" I ask with an audible gulp. "We don't know about that yet." Though I must say, Nathan isn't a strong advertisement for the notion. Erica smiles, passing me the gravy boat. A meaty smell wafts up from the lumpy, gelatinous mass, making my stomach lurch. Suddenly I don't feel very well. My mind is fluttering with images of Sofia's smile, Andre's bandaged hand, slice marks on Aubrey's wrist, and furry demons with a hundred ribs, moving up and down. I wobble in the chair as if I might fall off it.

Mike is on his feet. "Zoe, are you okay?"

"Um, yeah. I'm fine." But I'm not, and I vomit all over the dining room table.

All night I'm in and out of sleep.

After dinner, I was sent straight to bed to get over my flu thing. I'm not feverish, but I do feel as if I've been hit by a truck. Mike assured me he would clean up and that nobody hated me for ruining dinner. Since then I've been in bed, suspended in a half-dreaming, half-awake state, a fractured, sickly sleep. I am dreaming of Arthur stealing ornaments off the Scotch Pine (which seems altogether too realistic to bother dreaming about) when the unmistakable sound of my text tone awakens me. The clock says two a.m., though it feels as if I've been asleep all night already. I figure it's either Buffalo Psychiatric Center (which we kindly cover on the weekends) or the prison, so I reach over to take a look through one eye.

Razors, rope, gas or pills?

I stare at the message in dull confusion as my brain wakes up. The number is unfamiliar, a long-distance number. I think you are texting the wrong person, I text back.

No. It's a riddle for you.

I sit up straight in bed now, reading it again. Who is this?

Razor, rope, gas or pills. Can you guess?

The text looms on the screen while I decide what to do. My fingers tremble as I type. I'm not playing games. Stop texting me or I will call the police.

I'm not playing games either. But if you can't solve it, I'll give you the answer.

There is a pause then, and I find myself gripping the phone, waiting.

Razors, rope, gas or pills?

How many patients will you kill?

⤣

120

"What? What? Where did it go?" Mike yelps in panicked confusion as I shake him awake.

"Honey, wake up. Please." I am close to tears. "I need to show you something."

"Sorry," he mumbles, sleepily. "I was just dreaming..." Then he sees my face and sits up at once, fully awake. "What's wrong?" He moves toward me, and Arthur shifts in the bed. "What happened?"

I show him my screen, and he reaches over to take the phone. "Jesus."

"Do you think it's a prisoner?" I hear the desperation in my own voice.

"I don't know. It's weird, though. Did you try to call it?"

"Not yet. I didn't know what to do."

"Here, let me try." So he does, putting the speaker on. We both sit there breathlessly, like kids crank calling. No one answers. And there's no voice mail. "Is it a New York City number?"

"I don't know. I didn't recognize it." I take the phone back. "It seems more than coincidental, though, right? One by hanging, one by pills." I think further. "Though the heroin doesn't really fit in for that."

"And no one slit their wrists," he adds. We both sit there, staring at the menacing phone as Arthur starts snoring. "You think Sofia is behind this?" he asks.

I feel a chill tunnel through me, though it may be the flu. "The thought had struck."

He lets out an angry sigh. "You have to call the warden."

I shake my head in dejection. "He won't listen to me."

"Then I'll call him."

"No. Don't. That'll just make things worse."

He leans an elbow on one of his pillows. "Then what should we do?"

"There is someone." I think of the one person who could help me. The man who helped me find out Jane Doe's identity. The man who sent Sofia to prison. The burly, kind-hearted man who reminds me of my father, who died when I was in high school. "Detective Adams," I say. And I start looking up his number.

"Zoe?"

"What?"

"It's three o'clock in the morning."

So I wait until six o'clock to call him.

Mike is downstairs making coffee and chatting with his mom, and I hear the tip-tapping of Arthur, who has formed a deep and abiding love for Nathan and his mislaid Cheerios.

"A riddle?" The detective's voice is deep and hoarse, as I have clearly just awoken him. "I don't get it."

"It's about my patients, I think."

"What about your patients?"

I explain about the rash of "bad luck" among my inmate patients and how Warden Gardner is placing the blame squarely on me. I hear pages flipping in his notebook over the phone. "And you said you tried to call the number back?"

"Yes, but no one answered. And there wasn't any voice mail either."

His pen is scratching paper. "You've got my e-mail still?"

I lift the phone from my cheek to double-check. "Yes."

"Good. Send me a screenshot. I'll try to run the number, but we may need your phone."

The suggestion of handing over my primary addiction sends me into a minor panic attack. "Do you think that will be absolutely necessary?"

He exhales into the phone. "Yes, Zoe, it will be."

I pause. "I don't know. Maybe I'm just overreacting."

"You're not overreacting. At the very least it's harassment, quite possibly from a prisoner."

I pause, deciding whether to voice what has been budding in my head, and will surely sound like paranoid ideation. "This is going to sound crazy, but..."

"Yes?"

"Do you think the text could be from someone who's involved in this all somehow? Like, someone is out there, killing my patients?" There is long pause. "Barbara Donalds, for instance, the one who killed herself. She wasn't even on Elavil."

He yawns into the phone. "I'll talk to the warden, Zoe, but I gotta be honest. It sounds pretty unlikely."

"Yeah, but why else—"

"We'll look into it," he says, humoring me. "Send me the screenshot."

"Okay." I lay my head back on my pillow, fighting another spell of nausea. From downstairs rise up the sounds of doors opening and cheery voices, Nathan whining and racing feet. I still don't feel in tip-top shape, but I can't hide out in my room forever. "And there's one person in particular I was thinking about."

"Yeah," the detective says, "and I have a pretty good guess who that might be."

Chapter Seventeen

Walking down the hallway of the busy precinct, Detective Adams limps on one of his bowed knees. His burly frame has grown a bit burlier in the last year. "So it looks like a burner phone."

"A burner phone? What do you mean?"

"Pay as you go," he explains. "Untraceable."

"Oh." We sit down at his desk. "That doesn't sound good."

"No, you're right," he admits. "It's not very helpful."

"Can you figure out what cell tower it came from?" I ask, vaguely remembering this from a *Dateline* show.

"Doubtful. But we'll see. It'll help to be able to look at your phone."

With that unmistakable hint, I remove it from my purse. I hold it in my hand with great trepidation, like a crack addict being asked to hand over the pipe. "You said I could get it back first thing tomorrow, right?"

"Yes, Zoe. First thing," Detective Adams assures me, with minimal exasperation considering I have asked this question three times already. Scotty once told me, "You would get the shakes without that fucking phone." And he's fucking right.

"Okay." Though it pains me, I hand it to him.

"My tech team is fast, I promise," he says, placing it on his desk with care. "Any more texts, by the way?"

"No." A detective whistles down the hall to get someone's attention. "But when we find out who it is, we can charge them, right?"

Detective Adams shrugs. "We'll see. Fortunately or unfortunately, they didn't threaten you. So we might not have much of a case."

I bite my lip, not liking his answer. "It was probably just a stupid prank anyway."

"Probably. But it's worth checking out." He ushers me out of the building then, and it's a ten-minute drive over to prison.

Soon enough I'm waiting on the women's floor for a patient, feeling adrift without my phone tucked safely in my purse, when the desk phone rings.

"Zoe?"

"Hi, Jason. What's up?"

"Can you do another family visit? Abraham Green is here." His voice sounds stressed. "The warden wanted me to take all the families, but I've got a million patients left to see."

"Sure, I'll take him. Is Andre out of Medical yet?"

"Yup. His boo-boo's all better."

"Pretty bad for a boo-boo," I counter.

"Not as bad as Jimenez. Who *is* in Medical right now. And who I have to see next."

I'm thinking back at the name. "Oh, the penis guy? Don't tell me he got a hold of paper clips again."

"Nope," he says. "A safety pin this time."

We sit in the family conference room, the plastic veneer of the table reflecting a fuzzy version of Abraham Green's face.

"Andre is making some progress," I say. Andre himself looks down grimly at the table. He grips the edge of the table with red-gloved hands, his bandage gone.

"Good," Mr. Green answers, hopeful and smiling at his son.

"I've explained to him how important it is to take the pills," I say, more for Mr. Green's benefit than Andre's.

"But they make me cloudy," Andre objects, and the sentence does come out slow.

"It's okay, son. You'll get used to them." Mr. Green turns to me for confirmation. "Isn't that so?"

"Yes. And once you're stable, we can lower the dose, if the side effects are too strong."

"It's tough in here, though." Andre's eyes dart around the table, not focusing on either of us. "I gotta be on my toes."

"Don't worry about that." Abraham Green waves away

the statement. "You won't be in here for long. I'm working with the lawyer."

Andre subtly rocks back and forth in his chair. Scruffy hair is coming in under his chin, perhaps part of an effort to look older than his mere sixteen years. "Can I tell you something, Dad, if you promise not to get mad?"

"Of course, Son." Mr. Green takes hold of Andre's orange sleeve. "You know that. You can tell me anything."

Andre looks doubtful but pushes ahead anyway. "I got a warning."

"Okay." He turns to him. "A warning of what?"

"Beast Boy came by the other night. He said Violator's coming. He said to take care of things." There is a pause while Mr. Green looks down, then a slam on the table makes both me and Andre jump.

"Damn it, Andre." His father stands up with clear disgust. "That's fiction. I told you that before. These are stories, Son, stories. You're not a child anymore, Andre. It's time to grow up."

As he settles back in his chair, both father and son look embarrassed. A depressing silence fills the room as I finally get a glimpse of the not-so-perfect Mr. Green, breaking at the seams under the stress. And I can see Andre, too, as a little boy, being scolded by his father for reading comic books. But that's why we're here. To scratch the surface of this relationship. To mine out the cracks and hopefully start to repair them. "I'm sorry," Mr. Green says, to both of us. "I'm just at odds and ends here with all this."

"Of course," I say.

Mr. Green pushes the back of his hand to his mouth, holding back a sudden sob.

"He helps me, Dad," Andre says, as though to convince him.

His father sucks in air, trying to collect himself. "Who helps you, Son?"

"Beast Boy," he says. "And he would have helped Mom, too."

"All right, Son, all right." Mr. Green reaches over to massage his shoulder.

"I'm sorry, Dad," Andre says, leaning into him.

"It's okay." Abraham pulls a tissue from his pocket, and his wallet comes out, too. It falls open, revealing a crooked picture in a plastic shell. Behind the sheen is a young smiling boy with a front tooth growing in. At first I assume it's a picture of Andre when he was younger, but then I notice his skin tone is lighter, and his nose a bit broader.

"Is that Andre's brother?" I ask, openly staring at the photo.

"Oh no." He holds up the wallet for us both to see and smiles at the picture, which seems to conjure up a happier memory. Then he claps the wallet shut and shoves it back in his pocket. "That's his cousin, Jermaine."

"He's part of the coven," Andre whispers to me.

Mr. Green shakes his head in exhaustion. "What's he saying now?"

"A double," Andre whispers, even softer. "Like Steel Serpent."

The scent of coconut overwhelms me as I reach the office.

"I can smell that you're wearing your lotion."

"Yup. Love it." Jason sniffs his arm with ecstasy, as if he's on an air freshener commercial.

"Sure is beachy." I log into the computer and read over some patient notes. "So Fohrman is off his hunger strike."

"Yeah, turns out he's no Gandhi." He leans over my chair, the scent of coconut following him. "Hey, can you take Timothy Gordon for me?"

"The arm guy?"

"Yeah. You've seen him before, and I'm getting crushed here. Dr. Nowhere won't care anyway."

"No problem," I say, happy to get my census back up.

Jason goes to see another patient, and I wait in my clinic room until Timothy Gordon is led in. His arm is now out of the torture-device cast, the screws gone. "How is the arm doing?" I ask.

He lifts his arm as if it's a foreign object. "Okay. I guess."

"You guess?"

He gives me a small smile. "You're not gonna like my answer."

Tapping my eraser on the desk, I say, "Try me."

"I think I figured it out," he answers in a low voice, as if revealing a secret. "The arm isn't mine."

I pause. "Not yours?"

"Correct. But I figure, if it isn't harming me, I might as well just ignore it."

"Interesting." It is a coping mechanism of sorts, though it doesn't address the central issue of his ambivalence toward his limb. Standing up, I examine the arm, which is a touch atrophic and pale from the cast, but otherwise exactly like his other arm, softly freckled, with light-ginger hair. "How long have you felt this way?"

He scratches an itch at the wrist. "I remember it back in high school a little. My mom told the doctor, who said it was a phase. And it did go away for a while. But it seems like it came back."

"Have you been stressed?" I ask.

"Ma'am," he says with a wry smile, "no offense, but this place is practically the definition of stress."

"No offense taken." I do a brief exam. Normal muscle strength, no pronator drift. No extinction to double simultaneous stimulation, which could be a soft neuro sign of a sensory problem. His reflexes are symmetric. "Does it ever do things you don't want it to do?"

"No, not as I know." He extends and flexes it. "Only does what I tell it to do."

"Doesn't try to shut your book, or choke you, or something?"

The question elicits laughter. "Do people actually have that?"

"Alien limb syndrome. Often from a stroke."

"Well, I ain't had no stroke. Just a funny feeling about my arm." He rubs it again. "I'm not fully convinced that it's mine. But no one seems to agree with me, so I learned to stop arguing about it."

When he lifts his arms again, I catch sight of something. A fine line encircling the bicep in blue. So light that it would be easy to miss. "What's this?"

"Oh," he says, caught out. "A tattoo. It's supposed to be...therapeutic." He appears embarrassed at the admission. "Pedro did it for me." He pinches the skin around the tattoo line, then lets it go slack again. "Told me it would provide a physical separation for me. He said it's mystical. He's half-Navajo or something."

"Huh." I sit back down.

"Pedro's mostly full of shit," Timothy admits, "but I think maybe he's onto something."

I don't tell him that an SSRI probably wouldn't work any better. "Tell me if the tattoo doesn't work, okay? Before you try to hurt your arm again, you have to tell me, okay?"

"Yes, ma'am. Of course." He pulls his sleeves back up, and the guard leads him out, and I sit there wondering how I'm going to chart this one, let alone explain it to Dr. Novaire or the skeptical warden.

A mystical, therapeutic tattoo.

"Aren't we going out to dinner soon?" Mike asks.

"Uh-huh," I say, mouth full of peanut butter sandwich, while Arthur drools at my feet. "Why do you ask?"

"No reason," he says, extending his legs on the couch to check his e-mail. "Just that you're already eating dinner."

"No, I'm just fighting this flu still. It's weird. It seems to come and go." I wipe my hands on a paper towel, which Arthur grabs and trots off with into the living room. "There must be benefits to owning a dog, right?"

"Yes. But they're subtle at times." Mike puts his phone down. "Anything new at work?"

"Kind of. Got an interesting patient." I sit next to him on the couch, and he scoots over to make room. "He doesn't believe his arm is real."

"Excuse me?"

"Odd, I know. He doesn't think it's his own arm. At first I thought it was depersonalization, but now I'm thinking more body integrity disorder."

"You see some messed-up folks. Thank God for simple things like kidney stones." Mike turns the television on to the Sabres pregame show. He is the only one I know who watches the pregame show.

"I saw the detective today."

"Oh yeah?" He looks away from the game. "What did he have to say? Anything on the texts?"

"No, unfortunately not. He said it's a burner phone."

Mike looks troubled. "I was thinking about it," he says, as an ad for a bank comes on with smiling people shaking hands. "Maybe we should get you a gun."

The idea shocks me. "No way," I say, shutting him down immediately.

"Think about it. I could take you to the range, teach you how to shoot."

I gaze at him in a new light. "You know how to shoot a gun?"

He shrugs. "It's not that difficult, Zoe."

"Yeah, but I mean—"

"I know what you mean. My dad used to be big on that kind of stuff." He doesn't say anything more. Mike doesn't speak to his father, who left his mother for a younger model when he was in high school and left their family on food stamps.

"Anyway, no guns. End of discussion."

"Pepper spray?" he ventures.

I think about it for a minute. "Yes. Pepper spray I would agree to."

"Good," he says. "I'll pick some up tomorrow."

Chapter Eighteen

I was sick over Barbara Donalds. I'm no angel. I've done terrible things before, but this was different. She didn't deserve this. So I stalled. I came up with excuses.

And you punished me.

I wasn't sure at first. You hadn't brought me to the room in over a week. But I could explain that away. You were busy. You had a real life. You had other things to do.

But then when it was time for class, there was no denying it. You barely looked at me, leaning over the other girls, putting your hands on their shoulders. I doodled in my notebook, sketches of your tattoos, and you ignored me. You praised the other girls for their essays. You even chuckled when that fat bitch was flirting with you.

When class ended, I felt physically ill. It took everything not to cry. The girls scattered all over the room, looking through the stacks for the latest Danielle Steel or whatever. I went over to you, to our corner. I asked if something was wrong.

You were leafing through someone's journal and didn't look up.
I told you I'd help you if you helped me. *You're not helping me.*

I'm trying, *I said.*

Not hard enough.

I reminded you how I got on the computer and figured out her password. You were so happy when I did that before, I remember. You smoothed my hair.

But now you just looked at me, your eyes turned icy. I want another name. Either you get it for me or I don't need you.

I felt my lips tremble. I'll try.

You looked around then, and seeing no one was there, you leaned in. I thought you were going to kiss me and I relaxed but you grabbed me by the crotch. I gasped, feeling my pants pushing into me. You lightened your grip then, just a bit, and started rubbing. I groaned without meaning to, and you leaned into my ear.

You want more of this? *you asked, and like an idiot I nodded.* Then get me another name. *And then you dropped your hand and walked away, leaving me there.*

Furious, humiliated, and panting.

Like a fucking dog.

Chapter Nineteen

The next morning I have my phone back in hand, but no further word on the texting riddler. So I decide to take matters into my own hands. But when I get to Sofia's cell, it's empty. Checking the logbook, I find that she's signed out to "rec."

So I make my way to the yard. The rec area is depressing, "recreation" being a bit of a misnomer. The place is a mowed-down yard with a few pull-up bars, a cracked cement basketball court with no nets, and an ersatz walking trail, which is just worn-down grass from inmates pacing in circles around the outside. I catch up with Sofia on the trail, her breath coming out in little clouds. She is a shapeless blob in her oversize state-issued winter coat. As I walk beside her, she notices me.

"Ah, my long-lost sister."

"Nice place you got here," I say, looking around.

"Be it ever so humble," she returns.

I bury my hands deep in my coat pockets. "Perhaps you're wondering why I came to see you."

Her cheeks are red from the cold. "Figured my little sis just wanted to check up on me."

"Not exactly," I say, as we let two inmates holding hands walk around us. "I want to know why you're texting me."

"What are you talking about?"

"Don't play dumb, Sofia. I know you sent them."

"I'm not playing dumb." She kicks some snow out of her path. "I didn't send you any texts."

"Okay, fine, so you got someone else to send them, then."

She stops walking then. "I don't know what you're talking about, Tanya. I didn't text you anything. And by the way, need I remind you, I don't have a phone?" She starts walking again. "But if you tell me about it, I might be able help you."

"Oh, right. Tell you all about the texts so you can gloat over them? I don't think so."

She shrugs. "Whatever, Tanya. I'm trying to be straight with you here."

"Straight with me?" I let out a harsh laugh. "How is threatening to tell the newspaper about us being straight with me? How is worming your way into a research project being straight with me?"

"Please," she scoffs. "I could give a shit about that research project. CBT for psychopaths? I'm not a scientist, Tanya, but I can tell you that's probably not going to work." She kicks a pebble out of her path. "And why the hell would you put your sister in a research project?"

"What is it, then?" I ask, exasperated. "What do you want from me? Forgiveness, as you say? Because let me tell you, the texting isn't helping your cause."

"I didn't—" She doesn't continue, just shaking her head with annoyance.

"And don't tell me this is all about your conversion to Judaism. Because I know that's bullshit."

"It's not bullshit. Not that you would care." We walk for a while, our feet thumping against the trail in tandem. She blows on her hands for warmth. "You want me to be honest with you?"

"Honesty. I'm not sure that's genetically possible for—"

"I want us to be friends," she says, interrupting me.

Stopping right there, I almost laugh. A girl slams a basketball against the cement in front of us, the bang echoing around the yard. "Friends?"

"Yes," she says, standing with me, her voice small, almost shy. "Friends."

This time I do laugh, at the pure ridiculousness of the notion. "You need to read up on the friend thing, Sofia." I start walking again. "Friends don't stab each other, for instance."

"I already—"

"They don't text each other riddles. Sick-ass shit about razors and pills."

"I promise to God, Tanya, I didn't text you. I had nothing to do with that."

I stop walking then, digging my hands in my coat. "Let me tell you something, Sofia. Detective Adams knows about it. And if it's traced back to you, they'll be adding even more years to your sentence. If you're lucky, you'll be a Lubav-itcher by then." I start to peel off from the trail, then turn back to her. "And by the way, for your information, my name is not Tanya. It's Zoe. Actually, forget that. It's Dr. Goldman, to you."

After meeting with Sofia, I get a text from Jason that the war-den wants to meet with me. So straight from the frying pan into the inferno. I'm praying it's about the texts and not an imminent pink slip.

I knock on the office door, my stomach in ropes, but when I open it, the warden is beaming. "Dr. Goldman, thank you for coming." He stands up to greet me with such a wide smile that I think he's about to offer me a cigar. "And I presume you've already had the pleasure of meeting our reporter ex-traordinaire?" Seated in a chair across the room, Logan offers a hesitant wave.

"Oh yes, I've had that pleasure."

"So you know that he's been doing some interviews with our staff," Warden Gardner continues. "And he may have told you that after all of the…unfortunate events…as of late, we have worked out a situation with the *News* that we're hoping will be synergistic."

"Yes," Logan says, standing up for emphasis. "Synergistic. Full access, in return for a balanced story." His grin is unflap-pable. "As I told you before, I'm going to cover all the facts as well as the strides towards correcting some of the recent unfortunate events." He nods broadly at the warden, who nods broadly right back. "I believe in making bridges, not enemies."

"Uh-huh." I can actually see Logan running for president someday. "And how do I fit into this balance?"

"Excellent question, Dr. Goldman," the warden says. "Logan here says he's been trying to reach you for an interview. And perhaps it's just his perception, but he feels you've been less than forthcoming with him."

I loosen my fists at my sides. "I've just been very busy."

"Yes, well, that's what I told him. But we really do need you to make some time. We were hoping you could offer an interview from the fellow's point of view. You should be aware as well, Dr. Goldman. It might help to elevate your standing within the fellowship."

I straighten out my white coat, taking in the barely veiled threat. "Have you asked Dr. Chang? He might be a better candidate. He's been very successful in the fellowship."

Logan touches his sideburns thoughtfully. "I did get a limited interview with Dr. Chang." (Which means Jason probably propositioned him.) "But I was hoping for your perspective."

"Yeah, it's just—"

"Honestly, Dr. Goldman," Logan says, "or Zoe? Can I call you that?" He doesn't wait for approval. "Zoe, I'm not trying to make you uncomfortable here. I just want to paint the Buffalo Correctional Facility in the best light possible. I've already got some great stuff from the guards, some of

The Sandra Block

Sandra Block

the forensic patients, and the warden kindly gave me some time…" The warden nods in response. "But this would really make it complete." He runs his hands over his fashionably skinny mocha-brown pants. "If you would just think about it, that's all I'm asking."

"Of course," I say, happy to be off the hook on which I'm wriggling. "I will absolutely think about it."

"Great." Logan sits back down, apparently satisfied.

"Then we're agreed," the warden says, his smile plastered back on.

"Yes, we are agreed."

In the following silence, I realize the meeting has been adjourned. But I still didn't get to ask my question. Gathering up my purse and coat, I say, "I did want to bring up one more thing."

Warden Gardner looks less than enthused. "Yes?"

"Did Detective Adams talk to you about the texts?" Newsboy looks up with renewed interest.

"Yes, he did," the warden answers, shortly. "And all I can tell you is that we're looking into it."

"I'm glad to hear that. So," I ask, treading carefully, "you didn't find anything yet?"

The warden pauses, clearly not wanting to continue the conversation. "No, we haven't. We've done cell searches, the guards have been asking around. No intel as of now. But I will keep you informed, I can assure you."

"What kind of texts?" Logan asks with the perfect degree of nonchalance.

"Nothing that you need to be concerned about," the

142

warden says, in a manner that does not invite further questioning.

And for once I most unequivocally agree with him.

⌒

Scotty nurses his cappuccino as we sit near the blazing gas fireplace, me in my usual eggplant leather settee and Scotty in his usual threadbare French blue velvet chair. After my visit with Sofia, the cold seemed to burrow into my bones all day. In the glow of the fire, my body is finally defrosting. "So how did your visit with her family go?"

"Good, good. We've decided to have it at Westminster."

"That's where she wanted it?" I ask.

"Yup, which is fine." He doesn't sound so thrilled, though, looking into the fire. "I was hoping for TBZ."

Which is Temple Beth Zion, our temple. "It's just one day," I offer.

"Yeah, that's what she said." He looks away from the fire with a brighter look. "They're pretty into this whole thing. Huge room at the Hyatt, top-shelf liquor. Kristy even wants caviar and Smirnoff at the hors d'oeuvres table. She read about that in a magazine somewhere."

"Classy."

"I guess." Still, he doesn't look displeased at the thought.

"Who's going to be your best man?"

"Eddie," he says, pointing. Eddie hears him and beams at us in return.

"Thrilled to do it," he calls across the room, blushing a fierce red. Eddie is quite a blusher.

"Anyway," Scotty says, "I've bored you enough. Got to go back to work." He strides back to the cash register with a grin, and I find myself smiling for him and his happiness. Leaning back into the settee, I pull out my phone to squander a few minutes on Facebook before going back to my textbook. Mike has shared a post from Felicity of the ER office holiday party with him looking his rugged, handsome self and XO Serena leaning into him and laughing hysterically. I can almost hear her hyenalike laughter. Sean, the asshole PA, is staring right at Serena's V-scrubbed cleavage, which makes me actually laugh out loud, because that shit is *never* going to happen.

I skip over the "Only my true friends will share this" posts and rants against this or that. Then, for kicks, I type "Andre Green" in the search bar. I don't find any Facebook page and figure he's probably on something much cooler, Instagram, Snapchat, what have you, none of which I've had the energy to join yet. Next I type "Abraham Green" in the search bar. Like Andre, he has no Facebook page. Searching for Charmayne again, I find the same photos, same sentiments. Another one, a wedding photo, bride and groom holding hands and grinning at each other at some private joke. Then I scroll through the comments, which are to be expected.

You two look so gorgeous with ten likes.

You'll meet again in heaven with a heart emoji and twenty-three likes.

But at the bottom of the page is a comment I don't expect to see. With zero likes.

Abraham Green killed my sister and got away with it.

Just like he did his first wife.

Chapter Twenty

Mike is scrounging through the pantry. "Who ate all the peanut butter?"

"Oh, I did. Sorry. I meant to put it on the list."

He grabs cream cheese from the refrigerator as a second-place option and starts scraping it on his toasted bagel. "What's with you and peanut butter lately?"

"I don't know." I pour some more coffee into my "You don't scare me, I work with the criminally insane" mug that Scotty got me for Chanukah. "Don't you think it's weird, though?"

He takes a bite. "The Facebook thing? I don't know." He makes a sour face then. "I think this cream cheese is stale."

"Maybe I should check into it."

"Well, I don't know, it is or it isn't. I really wanted peanut butter anyway."

"No, not the cream cheese. The Facebook thing."

"No, maybe you *shouldn't* check into that," Mike says. "It's just Facebook, Zoe. Seriously, the poor guy's wife just died; his son is sick. He probably doesn't need any more stuff to deal with right at this very moment."

"Yeah, that's true. But I figured I'd ask the detective anyway." I don't mention I already set up a time to visit with Dr. Koneru, who did Charmayne's autopsy.

"Whatever." He rinses his plate off and puts it in the dishwasher.

"What do you mean, whatever?"

"It means you're going to do what you want anyway. But if you're going to talk to the detective, why don't you ask about the texts? That's the thing that's more worrisome to me." He shuts the dishwasher door with a squeak.

"I know. It's worrisome to me, too. But what more can the man do? He said it's a burner phone."

"I know. And stop saying *burner phone*. It's getting annoying."

"Burner phone," I repeat.

"Hey, did you remember to put the pepper spray in your purse?"

"Yes," I lie. I don't remember where the pepper spray ended up. Somewhere in the trunk of my car, I think.

"Don't forget, if you go to see Sofia again, make sure you have it on you. Okay?"

"Okay," I say. And I will, if I can find it.

⌒

The smell of formaldehyde stings my eyes.

Before work I make a quick pit stop at the Pathology department, in the basement of the county hospital. I already told Dr. Koneru how Charmayne was my patient Andre's mother. Dr. Koneru helped me figure out a tough case last year; I trust her skills implicitly.

"Nothing suspicious about it, Zoe," she says. A tuft of hennaed hair sticks out of the front of her scrub hat. "It was definitely cardiac."

I catch a glance at one of the splayed-out bodies and look away, fighting off nausea from my residual flu. "Odd, though, isn't it? A heart attack in a forty-year-old woman?"

"Not that odd." She moves over toward a metal table. "Heart disease is underrecognized in women, especially African Americans." Dr. Koneru positions her scalpel and unzips the chest with uncanny ease. "She'd had a silent apical MI in the past. Hypertension and prediabetes, probably sleep apnea. She's a pretty typical setup for this, to be honest."

I step away from the table. "But it's still routine to do an autopsy on someone this age?"

"Certainly. Unless there's an obvious underlying cause, like a known cancer or something."

"And if her husband had killed her, you would have seen signs of that?"

Bones crack as she pulls apart the chest wall. "I keep an open mind, Zoe. But when a horse comes in, I don't go looking for a zebra." She pauses, looking up from the body. "You have reason to suspect the husband?"

I unbutton my lab coat, snug around my thick sweater.

"I wouldn't say that exactly. But I was looking over her Facebook page, and there was a troubling comment from Charmayne's sister, blaming him for her death." Bile spills out of the abdominal cavity as her scalpel slices down, and I swallow back an involuntary gag reflex.

"Facebook, huh? An extremely reliable source," she jokes.

"Right, I know. But I just wanted to ask, at least."

"I reviewed her case thoroughly, of course. Like all my cases," she says. "But if it'll make you feel any better, I'll take another look."

It's early yet, so I drive through Tim Hortons and call the detective on my way into work. He answers on the first ring.

"What's up, Zoe? Any more texts?" he asks with a note of concern.

"Oh no." I peel off the lid and blow on the tongue-singeing coffee. "Nothing like that. I'm calling about something else, actually. A patient concern."

"All right. One second here, let me grab a pen." To his credit, he doesn't ignore my "patient concerns," seeing as one ended with my patient (sister) stabbing me and another in my patient being involved in an underground criminal ring. "Okay, go ahead."

I give him a brief summary of the Andre Green case and the aunt's Facebook comment and hear him scribbling notes again. "It was ruled natural causes, though?" the detective asks.

"Yes. Dr. Koneru is going to review it again, but she was pretty certain it was cardiac."

He pauses. "Did Andre say anything about his father killing his mother?"

"Well, Andre thinks his father is the devil and that he took her soul. But I'm talking about the literal devil here. As in he's hallucinating and delusional."

"As in he's not really a particularly reliable witness right now," he observes.

"No, you're right. But it got me to thinking. What if he's trying to tell us something all along here, and we've just been labeling him as insane?"

He pauses. "I don't know. I would say that's more your department than mine." A loud voice calls out his name in the background. "I'll see what I can dig up. But I don't have to tell you that Dr. Koneru's good. If she said it was the heart, it probably was. I wouldn't go by what you read on Facebook."

"Yes, I know. While I have you on, any more info about the texts?"

"No, nothing more, sorry to say. And I've been back and forth with the warden. They stripped down Sofia's cell more than once. There's nothing. I'm not saying she isn't involved, but if she is, she's done a damn good job covering her tracks."

"Well, she would." I slow down, seeing the prison up ahead.

"Anyone else that could have done this?" he asks. "People you work with, maybe?"

"I doubt it. But I'll think about it." When I showed Jason the texts, he got a horrified look on his face, saying, "That is creepy as fuck." I have to doubt it's he unless he recently took up acting. As I pull into the parking lot, we hang up. With just a few minutes before work, I check Facebook once more, heading right over to Charmayne's page.

The comment has been deleted.

I move over to the page of her sister who left the comment, Marion Thomas. Mining through it, I don't learn much. A sparse, rarely visited page. Googling her tells me she is a real estate agent and once went on a trip to Cancún. A scant digital footprint.

I know I shouldn't do it. And Mike, Sam, Scotty, and even Detective Adams would tell me I shouldn't do it. But I pull up a message box.

> I saw your comment, and I know Andre. Could you call me sometime?

Officer Maloney grabs me as soon as I get into the clinic. "Dr. Goldman, can I get your help?"

I quicken my steps to follow him. "What's going on?"

"Aubrey Kane. We have her in the hole. She's asking for you."

"In solitary?" I am jogging to keep up with him. "What happened?"

"Usual drama. But this time her nails are trimmed down, and she couldn't sneak anything sharp in. So she's biting instead."

"Biting who?" As he leads me into the freezing shoebox of a room, I am given the answer. She is biting herself. Aubrey is lying on the floor in a white, formless cotton sack, meant to prevent self-harm. Like a straitjacket, with fewer ties. Bite marks are bleeding through the cloth up and down her arms. She still has blood on her teeth. The room is illuminated by a single bulb hanging from the high ceiling.

Maloney says, "I tried to call Dr. Novaire like the warden recommended, but—"

"You couldn't reach him," I say, finishing his sentence. "Aubrey," I call to her. She doesn't look at me. She is shivering, her teeth clacking. "Aubrey," I repeat, softer. She turns this time, as Maloney backs up. I kneel down to her level. "What happened, Aubrey?"

"I need to get out of here," she whispers in a voice that's hoarse, probably from screaming.

"I understand. But they won't let you out if you're hurting yourself."

"I had a nightmare." Her eyes are squeezing out tears. "A bad, bad one this time." She rolls around in the cotton sack. "I'll die in here."

I put my hands on her birdlike shoulders, which are still quaking. "We'll get through this, Aubrey."

"The motel room," she moans.

"It's okay."

"Todd."

"You can tell me."

Her chest is heaving. "He came back that night. But he brought men with him. Men I didn't know." I sit beside her, rubbing her shoulder. "I was in and out of it, but the worst parts I remember. It went on for hours. Hours and hours," she says, hiccupping with crying now. "When I said no, they were laughing. And Todd, he was raping me, too."

I rub her shaking shoulder. "I'm so sorry, Aubrey."

"I begged them to stop, and they wouldn't." She shakes her head in angry disbelief. "They just laughed at me."

"I'm sorry," I say again, soothing her. "They should never have done that. That was a crime, Aubrey. It wasn't your fault."

"And the worst part is..." I can smell acrid sweat through the cloth. She is hyperventilating now, barely getting the words out. "The worst part is that I knew I would get punished for what I did, eventually."

"No one deserves that. You can't blame yourself."

"No, you're wrong," she cuts me off. "I did deserve it. I did something terrible." Her breath grows short again. "You don't even know what I did."

"That doesn't mean you deserved to be hurt, Aubrey—"

"After it happened, I thought, that was it. I'd been punished. It was over. I could stop feeling so bad about it then. That I would finally be forgiven. But I was wrong. It wasn't over. I keep dreaming about her. And she'll never forgive me."

"Who?" I ask. "Who won't forgive you?"

But Aubrey doesn't answer.

I sip my fruity-smelling herbal tea, having abandoned my usual cappuccino since my stomach is off yet again. I've already double-checked my Facebook messages for anything from Marion Thomas. Not a word.

"So you didn't find anything more?" I ask Scotty. I pleaded with him to put his mad computer skills to work searching out more information on Marion Thomas, Charmayne's sister.

"No, sorry." He straightens out the sugar box at a table. "We've been crazy. Went to see a bunch of bands last week."

"Any good ones?" I blow on my steaming tea.

"Yeah. Pretty good. I think we're going with the Underdogs. Mostly nineties and classics." He tidies the next table, a skip in his step.

"How about anything on his first wife, then?" I push my luck because he's in a good mood. "Like a marriage certificate or anything?"

"Who are we talking about again?" He smiles and nods at a regular customer coming in the door.

"Andre's father."

"No, sorry, didn't get a chance yet." His phone rings then. "Hey, babe." I hear twittering on the other end. "No, remember? I'm closing. Can they do it tomorrow?" The song changes to some snazzy jazz tune, and I try not to eavesdrop. "No, I already told you. It's not a big deal. Do it without me, then. I trust you." More yapping comes over the line. "Of course I care. I'm just saying I can't do it tonight." There is a pause then. "Babe? Babe." He shoves his phone in his back pocket with a grunt.

"Trouble in paradise?"

"Just about this stupid tasting thing. Who cares? It's between Tiddlybinks and Lucarelli's. Who cares? It's just fucking food."

"Yeah, well, the food is kind of important."

"I guess. Jeez, I never knew what a pain in the ass it was to plan a wedding."

I try not to laugh, considering he's probably doing less than an eighth of the planning. "I'm sure she's just stressed out."

"Probably PMS-ing," he grumbles, hopping back up to the register to wait on a customer.

I would argue against this as a sexist pronouncement, but he could be right. I feel as if I've been PMS-ing for two months straight now. As the next jazz tune comes on, a wailing saxophone, I open my forensic psychiatry text to get down to business. Just then a thought suddenly spears me. I actually gasp, out loud, and other customers look my way.

It's about Kristy PMS-ing. And me PMS-ing.

And nausea.

And the fact that I can't really remember the last time I got my period.

⤺

I am hiding in the bathroom, listening for Mike's snoring.

I maneuver the stick so I don't urinate on my hand, having verified ten times now that a cross means pregnant and one straight line means not pregnant. I am praying without apology for one line. It is my mantra.

One line. One line. One line.

But for all my concentration, I can't pee. I am in the process of willing my bladder to relax with all my might when a text comes through.

Grand Rounds canceled tomorrow because of snow. From Jason.

Thanks, I text back. Usually I would add a snowman emoji, but I am in dire straits at the moment and there is no time for emoji. Calm down, relax, and pee.

One line. One line. One line.

I'm tracing back to see how this could even be possible. Sometimes I forget to get my scripts exactly on time, and I've missed a birth control pill here and there. It's never been an issue before, but it *was* like a full week once. When was that? I'm trying to remember. Two months ago? Three?

One line. One line. One line.

Finally I am able to go, indeed splashing warm urine all over my hand, then put the stick on the windowsill and run over to wash my hands when I hear a snort. I pause to listen for more snoring but instead I hear footsteps and the doorknob being tried.

"Zoe? You in there?"

"Um…" I jog over to assess the stick, which still shows one line. But is another line fading in? "I'm sort of having some issues in here. Can you go downstairs?" I hear him grumbling, then footsteps receding.

I'm dying to look at the stick again, but the box admonishes testers to wait a full thirty seconds to be sure. The second hand crawls by for fifteen more seconds.

Still one line.

I hear the water running in the downstairs guest bathroom. Ten more seconds have passed on my watch. I count out five more slow seconds, then an additional five seconds for good measure.

Holding my breath, I walk over to the windowsill and pick up the stick.

Chapter Twenty-One

I *shouldn't have done it, but I was desperate.*

I have something for you, *I said, as the door to the room squeaked open.* But it's not a name.

Your eyes narrowed. What is it, then?

I told you about the boy I saw going to the clinic, all the while praying that nothing would happen to him. That I wouldn't have to hurt him. A black kid, young-looking, I said.

You scoffed. So what? That's ninety percent of the inmates.

He had red gloves on, *I added.*

This stopped you a moment. You got that faraway look, and I could see the wheels turning in your head.

I admitted that I didn't know anything about him, other than the gloves. But maybe it could tide you over until I could get back on the computer. You paused, deciding. You looked around the room with impatience and maybe a note of distaste for the dirty, barren place. My stomach was fluttering as you stood there, debating, un-

til finally you gave in. I could probably do something with it, you said. Then you pushed me down by my shoulders and told me I could give you a blow job, as if you were doing me a favor.

And who am I kidding, I would take what I could get. So I dove right in but you were soft and you shoved me to the side, snarling like it was my fault, and jerked yourself off until you were hard. Then you grabbed my head, holding me so tight I could hardly move, thrusting until my throat was burning, until finally you grunted and I could taste your salty come, gagging me. I stood up, my eyes watering.

You need to work on that, *you said.*

I didn't answer, but a little part of me hated you right then. The vile taste of you.

I used to love that storage room, you know, with every piece of me.

I know that sounds twisted and stupid. But I did. It was our little room. Our haven. And we had to make do. We had to take risks and take what we could get in this fucked-up, crazy place, and that was fine. That was better, even. We had to fight for it, not take it for granted. True love, real love.

We used to lie in that room for hours.

Do you remember that? Time just sailed by like it never does in here. Me, playing with your hair, watching your chest rise. You, tracing my collarbone with your fingers until I got chills. And then you would plunge your fingers in me, and I would be ready for you again. It was glorious.

But not that day. That day, you were zipping up and I touched your arm and you peeled me off like I was a poisonous vine. Don't be so needy, *you said, your lips curled.*

Why I didn't leave you right then, after that day? Why I didn't just tell you to fuck off, that I wasn't helping you anymore, and stop going to your stupid class?

I can't answer that . . .

All I can say is that I couldn't.

Chapter Twenty-Two

Arthur plants his entire body on me, hoping for a bite of bagel.

This is my second bagel with peanut butter, and I now see my peanut butter obsession for what it is, a check in the "craving" cliché box. Even Mike wondered aloud at the last grocery store run when I threw two more jars in the cart. *I never knew you were such a peanut butter fan.* Arthur dives in for a ninja lick with my every bite. Finally I put the plate down, and Arthur leaps off my lap with a complete lack of aplomb to get every morsel.

I've been waiting all morning for the socially appropriate time to call, and figure seven a.m. is close enough. So I pick up my cell phone.

"Hello?"

"Jack," I say, "it's Zoe."

"Zoe, hi," Jack says, his voice enlivened. "I'm glad you called."

I sit down on the couch, and Arthur checks to make sure I'm not offering any food, then resumes his licking. "Is this an okay time to talk?"

"Yeah, it's perfect. I don't have to be to work for another hour." A loud television news show echoes over the phone, then goes silent. "What's up?"

"I just wanted to ask you about something."

"First off," he says, "I'm sorry. I was way out of line in our last conversation. That woman just drives me crazy. And I don't like the idea of her manipulating you."

"Oh yeah, that. No problem. I don't think I'll be seeing her anymore anyway."

"Good," he says.

"I actually wanted to ask you about something else." Abandoning his now-polished plate, Arthur takes an oof-provoking leap back onto my lap. "I wanted to ask about our family history a bit. A health history." Arthur licks my lips, partly because he loves me and more because I taste like peanut butter, and I shove him away with a head pat.

A muffled cough comes over the phone. "Sorry, getting over something." He coughs again. "You mean, like diabetes and all that?"

"Exactly." I get out a notepad and draw up a little genetic family tree, and Arthur moves over to his blanket and lies down on his back. "So, starting with our mother. Did she have any illnesses, do you know?"

"I was so young when she died," he says, his voice pensive. "I don't even know. Dad had liver failure, but that was on account of drinking. And I don't think he had any siblings."

"Right." I look at my drawing, which is a spare family tree thus far.

"But Mom's sister died of breast cancer, I think."

I add a branch and write down "BREAST CA." "That sounds quasi-familiar."

"Grandparents." He murmurs to himself in thought. "No clue. Sofia might know. Not that I'm recommending you ask her. Oh," he says, interrupting himself excitedly. "I do remember one thing Dad told me, a while back. Right before he died. About his aunt."

"Maternal or paternal?"

"No idea."

"Okay, go on."

"I remember him saying she had a nervous breakdown. She was always a little off, he said. He wondered if that's where Sofia got it."

I add a dismembered branch. "Did he say anything in particular?"

"I vaguely remember him saying she would make these big plans, then go off and disappear in her bedroom for years. Basically the crazy old aunt."

Huh. Sounds bipolar to this psychiatrist. "How did she die?"

"He didn't say." He pauses, thinking. "He just said he was always afraid Sofia's genes came from her. From his bloodline. I don't think so, though. She seems like an animal all to herself." A gurgly cough escapes. "Why do you ask, anyway? You doing some project or something?"

"Not exactly..."

A long pause follows my conspicuous lack of explanation. He clears his throat, before a racking cough overtakes him, and I wait patiently for him to get back on the line. At last he does, taking in a deep breath. "Wait," he says, as if something just struck him. "Are you pregnant?"

Jason teases his forelock, a nervous habit that is also quite distracting.

"Transcranial magnetic stimulation has been used in various clinical situations, including Parkinson's, as well as seizure detection." He hits the next PowerPoint slide, and a multicolored bar graph pops up. "The newest data shows its real promise may lie in treating depression."

Twenty minutes into the psychiatry grand rounds, and I haven't heard a word. Every ADHD medication is out of my bloodstream, and I barely slept a wink last night.

"The technical components are simple…" Jason moves to the next slide, which whooshes onto the screen. He is big on animation; any more spinning, fade-ins and -outs, or dissolving images and I'm going to be motion sick, on top of my now-explicable nausea. Out of the corner of my eye, I see Dr. Novaire, his eyelids drifting downward. Pulling out my iPad, I write up a note to keep me focused: "TRANSCRANIAL MAGNETIC STIMULATION." Jason plays with his hair again. "TMS may be a safer, more viable alternative to ECT."

ECT, otherwise known as electroconvulsive therapy, which we almost gave to Jane Doe last year. Thankfully, we never had to. My foot is tapping, which wakes up Dr. Novaire. He pats a bit of drool at the corner of his mouth. I try my damnedest to concentrate, but it's impossible, as one thought keeps screaming inside my head.

WHAT AM I GOING TO DO?

I start a note on my iPad, in an effort to be objective about this.

Pros: Cute baby.

Cons: I don't want a baby.

Pros: Mike would be a great father.

Cons: He might not want to be a father.

Pros: I would have time to have the baby after the fellowship.

Cons: I'm not ready to have a baby.

I slap the keyboard case closed on my iPad. I can't do this right now. This isn't helping. I need to focus on Jason. TMS.

Focus, focus, focus.

My foot is going again, as if it's about to jump right off my leg, and I stand up and scramble down the long row of seats as unobtrusively as possible (wholly unrealistic at over six feet) and make it to the bathroom. After splashing my face with water, I look up in the mirror and notice that I appear oddly normal. Not as if my mind is peeling in a million directions. Not as if I have a secret the size of a cranberry bean lodged in my uterus. (Yes, a cranberry bean, straight off pregnantbabes.com.) I pat off my face with a paper towel, though the strong brown-paper smell makes me nauseous.

On the way back in, I nearly run into Dr. Novaire. "Oh, Zoe, quick word." I brace myself. "How is the pilot going?"

"Um, okay, I guess." My foot is tapping and he looks down at it. "I think Sofia may not want to continue the project, but that's okay because I've started with another patient, Tyler Evans. And I have some more on my list."

"Sofia doesn't want to continue?" he probes with concern.

"Um." My other foot is tapping now, trying to release the waves of energy trapped in my body. "I think she'd rather do it on her own, maybe. With her studies."

"Ah," he says, his face registering relief. "On her own terms. Well, that's just fine. It's unfortunate for the study, but you can't force her to, of course."

"Of course."

"And anyway, I do think her new Jewish outlook is helping her along nicely."

"Right." *And she's playing you quite nicely, too*, I want to say.

"How is the other patient doing so far? Do you think he's recovering?"

"Recovering?"

"His sociopathy, is it responding to CBT?"

"Oh, I'm…not certain yet. Still in the early stages."

"Is that so?" He frowns. "I'd hoped we'd be further along by now. But oh well. You can't rush genius, right?"

"No," I say. "You sure can't."

"Well, keep up the good work. Keep tracking those Hare scores. The final research project is due in May, don't forget." Then he heads into the men's room.

And I take a deep breath and head back into the conference room, to see Jason clicking to another spinning slide. Getting to my chair, I sit down, trying to decipher the pie chart, but my brain won't shut up.

Pregnant baby cranberry bean Mike baby pregnant cranberry bean baby pregnant.

I drop my head into my hands, feeling nauseous again.

What am I going to do?

"Hello," says the polite, but officious, voice over the phone. "This is Dr. Marchand's office. How can we help you?"

"Hi, this is…" I stutter, my body in a sudden hot sweat and my brain turned to putty.

"Hello?" the polite voice repeats.

I hang up the phone, and in seconds it seems to come to life again, vibrating in my palm. I stare at it in discombobulation, with the paranoid, fleeting thought that Dr. Marchand's office is now tracking me, but then I see it's a number that I don't recognize. "Hello?"

"Hi, this is Marion Thomas. Charmayne's sister." Her voice sounds unsure.

"Oh!" With the cranberry bean on my mind, I had forgotten about her. "Yes, yes. Thanks for calling me."

This is followed by another uncomfortably long pause. "Did you know my sister?"

"No, no, I didn't. But I do know Andre. He's my patient." I explain as much as I can without breaking HIPAA, which means I am definitely breaking HIPAA. "He's not well, Marion. I'm trying to help as much as I can. But he needs to be in a hospital, not jail."

"Andre ain't like that," she mutters. "I don't know what's going on with him. But he was never like that."

"Schizophrenia can be a very difficult disease."

"Yeah, I don't know about all that. The schizophrenia thing. He wasn't like that a year ago."

"Things can change pretty quickly, though—"

"Which is why I want to see for myself," she interrupts. "But of course, he won't let me on the list."

"Who won't let you?"

"Who do you think? His father," she says this like a curse. "I just don't believe what he's saying. It's not like Andre to do that, to go and stab his father. He's very smart, a good boy. He wouldn't have done that without some reason."

"About Mr. Green," I start, then hear rapid, rhythmic footsteps down the hall, which sound like Officer Maloney coming to peek through the cracked-open door. I catch his figure walking by, but he has no patient for me yet, and the footsteps fade off. "Why did you say he killed your sister?"

"Because he did." She says this with absolute certainty. "I don't know how he did it, but he did."

"What makes you think that?"

"Here's the thing. I talked to the coroner," she says with

derision. "She said it was natural causes. But I'm sorry. I just can't believe that. We don't have any heart disease in our family, and Charmayne was fine the week before." She pauses. "Well, I didn't see her myself, but my family saw her. Said she was maybe coming down with the flu, but that's it. Nothing to do with her heart."

"The flu, you say?"

She huffs into the phone. "Oh, I don't even know about that. She was fine, that's the point."

"So you didn't actually see her?"

"Well, we were in a bit of a tiff," she admits. "We hadn't talked in a few months. I mean, it's not like we weren't talking, we just weren't talking. Sometimes Charmayne could get like that. Very stubborn."

"Can I ask what was the tiff over?"

"What else? Him. I told her straight out. I didn't like the way he treated her. I didn't trust him. And she said it was none of my business."

I smooth my hand over my desk. "Was he abusive?"

She pauses. "I wouldn't say that. He was just controlling, is all. She wasn't the same when she was with him. She wasn't herself. It was like she was watching every word, trying not to upset him."

"Uh-huh." So this could be a controlling husband or an overprotective sister. Or both. "And you said there was another wife?"

"Well," Marion hedges. "I didn't know her, but he told us about her. His first wife. April Green. He said she died of a heart attack, too, age thirty-five."

I'm writing this down on a spare pad in the drawer. "That does seem coincidental."

"It sure does," she says. "But no one believes me."

I draw arrows between "April Green," "Charmayne Green," and "MI" with a red pencil. "Did you go to the police about your concerns?"

"Yes, I did. And I got the same runaround as I did with the coroner. They see a plus-sized black lady like my sister, and of course she had a heart attack. Or whatever they called it. Some rhythmia thing."

"Hmm." Dr. Koneru had a point. Some plus-size black ladies do in fact have heart attacks or arrhythmias. "I have to go, but I'm going to look into this some more," I say, as I see Maloney coming again, but this time with my next patient.

"I appreciate that," Marion says. "I'll give you my cell. Let me know if you find out anything."

"Oh, one more thing, before I forget. Abraham had a picture of another boy in his wallet. Jermaine, he said. Does Andre have a cousin named Jermaine?"

"Jermaine?" Marion sounds baffled. "No. Not that I know of. No Jermaines in our family." Her voice softens. "But I wouldn't blame Andre if he told you that. Could be a hallucination or something."

"Could be," I say. But it wasn't Andre who told me that.

Officer Maloney leaves as my next patient comes in. Janaya Jones.

Janaya's nickname is Ol' White Lady, which is odd because she's fortysomething and not white. She smells as if she hasn't showered in a week, her orange jumper is sweat-stained and straining over her double-D chest, and her hair is standing in a million directions, like Medusa without the snakes.

"Have a seat," I say.

"I prefer to stand," she answers, holding herself staunchly upright. "And if you please, I'd like to know why I've been sent here." She enunciates every word, sounding like a headmistress of a posh private school. I'm starting to get the nickname.

"Why do you think you're here?" I stand up as well, to match her posture.

"I was trying to explain to the guards my extremely valid concerns about the goings-on in my cell."

"Which are?" I glance at my computer to cut to the chase here.

"It's unhygienic. Thoroughly."

"What's unhygienic?"

"The pile in the room. They've been stacking them there all week, and I've had quite enough of it."

"Stacking what?"

"Dead people," she complains. "I've told them again and again. There's flies everywhere. They're starting to topple over, and on top of that, they're a health concern," she says with a disdainful sniff. "This is how the bubonic plague started. Are you aware of that?"

Right. A minor issue, just a few stacks of dead people that the guards must have overlooked. "Have you been taking your medication, Janaya?"

"Miss Jones, please."

"Sorry, Miss Jones. Have you been taking your medication?"

"Of course," she huffs.

"Not palming them at all?"

"Now why on earth would I do that?"

"I don't know," I say, sitting down now because I missed lunch somehow and am getting a bit light-headed. "But it might be the same reason you did it last year and the year before that."

"Now that's a damned false accusation."

I start typing orders in the computer. "I'm thinking we might need a blood lab. Just to check your levels."

"Oh no," she says, a bit less strident now. "I don't see as that will be necessary."

"Fine, then. I would like you to take your medications, every single day. Then we'll check in with you next week. And if the bodies haven't been cleaned up by then, we'll probably need a level."

She pauses to consider. "Okay, Dr. Goldman, I will accept your offer."

"Excellent."

She reaches out to shake my hand, sealing the deal, and leans in to me before Maloney steps into the room. "Sofia says three thirty in the library," she whispers. "She's got a gift for you."

Chapter Twenty-Three

I have no idea why I go there, but I do. Maybe I'm pathetic enough to wonder about the gift. Or maybe it's because Newsboy hasn't written his article quite yet.

"I figured we should go for the library today," Sofia says. "Too cold for the rec area." She puts down her book, some thriller with a girl in a red coat standing by a fogged-out iron fence on the cover.

"So what's up?" I ask. "You decided to come clean about the texts finally?"

She shakes her head. "I'm not lying about that, Tanya. I didn't text you anything."

"Dr. Goldman," I remind her.

"Right, Dr. Goldman." A couple of inmates laugh behind us, shoving each other playfully, and the guard scolds them. "The truth is, I felt bad about how our last meeting ended. So I wanted to give you something, as an apology."

"You don't have to do that."

"I know I don't. But I wanted to. Here." She hands me a little metal tube with a paper stuffed inside, and scratch marks on it, like hieroglyphics. "Made it in shop class. I wasn't supposed to, but a friend helped me. And I figured it was worth getting in trouble over if we got caught."

I turn the cold metal in my hand, fingering the scratch marks, which suddenly pop with meaning. "Are these Hebrew letters?"

"Yes, it's a mezuzah." She points to the top. "I left a little hole in there for a nail. You put it on the doorpost so—"

"I know what you do with a mezuzah," I shoot back at her. But in her ensuing silence, I clear my throat in remorse. The mezuzah is a big thing. The Bible commands that we have it on the doorpost to remind us of our bond with God and to let others know that a proud Jew lives in this house. But there's no way I want to be reminded of Sofia every time I walk into my house.

"I can't take it," I say.

"But... why not?" Her face is crushed.

"I just can't. I'm sorry. It's against the rules." A couple of prisoners stand by us, perusing the mystery bookshelf. I hand the steel piece back to her, and she takes it. "But thank you. It was a nice thought."

She bites her lip in thought, then nods. Glancing around at the lavender Formica computer stations and the rows of creased paperback books, I suddenly wonder what I'm doing here. All I want to do is go home and sleep. And talk to Mike. "You okay?" Sofia asks, looking at me with curiosity.

When I look at her face, her eyes are questioning, caring even. "Oh yeah, I'm fine."

"You seem distracted or something."

"Just a lot on my mind."

"Do you want to talk about it?" she asks, then laughs at herself with glee at parroting the psychiatric cliché. And all at once I am struck by it, the sudden urge to talk about it. Indeed, to tell her everything. As the silence grows, her look transforms from one of mischief to one of bemusement.

"Dinner in ten," the guard calls out, saving me from myself. "Lockdown time."

Sofia appears to deflate at the announcement. "Time for some more atrocious food. Four p.m., early bird special."

We both stand up. "Worse than hospital food?" I ask.

"It's a fractional difference," she admits. "But there I could go to the gift shop, at least."

I point to the ATM-like screen mounted to the wall, where prisoners can check their accounts, court dates, et cetera. "You can't get anything from the commissary?"

"No money." She stretches out her back. "But I'm working on it," she adds with her inimitable sly smile, and I try not to contemplate what she might mean by that. We are heading out of the library when Newsboy passes us.

"Oh, hey, Zoe," he says, touching my arm. A stray sky-blue string sticks out of his sweater cuff. I have the strong urge to yank it and unravel his whole sweater.

"Sorry, gotta go," I say, tilting my head toward Sofia in explanation.

"Oh, sure. Call me, okay? To set up a time?"

175

"Definitely," I say, and I may be mistaken, but I could swear he and Sofia exchange a glance before we lose sight of him in the library.

Andre erases something fiercely, his pencil almost tearing through the paper.

"Tough subject?" I ask, as the guard leads me into the cell.

"No," he grumbles, "easy subject. My brain's just fucked up." Sitting on his bed, he turns back to his paper, which is on his lap on top of a comic book.

I glance over at the work, which is filled with x's, y's, and equations I was never any good at. "Doesn't look easy to me."

He scoffs. "I was doing this stuff two years ago. I can barely add two plus two right now." He puts the paper and comic aside with some frustration.

"Give it time. You'll be back to yourself eventually."

"Maybe." He leans down, his back against the wall and his lower body on the bed, as if he's at a right angle.

"You seem like you're doing better," I observe. "What do you think?"

"Kind of. They're still there sometimes, out of the corner of my eye."

"The devils?"

"Yeah, but they don't bother me as much. They keep pretty quiet." He is playing with his pencil now, twirling it between the fingers of his gloves.

"You feel like you still need those?" I ask, pointing at them.

He shrugs. "Maybe, maybe not. I'm keeping them on for now. Just in case."

We sit a moment in silence. "Can I ask you something, Andre? Not related to your condition?"

He shrugs. "What about?"

"It's about your Aunt Marion."

He twirls his pencil again, like a baton. "Okay?"

"How should I put this?" I drum my fingers on his desk. "She doesn't seem to have the warmest feelings for your father."

Andre chuckles. "Hates him, you mean."

I smile at his honesty. "Why is that, do you think?"

He sits up on the bed now. "I don't really know. I think she felt like my mom could do better, maybe. Like he wasn't good enough for her."

I adjust myself in the chair. "Do you think your aunt was afraid he was hurting your mother?" As soon as I say it, though, I'm afraid of planting thoughts in him.

But he shakes his head. "I don't think so. Just oil and water, you know. They didn't get along. Which meant she and my mom didn't get along." His eyes wander over to his math paper again. "Just lots of drama, I guess. I never really got it."

I stand up from the chair. "Thanks. Well, I'll let you get back to work."

He nods. "You could talk to my other aunt. Auntie Zena. She might know."

I jot this down on his sheet. "Aunt Zena. Is that your mom or dad's sister?"

"Mom's. She had two sisters. Marion and Zena. She always got along better with Zena."

I tuck the paper in my lab coat pocket. "Okay, great. Maybe I will talk to her," I say, and then, pausing at the bars, I turn back to him. "Would you happen to have her number?"

⌒

"Did you have a good holidays?" Sam asks politely.

"Yes," I answer politely, mentally editing out the less than rosy parts. The vomiting, the screaming three-year-old. And, of course, the cranberry bean. I fiddle with the squeaky knobs on the liquid motion toy.

"You seem a bit out of sorts today."

"Not really." My foot is drumming the floor of its own accord, which belies my denial of any problems. So I focus back on the toy. "Maybe a little. A lot of stress."

"Care to elaborate?"

"Just life," I say, which is rather lame and a thing I hate when my patients say, leaving me to guess at what might be ailing them.

"I got some weird texts," I offer, remembering I haven't told him yet. After I explain about the riddle and the burner phone, he looks concerned.

"What did Detective Adams say?" he asks.

"They've tried to track it down, but they can't. And Sofia is denying any involvement, for what that's worth."

"Anything new on that front, with Sofia?"

"We're still communicating a bit."

"And how's that going?"

"Okay, I guess. She keeps insisting she's changed, but I keep thinking she's up to something. Jack thinks I'm nuts to even talk to her."

He adjusts his yellow pad. "I understand his concerns. But you're not beholden to Jack."

"I know. And I think he's got a blind spot when it comes to her." I glance up from my toy. "Oy, that's terrible. Really, that pun was not intended." Sam betrays a glimmer of a smile. "Anyway, she might actually be genuine about this conversion thing. I'm still not sure."

"Nor is it your burden to decide."

"That's true." I try to hold off a yawn, and find my foot jittery again.

"How are you feeling about your medications?"

"I think they're okay."

As he turns his head, the bright-red temple of his glasses flashes in the sun. "If you aren't noticing any problems, we'll keep everything the same for now, but let's watch it, okay? I want to see you back in a week."

"A week?" We've been monthly now or even less, unless some crisis pops up.

"You're obviously under a great deal of stress." He takes off his glasses, holding them between two fingers. "And I can sense something isn't quite right."

"Uh-huh." Sam has a keen nose for this. But he might not be able to guess *what* isn't quite right. Or that I flushed all my pills down the toilet. What isn't quite right is that I'm pregnant, and I haven't told Mike. That I'm pregnant and have no idea what to do about it.

But I don't say any of this.

We spend the remaining minutes wrapping up, he pushing issues and I avoiding them in an uncomfortable tango until finally I am released.

I sit in the car a moment, enjoying the enveloping heat of the sun through the windshield. Then I turn on the engine and dig out of my satchel the paper with Andre's aunt's number on it. I sit through about eight rings and am about to hang up when a voice mail message comes on. She states her name, so I know I got the right number, at least.

"Hi. I'm Dr. Goldman," I say, sounding young and nervous. "I'm working with Andre, and I just wanted to go over a few things, if we could." I give her my cell number and hang up, hoping that she doesn't run this by her brother-in-law. Though certainly she might. I stare at my phone with a sigh. It's only six in the evening, and Mike's on late tonight.

So I do a quick Google search on my cranberry bean. I find out that "your jeans might not be fitting much longer!" and "your womb is already twice the normal size!" which actually astonishes me. I turn back to my pros-and-cons list.

Pros: Cranberry bean looks pretty cute at
2 centimeters.
Cons: Not ready to have a baby.

I shove the phone onto the passenger seat in exasperation. The truth is, I have to talk to Mike.

She gives me the thinnest smile, but it's clear XO Serena isn't thrilled to see the likes of me back in the ER. But I can't face dinner alone tonight. Mike spots me right away. "Hey, hon." He kisses my cheek.

"It's Zoe, the master psychiatrist!" Sean says.

"I thought you were in Derm," I remark.

"They told me they had too many PAs this month. Sent me back to ER."

"Too many PAs, I'm sure," I say.

"Anything in there for me?" Sean asks, eyeing the Chinese food bag like a hungry puppy.

I plunk the bag down. "Well, I got an extra egg roll, if you want it. And one for Serena, too."

"Nice." Sean scoops it up.

"Oh." She squinches her nose. "Is it, I mean, vegetarian?"

"No, it's not." I turn to Mike. "Chicken lo mein for you."

He lays out a napkin and the container. "Perfect timing. I was starved."

I pull the lid off my wonton soup (which is also, I mean, not vegetarian) and start in. We all eat in silence for a bit, and Sean takes the next patient. Serena doesn't stray an inch from her spot at Mike's side. She would use surgical glue if she could.

"So, what's new?" Mike asks, wiping some soy sauce off his face.

"Not much, this and that." *I'm pregnant, not so sure how far along or what to do about it.* "Had grand rounds today. So that was good."

"Uh-huh. What about Newsboy?" he asks. "Is he still stalking you?"

"I held him off for a bit longer, at least."

"Who's Newsboy?" Serena asks.

"Some asshole from the *Buffalo News* who wants to interview me," I answer.

"Oh," Serena says, flinching, as if they don't use profanity in her world of beautiful, skinny, not-too-tall people.

A nurse flashes by then. "Trauma coming. MVA." A burly EMT bustles down the hall with a gurney, and a group of staff starts gearing up for the trauma room.

"See ya in a bit," Mike says.

Serena puts her water bottle down. "Here we go again," she says, as if she's auditioning for a new TV doctor drama. She grins at Mike, establishing ownership for the next few hours. Then they race off, and the ER suddenly goes dead, devoid of the usual bustle. A nurse gets a med here and there, a doctor looks after a broken hand.

All at once I feel terribly out of place and alone. Mike and XO Serena are out saving lives while I'm losing them, just barely scraping by in my fellowship. And I'm pregnant. And I haven't told Mike. The sound of a text breaks up my dark musings.

Did you miss me, Angel of Death?

My spoon falls from my hand.

How about another riddle? I examine the number, which

is a different one from the last text. No, I type in. I'm not playing your games.

Come on, you're so clever. You must love riddles.

Seems like you think you're pretty clever too, I answer back, figuring the more I can get the riddler to talk, the better the shot I'll have at catching the person.

Ready or not here we go.

Razors, ropes, pills or all of the above.

Who's the next one you'll get rid of?

I told you I'm not playing, I answer.

A nurse in lavender-heart scrubs leans over me. "Smells good. I could really use some Chinese food right now."

"Oh, I know. It definitely hits the spot," I say, covering the phone, and we smile at each other before she walks down the hall. As soon as she's gone, I take my hand off the screen.

How about the boy with the bright-red gloves?

Chapter Twenty-Four

I call the detective about a hundred times but can't get a hold of him, and Mike won't be home for a few more hours. So I lie down in bed, trying to sleep, but the riddle keeps me awake.

It must be someone who knows about Andre. Not just his name, but this particular detail. Someone with more than just a passing knowledge of the case. The texter has to have seen Andre. Could it be someone from work, as Detective Adams suggested? Who, then?

Jason? No way. Dr. Novaire? Too busy collecting his ducats. It could be one of the guards or another male inmate. But my brain keeps landing on the most obvious candidate: Abraham Green. But I don't understand why he would be texting me.

Exhausted with these thoughts swirling in my head, I finally start to drift off as Arthur snuggles beside me. I descend into a broken sleep, dreaming of beans. Lima beans, red beans, cranberry beans.

Then I dream of a baby bean whizzing against my palm, like a trapped fly. Teeny, delicate. A slippery Mexican jumping bean.

I'm cupping my hands together, trying to hold it but not smother the thing. "Stop it," I say into my hand, with consternation. "I don't want to hurt you." But the bean finds a space between my fingers, tunneling out, and I am chasing it, this Tinker Bell of a thing. It is looping up and down, playing with me. The thing darts up the stairs, and I run after it.

"What are you looking for?" Mike says, suddenly materializing on the steps.

"Our baby."

"Oh," he says, nonchalantly, "I think it went into the baby room."

A baby room? I scramble up the stairs with an exquisite relief. Mike knows, of course he knows. He always knew. Mike set up a baby room for us. I enter from the hall, expecting soft pastel colors, a stenciled runner. Winnie-the-Pooh, maybe.

But the room is painted hot red and smells of something rotting. Piles of corpses line the walls, surrounded by buzzing clouds of flies.

Charmayne stands in the middle of the room in her wedding dress.

"He killed me," she says, and reaches out to me with bloody fingers. Backing away, I slam the door shut and turn to go down the stairs but find myself floating off the staircase instead. I am flapping my arms, madly, trying to fly, and I land on a hospital gurney being rolled down a hallway.

Prisoners' faces hang over me in a line, menacing.

"Bitch. You wanna fuck me now?"

Globs of saliva fly past. Urine falls like raindrops on the hospital bedsheets.

"Come over to Big Daddy. Let me show you how we do it."

"I bet you like it rough, don't you, whore?"

At last we motor past them and into a brightly lit hospital room. A doctor removes his scrub mask, revealing the face of Dr. Novaire. He places a gold coin in my hand. "It's a magic coin," he says. "Don't lose it."

But right then a grinding in my belly takes my breath away. "Help me."

Mike appears beside the gurney. "It's okay. You can do it, Zoe. Push." His kind, handsome face. His hand gripping mine. The gold coin is sweating in my palm. A pain wrenches in my belly. "Push!"

And I can feel the relief then, of the baby coming out. And the pain is gone, and I look at Mike with pride and anticipation, but his face is distorted in shock.

"What?" My voice is hollow. "What's wrong?"

As Dr. Novaire smilingly lifts the baby in victory, I can see its muddy-brown fur, its double tongue slithering in opposite directions.

And a hundred ribs, moving up and down.

Chapter Twenty-Five

Checking my phone, I see the detective still hasn't called back. I toss the drugstore bottle of prenatal vitamins back into my purse as Aubrey is led into the room.

She doesn't look bad, after her solitary stay. She's lost a few pounds she couldn't afford to lose, and her sumptuous strawberry-blond hair is on the stringy side. But her smile is warm, and her bright-green eyes are no longer haunted. Considering I hardly slept after the dream last night, she probably looks better than I do. "How are you?"

"Getting there," she answers with some relief.

I check her chart. "We went up on the Prozac. Do you think it's helping?"

"Maybe?" She answers it as a question while playing with her bracelet, which is a new one, a light-green thread now. "I think it's more than that, maybe. I think, in the end, you were right after all."

"About what?"

"Just talking about it. Getting it out there." Aubrey tugs at her bracelet. "It's like, it made it less terrible, somehow. Well, it's still terrible. But, you know, I could deal with it."

"Instead of running away from it."

"Yes." She releases the bracelet, looking at me. "That just made it worse."

"I know," I say, nodding. "Secrets can fester and bubble out in different ways, usually negative ways." As I say this, I am pierced by the truth about my own festering secret. Physician, heal thyself.

"You're smart, you know. You remind me of my sister."

"Oh yeah?" I want to laugh. *Because you're not at all like my sister.*

"Yeah. She's smart, too." She taps her thin fingers on the table. "She's older. Really smart. She always kind of protected me."

I check the computer family history for a mention of her. "Does she come visit you?"

"At first she did." Aubrey shrugs. "But not so much lately. She's got kids and all...so it's hard."

"Anyone else come to see you? Your mom, dad?"

Her eyes grow red, but she doesn't cry. "My mom died."

"Oh." I reach over and touch her arm. "I'm sorry."

"Thanks." She blinks back tears. "I was already addicted, so...she didn't get a real pretty picture of me, before she went."

I nod. "I'm sorry about that, Aubrey. But I'm sure she loved you."

"I don't know." She takes a quick breath. "I wasn't very lovable."

"Parents love their kids, no matter what."

She rolls her eyes, letting out a surly laugh. "Why don't you tell my dad that? He's certainly not on my visiting list. He hates me."

I lean in toward her. "Why do you say that?"

"Because it's true." Her hand turns into a fist, and she rubs her knuckles on the table. "He blames me for my mom's death. Though I don't get that one," she grumbles. "I might be an addict, but I didn't give her cancer."

"No. That's not right of him." We sit in silence for a while.

"Anyway." She puts her hands on her knees with an expression of renewed hope. "My sister did say she'd help me once I get out. So that's something. As long as I'm clean."

"Hey, then that's motivation right there," I say, building on her positivity.

"Yeah, until I screw it up again."

"Look." I pull my own faded pink friendship bracelet out from under my sleeve. "There's a lot of people rooting for you, Aubrey. Don't forget that."

Aubrey grins at me, then reaches over to touch my bracelet, before pulling away with some embarrassment at the closeness of the moment. "You know what I wish?" she asks, her tone hushed.

"What?" I turn from the computer chart to look at her.

"That I had met you when I was sixteen. Instead of Todd."

I search for the wry smile, the false tone of flattery, the hint of manipulation in her eyes. I search for it, and maybe it's in there somewhere, but I don't see it. All I see is such bald approbation that it's almost discomfiting. So I decide to accept this compliment. To add it to the win column, negating the longer list of names on the other side. As Sam said, you have to remember the good cases, too.

"You know what?" I say. "I do, too."

Tyler Evans struts into the room as Harry mans the door closely again. I am inches away from the red button. With Tyler in the room, I never let that button out of my sight.

"So I did my homework, Dr. Gold-Jew." He lays his chained hands on the table.

"How did it go?" I ask, deciding that ignoring his jibe is the best play.

"Good, real good."

"Is that so?" I ask, pleasantly surprised. "Why do you say that?"

"Some of the things they asked." He looks up at the ceiling, trying to remember. "Like about manipulation. That was one of them. Do you use manipulation to get things you need? And hell yeah, man. I'm really good at that."

"Oh." This is not exactly the insight we were after, however.

"And lying," he adds. "I'm a great fucking liar. This one time"—he cackles at the memory—"my cousin Jonesy got all upset that someone took his shit. You know, a little crystal he had laying around. And I told him I didn't know for sure, but I saw Hunts in that room earlier. And maybe he could've took it. Hunts is our nickname for my other cousin. His real name's Hunter."

"Right. Hunts, I got it." I bite back a yawn. "And I'll bet Jonesy is actually Jones."

"Yeah. How'd you know that?"

"Lucky guess."

"So, anyways, Jonesy goes after Hunts who's all like, yo, I didn't touch your shit, man. And I'm, like, fucking laughing inside because I *know* that Hunts had nothing to do with it, right? And you know how I know?"

I pause. "Because *you* took it?"

He looks at me with approval. "Damn, girl. They're right what they say, you know. You Jew bitches are pretty smart."

"Uh-huh. Well, thanks."

"So Jonesy goes after Hunts, actually ices the dude. And I'm like, fuck, man, I better hide that shit and quick, right? So I go sell it to some guy from out of town, and Jonesy never even heard about it." He crosses his arms, shaking his head at the memory. "He would have killed me, too, for sure. Jonesy, he's a fucking psycho." He laughs then, looking like a little boy in his glee at sharing his funny story. "Whoo-ey, that shit was close."

I stare at him in silence. "So what happened to Jonesy?"

"Oh," he says, as an afterthought, "he got locked up here, too. Caught fifty for murder. For Hunts. We boys in here, though. It's all good."

I shake my head. "Okay, then. I'm glad you got something out of the homework. You keep working on it. We'll have one more session to wrap up."

"Cool. Cool, yeah." He stands up, his chains clinking. "You do any courses in here? Like on war and shit? My friend is always going on about some book he's reading about how war is like art. And I was thinking maybe I could do some homework on that."

"Sorry, no. I don't have that particular book."

"Oh, okay. Cool." Harry immediately steps in to take Tyler back whence he came. I am finishing my note about Tyler's happy little story when Detective Adams finally calls me back. Just seeing his number fills me with relief.

"Hello, Detective."

"Hi, Zoe. I saw that you called. Sorry, I've been stuck in meetings all day." I hear the buzz of his office in the background. "And I do have some more information for you, but first...you said you got another text?"

"Yes. I sent you a screenshot. Did you see it yet?"

"No, sorry. I saw you e-mailed but didn't get a chance to read it yet. Wait, just a second, I'm pulling it up right now." There is a pause while he reads it. "Who's the boy with the bright-red gloves?"

"Andre," I say.

"Oh." The word is weighted with worry. "That is concerning." Keyboard tapping sounds out over the phone. "I'll put a call in to the warden ASAP. We need a record of everyone who's accessed Andre's file."

"Yes, good plan. But I also have a strong idea about who could be texting me now." I brace myself for his protest. "Abraham Green."

The detective pauses. "He certainly would know about

the gloves." I hear more typing. "But on the other hand, it doesn't make sense. Why would he be texting you about other patients?"

"I don't know," I admit. "Unless he was just trying to cloud the picture. Throw us off the trail a bit."

"And what trail is that?"

"The trail of his killing Charmayne, maybe? And maybe Andre knows about it?"

There is a long pause. "I should go ahead with my news. Because it may be more of an issue now."

"Okay." Out of the squeaky drawer, I grab a notepad.

"I couldn't find anything on April Green. It's not a real common name to begin with, and there wasn't anyone linked to Abraham Green anyway. So I decided to be creative and try some other months."

I tap my pen on the pad. "What do you mean, other months?"

"You know, how people are named May or July, for instance."

"Okay, right. I got you."

"It turns out there was a *June* Green," he says, "who was married to Abraham ten years ago. In Atlanta."

Footsteps sound down the hallway, then a knock before the door is opened. It's Destiny with my next patient. I mouth, "One sec" to her through the crack of the door. "And what happened to her?"

"It was ruled an accident, Zoe. So do me a favor and don't go jumping to any conclusions here." Destiny is laughing politely at something my patient said.

"I won't," I say. "What happened to her?"

"We're still looking into it. But it appears that June Green didn't have a heart attack after all. She fell down the stairs." He pauses. "And Abraham was the one who found her."

Mike sips his sake. "You sure you don't want any? I'm happy to share."

"Yeah, I'm sure."

"Stomach still off?"

"A bit," I answer, eating a California roll. I hold off on my usual sashimi, as I heard it could hurt the cranberry bean. Though I'm still not sure if I'm keeping the bean, I figure better safe than sorry. We sit a while not talking, listening to Japanese music with rolling flutes.

"You seem quiet."

"Just tired," I say, which is in fact true. "Had a nightmare last night."

"Oh, about the fire?" he asks, concerned.

"No, no. Not about that." I had nightmares for most of my life about the fire that killed my mother. When I learned the truth of what really happened, the nightmares stopped. "I don't even remember what it was about," I lie. "Just a bad night."

Mike frowns into his little white sake cup. "You sure you got that pepper spray?"

"Yes. Right in my purse."

"I was thinking." He reaches for a tuna roll. "Maybe this weekend we could go down to the gun range. Just for fun."

"That sounds like the opposite of fun."

He shrugs. "Don't knock it 'til you've tried it."

"Anyway, I have big plans to sleep all weekend," I say with a yawn.

Mike pours another minicup of sake and assesses me. "Maybe you're anemic."

"I'm not anemic."

He stares up at the soft recessed lighting. "Hard to tell if you're pale in this light."

"I wasn't pale yesterday," I remind him, dipping my roll in the soy sauce. "And my blood work was perfectly fine this summer."

"Well, don't get all defensive."

"I don't mean to be." I offer a California roll in apology, which he accepts. "It's just...I'm fine. Don't worry about me." Though part of me is chuckling. I may be a crap psychiatrist, but it turns out the ER doc is not much of a diagnostician either. The flute starts up again, and our phones ring at the same time.

"That's weird," I say, as we each look to see who's calling.

"Scotty," I say.

"ER," Mike says. I scoot out of the seat and walk toward the lobby as Mike lowers his voice to take his call.

"What's up?" I say, entering the vestibule.

"Got something for you on June Green. She...Wait just a second." I hear yelling, then the phone is muffled. "They both look great," he yells out. "Sorry, she can't decide on a font for the invitation. She's driving me nuts. The two look exactly the same."

"Pick one."

"Huh?"

"Pick one," I advise him. "You have to at least feign some interest in it."

"Oh," he says, puzzled. "You think? Maybe you're right, one sec." The phone is muffled again. "I like the one on the left," he yells, then after a bit returns to the phone. "Thanks, that did seem to work."

"Good. Okay, back to June Green."

"Yes." I hear him rummaging around, the sound of paper flapping. "This wasn't easy either. I'm losing my chops. Took a friend to help me hack into their system." More papers are shifted. "Here it is. You want me to e-mail it to you, or do you want plausible deniability?"

"E-mail it. But tell me first, what am I looking at?"

"The cover page of her life insurance policy. Bought six months before her death."

A couple walks into the vestibule, letting freezing air blow into the room. They peel off their scarves and stamp their boots on the rug.

"How much was it for?" The couple opens the door to the restaurant, and I catch a snippet of flute before the door closes again.

"I hate to admit it, but you might be onto something."

"How much?" I repeat.

"A million dollars," he says. "I just sent it."

Chapter Twenty-Six

It certainly is suspicious," the detective agrees.

"Talk about motive," I say. "But I'm surprised that they didn't look into it. Wouldn't that be the first thing they do? Check life insurance? That seems like Detective 101."

"Usually," he admits. "But it's hard to make assumptions about someone else's case. Who knows what investigation they did? I'm sure it wasn't obvious, or they would have gone there. They always look at the spouse first."

I shift lanes. "How about the latest text? Did you find out anything more?"

"Nope. Another burner phone."

"Damn." I speed through the yellow light. "Maybe you should talk to Abraham?"

"No," he answers, definitively. "If he is the texter, which is a big if, we don't want to spook him. We want to let them keep texting, until they make a mistake."

"Or until they kill another patient. Or me."

"That's a leap, Zoe. It's more likely this person is tormenting you over cases for some reason, rather than actually killing your patients. But we're looking into it, believe me. The warden is taking this very seriously. He's pulling the names of anyone who's laid just one finger in those charts."

"So what am I supposed to do, then, just wait?" I tap my hand on the steering wheel, softly at first, then smacking it with frustration. "Can't we just arrest him?"

The detective sighs. "First off, we don't even know that Mr. Green is doing this. Just because he may be involved in June Green's death doesn't mean he's doing anything to Andre. Who knows? It could just as well be Sofia, or someone linked to her."

"Though you haven't found evidence of that."

"No," he admits. "Not yet. And the other thing is, he hasn't actually threatened you, Zoe. It's harassment at best."

"Oh, just harassment."

"Listen. I know you're upset, and you have every right to be. But I promise you, we're doing everything we can. I'll put another call in to Atlanta. But that might take a while. I have no jurisdiction over there." The sound of yelling breaks over the phone, then he is back on. "Sorry, it's a bit crazy here today."

"That's okay. I know this isn't your only case. And I appreciate everything you're doing, I really do. I don't mean to get riled up, I'm just a little..." I'm about to say *hormonal* but decide to let it hang at that.

"It's okay. I'm on it, Zoe. Trust me, okay?"

After we hang up, I realize I've accomplished nothing except possibly pissing off my one ally. The texter is still out there, taunting me, and I have no more information. I've already put June Green's name through every search engine I can think of and found nothing. Photos from her gardening club, a black-tie event with Abraham, and her obituary. No kids that I could see. I drive a few more miles, dreading every inch of the way, until I finally pull into the parking lot. My stomach is in knots. Back to the reason I'm feeling hormonal right now.

"Time to face the music," I say to myself, and cut the engine.

I try to focus on the mellow pink clouds outside the window instead of her hand reaching inside me or my heels in the rock-hard stirrups.

Dr. Marchand sits up suddenly, snapping off her rubber gloves and tossing them in the bin in a well-practiced maneuver. She shoves the stirrups back in, and I sit up with relief, though goo is leaking from me. I hate seeing the gynecologist. Even when I'm not pregnant.

"So what do you think?" I ask.

She leans over and taps off check marks on her tablet for my visit. Two paper-wrapped tongue depressors stick out of the breast pocket of her lab coat like bunny ears. "You're probably twelve weeks by now, but we'd have to do an ultrasound to be sure."

"Twelve weeks?" I ask with a gasp. "So that means an apricot, not a cranberry bean," I say, thinking of the pregnantbabes.com illustration.

"A cranberry bean?" She gives me an odd look.

"Nothing, forget it."

"Yes, well, we have to verify it, of course. But do you keep track of your menstrual cycle?"

"Obviously not well enough."

Dr. Marchand turns to her tablet again. "And you were on all these meds before pregnancy?" She makes it sound as if I'm some kind of dope addict.

"Yes."

"And you stopped them when?"

"Right after I found out."

A frown pokes through her professional demeanor, and my stomach sinks. "Then I'd definitely recommend an ultrasound at this point to rule out any neural tube defects."

She's speaking to me doctor-to-doctor, which I appreciate. But don't appreciate. Neural tube defects, meaning spina bifida or worse. "The thing is…" I begin, licking my suddenly dry lips.

Dr. Marchand looks up from her tablet. "Yes?"

"I'm still not positive I'm going to keep it."

"All right." She nods, businesslike. "You're past ten weeks now, so we'd be talking surgical termination. You're still in the window for an aspiration." Her tone betrays no opinion on the matter one way or the other. I'm not sure what I expected. I see her every other year for a cervix check. It's not as if we're friends.

Of course she can't tell me what to do. It's my decision. I just never thought I would have to make it.

"You can talk with your...partner," she says, uncomfortably. "And make your decision. Just give the office a call. Again, I would recommend sooner rather than later."

"Uh-huh," I respond, blankly. It might help if I actually *told* my partner. My gown crinkles as I sit there in shock. Twelve weeks.

"Anything else?" Dr. Marchand asks, briskly.

"No, I guess I'm good."

"Fine, then I can send your prenatal script to the pharmacy and—"

"No, please. Just give me the hard copy, if you would." The last thing I need is Mike finding it when he picks up his blood pressure medication. She scribbles it on a pad, and I am sent out to the waiting room, packed with more obviously pregnant ladies. Walking to the parking lot, I try to put the visit out of my mind and glance through my texts to make sure I haven't missed anything. Again I come upon the riddler's ugly text.

How about the boy with the bright-red gloves?

I sit down in my car, feeling low. But then it hits me. The detective may not want to meet with Abraham Green.

But that doesn't mean that I can't.

I stifle a yawn as Janaya Jones, aka Ol' White Lady, comes in.

She takes a seat with her head held high, as if waiting for me to offer her crumpets. Performing a quick appearance check, I note her orange sweatshirt is spotless today, and she smells as fresh as a daisy, so the medications must be taking some effect. "How are you?" I ask.

"Very well," she answers with a genteel smile. "They have cleaned up the putrid bodies in the room. Thank you."

"Good, good. I'm glad."

"It was an unacceptable living environment, as you can well imagine."

"Certainly."

"But it's been rectified," Janaya says.

"And you're taking your medications?"

"I am. For hypertension and diabetes mellitus type two."

"And for..."

"Schizoaffective disorder, yes," she says, as though speaking of someone else. "Minimal side effects," she adds, pre-empting my next question. "Mild dizziness upon standing. I think they call that orthotics."

"Orthostasis," I correct her, only God knows why.

"There are several words for it," she returns, icily.

"Yes, of course. Either one." *Although one is for sneakers*, I just hold myself back from saying. We run through her labs and verify to the best of my abilities that she is in fact taking her medications and is stable. "So I'll see you in one month, then." I toggle up the appointment calendar.

"Six months should suffice," she says.

"I'm thinking one," I say, not negotiating.

She sits up, more primly. "As you wish." She waits then, though the appointment appears to be over.

"Is there something else I can help you with?" I know full well that there is. But I don't have the time or energy to deal with my sister right now.

"I have a message from Sofia."

"You can tell her I'll call her this time, when I'm ready to meet."

"No, she just wanted me to tell you something. About Ruth."

"Ruth?" I ask, thrown for a minute. "Who's Ruth?"

"Wait a moment, I wrote it down." She opens her palm, where she has scribbled something in black ink. "'Don't ask me to leave you or turn back from you. Wherever you go, I will go.'" She shuts her hand into a fist. "The book of Ruth."

"Andre's not coming?" Mr. Green asks. He folds his black wool coat in half and lays it on the table, next to his black leather briefcase and the smartphone at his elbow. "Is everything okay?"

"Everything's fine," I say. "Sometimes I like to meet without the patient present so everyone can speak more freely."

He seems to weigh this and nods. "So, how is he doing?"

"Stable," I answer. Though in this case, *stable* is barely functioning.

"That's good to hear." He surveys the conference room, which is austere, walls painted a forbidding gray without any pictures to dispel the gloom. "Is there anything I can help you with, then?"

"Yes, there is. I wanted to ask about your wife, Charmayne."

"Okay," he answers warily.

"Were she and Andre close?"

"Close?" he repeats with relief. "Oh yes. Certainly they were close. She was his mother." He frowns then, which may or may not be for show. "It was so sudden, when she passed. It was a shock for everyone."

"Yes, I'm sure." I put on a soothing voice. "Another question. Can you tell me more about your first wife?"

Mr. Green backs up in his chair. "I don't see how that's relevant."

"It may not be, but Andre mentioned her. Did she have any relationship with him?"

"Andre mentioned her?" he asks, and I nod. "I'm surprised by that. We didn't really talk about her much. She died ten years before I even met Charmayne." He looks off into the distance at the bare wall. "Heart attack," he says.

Which I now know is a lie. "Andre mentioned her name, I forget, it was a month, I think—"

"April," he says.

Which is another lie. I wait him out then, tapping my

fingers on the table through the silence to unnerve him. It appears to be working, as he starts squirming in his chair. "Her name is June, though, right?" I ask. "June Green. Not April Green."

His eyebrows shoot up, then he leans back with an eerie calm, assessing me. "May I ask, Dr. Goldman, what exactly are you playing at here?"

My fingers keep drumming. "I just want to know why you're lying to Andre. And to me."

"This is of no concern to you," he barks. "You were supposed to help my son. That's all. That's all you need to be doing here." He stands up then, launching an offensive. "But you don't seem to be capable of that. And now you're going on about my first wife?"

I shift away from him. "I'm just trying to understand—"

"You said it was schizophrenia. You promised you would help him. And now you're trying to blame this on me somehow? Nuh-uh. I don't think so."

"I didn't mean to upset you," I say, to calm his explosion.

"Well, you have upset me. You have most certainly upset me. Dragging up the memory of my poor first wife. She doesn't deserve that. I don't deserve that." His hand is resting against the tabletop, trembling. "You know, Dr. Goldman, I've had my doubts about you. Since day one I have. When my boy wasn't getting any better, but you convinced me. Conned me, maybe, that you could help him. But now I think my doubts were well served, and I'm going to talk to your attending about switching him from your care."

I lace my hands together. "I'm sorry again that I upset you. But we're both on the same team here."

"I'm not so sure about that," he thunders, and then a ringing sound interrupts us. I look down to his phone, but it's face-up with a dark screen. The ringing stops, but after a few seconds starts up again, and appears to be coming from his briefcase. Again the ringing stops.

We are both staring at the briefcase.

Still standing, Mr. Green grabs his belongings, throwing on his coat, slipping his phone in his pocket, and taking his briefcase in his hand. "I'll be going now," he says, "as this was obviously a complete waste of my time. And you can be sure, Dr. Goldman, that you will be coming off Andre's case. Or you will be hearing from my lawyer."

With that he storms out of the room, and I sit there, trying to figure out my next step. That has to be the burner phone in his briefcase, and I have to get a hold of it somehow.

So I count out thirty seconds, and then I follow him.

Mr. Green strides over to a dark-gray sedan in the visitor's lot.

It looks old and possibly used, certainly not like the flashy car you'd expect a millionaire to be driving. But then again, June Green died ten years ago, and maybe the money's all gone by now. And if the coffers were empty, perhaps Charmayne was the next deposit.

As he backs up his sedan, I dart into my car (a conspicuous red MINI Cooper) and follow two cars behind him. I don't have a plan at all, except to follow him, and, if possible, call the phone while he's in earshot. I already called both text numbers and got no answer. But that may not mean anything. I wasn't close enough to hear if the phone was ringing.

A late-afternoon flurry hasn't been plowed yet, and the streets are caked in snow. All the cars are crawling and skidding, and I have no idea where we're going.

We drive past the city in a painfully slow slog down Main Street, past old, faded storefronts with peeling paint and hand-lettered signs. The night darkens, the streetlights casting an orange glow on the street. As we snail toward the suburbs, the storefronts change, turning richly colored with confident bold signs and pricey restaurants on either side. I am monitoring the progress of the car crawling on my bumper in my rearview, when suddenly Abraham's car makes a sharp left turn.

I slam on the brakes, fishtailing the MINI Cooper, overcorrecting and then undercorrecting my steering, and finally end up an inch away from the car in front of me. My heart trots in my chest as the driver behind me lays on the horn, then passes me. At last I get the chance to make the left turn and park in a dark corner in the front of the parking lot.

Powering the grimy car window down, I let cold air blow in but keep him in sight. I'm rewarded with a view of his thick form sauntering toward the entrance. His keys jingle in black leather gloves, and he is whistling some carefree ditty.

No briefcase.

I hear the bells of the door as he opens it to the gold-lit

doorway of an expensive Italian restaurant. Someone stands up to greet him in the front window, a pretty African American woman in a dark-blue, work dress–type outfit. They kiss on the lips briskly, then sit down at the table. I have a perfect view of them, picking out a wine on their tall menus and laughing, their breath fogging the window. He puts his hand on hers, and they beam at each other like actors in a Viagra commercial.

I take a blurry but unmistakable picture with my phone, in case no one believes me. I wait a while, watching them, but nothing happens. They just keep making lovey-dovey faces at each other. And then, because I am freezing and hungry, and wouldn't last ten minutes on an actual stakeout, I carefully pull the car out, make a slow, skidding turn out of the restaurant, and drive home.

Chapter Twenty-Seven

You told me you were putting together a plan, and I could help you. I leaned back, the heels of my palms scraping against the cement floor, and asked you what kind of plan.

You gave me a serious look. Can I trust you?

Of course, I said.

You said I could help you, be your soldier. But I'd need to follow your every order, without hesitation. You asked if I would be able to do that and I nodded, but I wasn't so sure. My wrists were getting tired of leaning, and I sat up and crawled on top of you. What's my first order, sir? I asked, in a joke-sexy voice, and you didn't smile. But you didn't push me off either.

You said we needed two more patients, then we could go on to the next step. I started unbuttoning your shirt. I remember marveling at the pearl sheen of the buttons. We don't get anything pretty in here. You asked if I had a name for you right now, and I was ready this time.

They call her Ol' White Lady, I said.

You smirked at the name and I circled my fingers around your chest. I said she was crazy, and I could probably get her to drink something like Barbara Donalds, but you said that was too obvious, and we needed to do something different. You pushed my hand away, but gently. Let me think about it.

I nodded, but the idea made me apprehensive. Giving someone a drink was one thing. Killing them with my hands was something different. But you were happy that I got you a name anyway, and said we just needed one more, then we could go on to the final stage. I asked what the final stage was, and you told me I wasn't ready for that yet.

I can see now that you were right. I wasn't ready. Maybe in your heart you knew that I would have left you then. I would never have agreed to do that.

You ready for your reward now? *you asked with that grin. That wicked grin I have grown to love and to hate in equal parts.*

I smiled in answer and you told me to get on my hands and knees. So, awkwardly, I shifted off you. I wish I could say I felt turned on, but I didn't. It was just playing games. I didn't want that. I wanted to hold you again, to be held.

But instead I waited for you, feeling stupid and anxious with my knees getting sore on the hard floor until you pulled down my pants and positioned yourself so it became very clear what you wanted. Because you're not original, Professor. It turns out you're just like every other man out there, wanting to fuck some girl in the ass. I tried to relax because I knew what was coming, and you whispered, almost tenderly, Is this okay?

But before I could answer, you rammed into me so hard that I fell to the floor. I lay there, my face scratching against the cold cement, just wishing you would finish already. But you took your time. Then finally, after what seemed like forever, you were done. I was on my stomach still, exhausted and hurting. I stared at a patch of mold on the wall, trying not to cry. I remember thinking, This is it. It's over this time, for good. He doesn't respect me, and I don't need this from him, or anyone. But then you rolled next to me, surprising me with a deep, warm embrace. You held me for a long time, until I relaxed into your arms.

Then you sighed right into my ear, I love you.

Chapter Twenty-Eight

Come on, Zoe," the detective roars into the phone. "It was a date!"

He is responding to the picture of Abraham and the mystery woman that I e-mailed to him. Though I didn't necessarily expect gratitude for my initiative, I also didn't expect outrage.

"Yeah, but what about the other phone, in his briefcase?"

"I told you, I don't know. We'll look into it. But there's plenty of reasons people might have a second phone," the detective says. (Which is what Mike said when he came home late last night. Though I failed to mention the part about following Andre's father to the restaurant.)

"You don't think it's suspicious?"

"No, Zoe, I don't," Detective Adams says, not sugarcoating it in the least. "His wife's been gone for over a year now. So he went to dinner with someone. Last I checked, that wasn't illegal." I hear papers shuffle over the phone. "And by the way, how did you even know he was going to be there? You just happened to be eating at the same restaurant?"

I tap my pen on my desk and don't say anything.

"Please don't tell me you were following him." Again I don't have a satisfactory answer. "Okay, Zoe, this conversation is ending here and now. I understand that you care about your patients, and we will get to the bottom of the texting thing. But this isn't helping," he says, stressing each word. "If Abraham Green is involved in his wife's death, and that is an *enormous* if at this point, then he is a dangerous man, and you could be putting yourself in harm's way by going after him. Not to mention messing up any investigation we might end up doing."

Jason sits down at the computer next to me, smelling strongly of coconuts.

"Could *you* do something, then? Search his house, maybe?"

"We're nowhere near a search warrant, Zoe." He sighs into the phone. "Listen. I agree with you about the life insurance, it's suspicious. And the second phone is...*possibly* suspicious. But here's what we have right now. June Green was ruled an accident and Charmayne a heart attack. Both natural causes."

"But what about the text about Andre?"

"Zoe," he says, his voice low on patience. "Please. Please don't play detective anymore. I'm sure you must have a million other things to worry about."

"Yeah," I answer. He's wrong, though. I don't have a million things to worry about, just one thing. About the size of an apricot. "I'm sorry. The whole thing just has me worried. And I do appreciate all you're doing to investigate it."

"Okay," he says, mollified. "Promise me something, then. Stay away from Abraham Green. Remember what I said. If it's him, we don't want him to catch on that we know. Let him tie his own noose."

"Okay," I say with a shiver, thinking of my patient on that hot day in July, hanging from his own noose.

"'Sup?" Jason asks, unzipping his sweater a bit.

"Nothing much, you?"

"Saw Red Gloves in the hall."

"Oh yeah?" I pull up something on my computer.

"Yeah. I don't know what cocktail you guys have him on right now, but I gotta say, the kid looked half-dead."

I rush off to see Andre while I have the chance.

If Abraham does speak with Novaire, this might be the last time. It takes me a while to find Andre but I finally catch up with him in his classroom. The teacher is talking about Darwinism, in a place where survival of the fittest surely has its advocates.

Jason is right. Andre looks bad, worse than when I saw him last. He is seated at the back of the classroom, slumped in his chair and barely focusing.

"Andre," I whisper. "How are you doing?"

His eyes are glazed over. "Okay."

"Have you had any more visions?"

"Huh?"

"Visions, demons. Have you seen any?"

He shakes his head. "He's hiding." The words are slurred.

The Haldol appears to be doing a number on him today. Though last week he seemed to be acclimating to it. It doesn't make sense. He shouldn't be going backward at this point. I make a note to check his Haldol dose. "Who's hiding?" I ask.

"The devil. Getting reinforcements." Chalk smacks against the board, echoing around us. "Sgt. Fury is coming, though. He told me. He's gonna help me."

The teacher speaks louder now, glancing pointedly at us. He booms the next question out, and a teenager in the front half raises his hand. "Andre, I need to ask you a question," I whisper, softer. "Did you know your father was married before?"

He nods, slowly, robotically.

"Do you know anything about her?"

"April." He grips a yellow pencil in the palm of his red glove. "She died, too."

"Do you know how she died?"

"The heart. Devil always goes for the heart."

"Uh-huh." I scoot my chair toward him as the teacher blares on. "I called your Aunt Zena, by the way. I haven't heard back from her yet, but I'll let you know when I do."

"The devil always goes for the heart, but it's okay. Sgt. Fury's gonna help me."

215

"Okay, Andre." I'm realizing that real conversation is fruitless at the moment but take one last stab at it. "One more question. Do you have a cousin named Jermaine?"

Andre whips his face toward me, the absent look gone. His eyes are a force field. "That's him. The double." The pencil is trembling in his gloves. "They sent him to replace me."

I dab my lips with toilet paper.

I was in the clinic already when a wave of nausea came out of nowhere, and I made it to the bathroom just in time. Lumbering back to the clinic, I sit down across from Aubrey, praying it doesn't happen again.

"You okay?" Aubrey asks.

"Yeah. A little food poisoning, I think."

"Yuck." She scrunches her face. "That's the worst."

"No fun at all," I say, guilty at the lie. "So, you thought things were going a bit better?" She is looking better, brighter. Her hair is wet and smells freshly washed. She has a bit of lip gloss on, if I'm not mistaken.

"Definitely better. And I think I know why."

"Tell me."

She leans over toward me across the table, sharing a secret. "I wrote to Todd."

"Really?"

"Yes," she says with finality. "I told him it's over. I told him

216

he was a pig and an asshole for what he did to me. And I told him I was never ever speaking to him again."

"Wow." That serotonin really is kicking in. Surveying her arms, I see no new cuts either. "And have you been working on the stress relief measures we talked about?"

"I have." Her voice is proud. "Working out with my friend." Her pale skin blushes a tinge at the word. "Doing more reading. Writing poetry."

"Poetry?" I add this to her chart for future reference. "I didn't know you were a writer."

"I wouldn't say that, exactly," she backtracks. "I'm in this little class thing. I don't even go all that often, but it isn't bad." She pauses a second. "There's a girl in there, says she knows you."

"I do see a lot of patients."

"Not this one. She said she was your sister." The line is delivered with scorn, and she watches me, gauging my response. When I don't respond, she shrugs. "That's what I figured. She lies about everything. And she's all over the teacher, like, please, as if you have a chance with him. She's very into herself."

"An inflated ego," I say, in psychiatry-speak.

"A *super*inflated ego," she returns.

After ten more distracted minutes, I ascertain that she does in fact seem to be doing better and make a note to ask her about her new workout friend at the next visit. Aubrey has borderline tendencies, a point on which Dr. Novaire agrees with me. When this new relationship ends, she could go spiraling downward again, and damn it, I'm determined to keep this one in my win column.

Out of the corner of my eye, I catch Maloney sidling up to the door, and I give him a thumbs-up to collect Aubrey. "Hey," I say, "can you get Sofia Vallano for me?"

He consults his tablet. "I don't have her on for today."

"Add-on," I say.

⌐

Sofia plops down in the chair. "So what's up? The hours were crawling by without me?"

"Have you been telling people about us?" I demand.

"What, about our affair?" She lets out a throaty laugh, and right then a wave of nausea hits. I grab for a packet of saltines in my lab coat pocket and stuff one in my mouth. "I'm just kidding, Jesus." She leans back in her chair, checking me out. "You sick or something?"

"Just getting over a bug," I mutter.

"Hey, wanna see my new tat?" She whips up her pant leg to reveal a dark-blue verse in pseudo-Gothic lettering. Pseudo apparently because the jailhouse tattooist is in the apprentice stage. "A time to love. A time to hate." I get a flashback of her other tattoo, which she got after sneaking off on a field trip from her previous mental hospital. It is more artful as well as more sinister, a black-and-white tattoo of a knight on his horse, the tarot Death card.

"That's something," I say, as she pulls her pant leg back down. "Ecclesiastes. Or is that meant to be the Byrds version?"

"Fuck off," she says, not unpleasantly. "I like it." She pulls the pant leg up for another glance. "Anyway, what's up? You're the one who wanted to see me this time."

"Yes, this is true." I polish off the second cracker and wipe the crumbs off my lab coat. "One of my patients had something interesting to say. That you told her I was your sister."

"Doubtful."

"So...it just came to her out of nowhere?"

"Who was it?" Sofia asks with curiosity more than annoyance. "Maybe someone else told her."

I pause. "You know I can't tell you that."

"Then we're at a stalemate, aren't we?" The silence grows, and Sofia taps her polka-dotted nails on the table. She catches me staring at them. "Someone stole some Wite-Out," she explains.

I nod. "She was in your writing class. Implied you were very close to the teacher."

"In his dreams," she scoffs, but the way she swallows makes me think I've struck a nerve. She runs her polka-dotted fingers through her hair, seductively. "I could have any man in this place in a heartbeat. I don't need him. Plus I have enough bitches trying to service me anyway."

"Of course." I try not to snicker.

"Ridiculous class. I'm only doing it for good behavior. Bunch of drama queens sobbing about their mommies."

"Right. Though most of them probably didn't kill their mommies."

Her jaw muscle pulses in a clench. "That's pretty low," she says, quietly. "Even for you."

Right then I wonder what I'm even doing here, fighting with my sociopathic sister, stooping to her level. "I'm sorry, Sofia. Anyway, I'd appreciate it if you didn't go around telling people."

"I won't. Trust me, Tan—" She catches herself. "Dr. Goldman. As they say, blood is thicker than water." Her hint of a smile is back.

"Right." I stand up, and she stands, too, at the cue to leave. "By the way, Sofia, you might want to know something. Jews don't get tattoos."

This gives her pause. "How do you know that? The rabbi never said that."

"Well, they don't. Maybe you didn't get to that part of the Bible yet, but it states it pretty clearly. 'You shall not etch a tattoo on yourself.' I call the guard over. "Leviticus. Look it up."

That night Mike is finally home for dinner, and I decide to tell him.

He bites into a chicken wing, the aroma of spicy heat pouring over the kitchen table. They smell wonderful, and I steal one from the box.

"Hey," he says, guarding the rest with his arm. "You said you didn't want any. Just pizza, you said. I would have gotten twenty."

"I changed my mind," I say, reaching for another.

"And you're taking all the drumettes," he complains.

"They're the best ones."

He sighs. "Fine, just leave me the carrots, at least." We sit, munching away, with Arthur darting from side to side for the chance of a dropped morsel. It's a pleasure to have Mike home for dinner again, though my nerves are on edge with the thought of telling him.

"So, how do you think my patient found out about Sofia?" I ask, retreating to the barely safer territory of work.

"About Sofia?" He reaches for another wing. "It was bound to happen eventually."

"I suppose," I say, dipping celery in blue cheese. "I just don't want Newsboy to catch on if I can help it."

"*Mmmph*," he says, nodding with commiseration as he bites into another wing.

In the pause I take a breath. "Mike, I wanted to talk to you about something."

"Okay." He wipes grease off his hands, turning his napkin orange. "What is it?"

"It's about something that…" I find myself breathing funny as the silence builds. Mike looks at me, perplexed. Instead of talking, I wipe my hands off, too.

"Zoe, is everything okay?"

"Yeah," I say, trying to breathe normally. "Everything's fine. I just—"

"You're taking your meds and everything?" he asks.

"Of course," I answer, offended with the question by instinct, though I am, in fact, not taking my medications.

"I shouldn't have asked that," he says. "You just seem more distracted lately or something."

I don't answer but busy myself by throwing out the box the wings came in.

"Of course, you've got a lot on your mind," he continues. "With that idiot texting you."

Mike gets up, too, and we both wash our hands and sit back down at the table. He takes a long sip of his beer. "You sure you don't want one? It's hoppy."

"No, no, I'm really fine," I say, practically drooling at the thought of a hoppy beer right now.

Then Mike scoots his chair next to me. His skin smells like the lemon soap by the sink. "All right. What is it you wanted to tell me?"

I pause, feeling a squeeze in my chest. "Nothing really," I say, weaseling out of my confession. "Just about Sofia. I was thinking maybe I should stop seeing her."

"Definitely," he agrees, readily. "There's no reason to see her at all. She just upsets you."

"Right."

"You don't owe her anything, no matter what she says." He takes my hand and starts tracing his finger around my palm. "And try not to stress about the texting thing. The detective will find them eventually, okay?"

"Okay," I say, but I can't concentrate very well because now Mike is kissing my neck, which is a bit of a distraction.

I mean to tell him about the apricot. I want to tell him about the apricot.

But it's not the right time. His fingers are running through my hair and it feels so good and I'm kissing him back and pretty soon our shoes are thrown off and we've landed on the couch.

And then we don't talk about Sofia, or the texts, or the apricot. Or anything at all.

Chapter Twenty-Nine

The next morning I get an urgent call to see Ol' White Lady.

Destiny takes me cell-side, then goes back to her desk two feet away in the hallway. Janaya is sitting on her bed in her depressingly small cell, which just barely fits the bed, a toilet, and a couple of library books. (As Maloney is fond of saying, it's prison, not a hotel.)

When she sees me, she stands up, and I lean into the red-and-white cage that separates us. "Listen," I start. "I know this isn't your fault. But just tell Sofia that I will see her when I see her."

Janaya shakes her head. "This does not pertain to Sofia."

"Oh, okay." I relax. "What's going on, then?"

She looks both ways down the hall for any eavesdroppers, and at Destiny, who smiles at us. Sappy tunes from a late-afternoon soap opera play on the flat-screen television mounted on the wall. "Someone's after me," she whispers, leaning right up to my face. I can smell her fetid breath, and her hair is looking like a rat's nest again. So this visit is more about her palming her meds than about my visiting with Sofia.

"What do you mean by that, Miss Jones? Who's after you?"

"I heard it," she whispers, urgently. "It's in the milieu. Someone is trying to get me. It's murder. Out-and-out murder."

"Do you know who?" I ask.

She grips the cage bars. "I don't know. The who or the why, I don't know. But the truth is out there. In the walls. People are talking."

"Are you hearing the voices in the walls?"

"No," she says with disdain. "It's an expression. Not the actual walls talking. People talking. Saying things about me. They get quiet when I come over, but I know that they're talking about me. I am certain of it." She glances up and down the hall again, as if the potential killers might be lurking out there. "I'm scared," she whispers. "Janaya is scared."

"Have you talked to the guards about this?"

She nods, glumly. "I tried. Lord, I have tried, but they won't listen to me. They just think I'm crazy. They...they lack perspective."

I'm sure she's right that the guards won't listen to her, and they may indeed lack perspective. But I'm also sure that she is quite paranoid right now and also lacks perspective. "I'll talk to them."

"The guards?"

"Yes."

Her smile is relieved. "You'll do that for me?"

"Yes. Of course."

She bows her head toward me. "I knew you would. I knew I could count on you." She gives me a gratified smile. "You're accountable, Dr. Goldman. Not many people in this world are accountable. But you are accountable."

I look around her cell. "Everything else okay? The bodies gone?"

"Indeed." She nods with approval, glancing around at her cell. "Absolutely pristine."

"Good," I say. "So I'm just gonna…" I point my head toward Destiny, and Janaya nods. "Oh yes, by all means." So I head over to tell Destiny that my paranoid patient is paranoid and thinks someone might be plotting to murder her.

"Noted," she says, raising her eyebrows conspiratorially. On the way out, I tell Maloney and Harry, too, for good measure, then sit down at my clinic desk. I'm starved, and exhausted, and quite sick of thinking about apricots. So I grab my phone.

"What up?" It's Jason.

"Did you eat lunch yet?"

I take a slurpy bite of my ramen, which was the only thing that didn't turn my stomach when I packed my lunch today. Jason is inhaling a taco that smells disgusting.

"Don't you think that's weird?" I ask, showing him the newest text.

"It's not weird, Zoe. It's totally freaky-slash–fucked up."

"Thank you," I say, validated. "You're the only person who seems to appreciate how bizarre this whole thing is."

"What did Gardner say about it?"

"Not a word," I say. "I guess he's talking to the detective or whatever, but I don't really want to bother him if I don't have to."

"Yeah," Jason agrees. "That's probably wise." He bites into his taco, getting sour cream on his chin. "So what else is new? I feel like I haven't talked to you in forever. What's up with Mike? Any rings flying yet?"

And then, distressingly, I start crying.

"Oh shit." Jason's eyes get wide. "Men are stupid, Zoe. I'm sure he'll ask eventually." I shake my head to let him know that's not it, but can't speak without sobbing.

"Did you break up?" I shake my head again, still mute.

"Um." He puts his hand on my shoulder. "I'm running out of guesses here."

Wiping my eyes, I breathe in deeply to steady myself while he watches me. I take another deep breath and release it. "I'm pregnant."

"*What?*" His eyes practically pop out of his head. "You're...Seriously?" he whispers.

I nod.

"You're fucking with me." I shake my head. "You're not fucking with me."

"Not fucking with you."

227

"Oh my God. When did you find out? What are you going to do? Does Mike know?" he asks in rapid fire.

"I found out a couple weeks ago. I'm not sure what I'm going to do. And no, Mike does not know yet."

"But you're going to tell him," he says, as if advising me and not asking me.

"Yes," I say. "Eventually."

"Holy shit." Jason pushes his plate to the side while I take another sip of my soup. "I thought you were looking a little rounder lately."

"Thanks, Jason. That's actually not helpful."

"You still look good," he says, backtracking. "Some guys like that. I hear."

We both chuckle a bit at that, and then he puts his hand on my shoulder again. "I'm here if you need to talk, okay? I mean, I know you've got Mike, but I'm happy to do whatever. If you want me to. Now I'm sounding stupid."

"Thanks, Jason."

"I mean it," he says.

"I know you do," I say.

Jason checks his Apple Watch. "I gotta go. Hang in there, okay?"

I nod, trying not to tear up again, and go back to my soup with great fervor, realizing all of a sudden that I'm famished. As Jason walks away, I wonder why on earth I chose to tell him. And not Scotty, for instance. Let alone Mike. With a stab of sadness, I realize that I would have told my mom, if she were still here, before her dementia. And if I had a sister, maybe I would tell her. And then I remember that I do have a sister. And this makes me want to cry even more.

My phone rings then, and I note with some surprise that it's Dr. Novaire's number. Maybe he wants to discuss some patients. Will wonders never cease? "Hello?"

"Dr. Goldman, are you available to meet?"

"Yeah, I have a couple more patients to see but…"

"No." His usually jovial voice is frigid. "Now. In my office, right now. I just got a call from Abraham Green."

"I can explain," I say, sitting down across from him at his natural disaster of a desk.

"Yes, Dr. Goldman." Dr. Novaire is gripping a stress-reliever brain model, squeezing with some vigor despite his age. "Please do. Please do explain why you've been harassing a poor man who just lost his wife and is now dealing with a very sick child in prison."

I swallow, rapidly realizing that this meeting may not go well. "See, I got this text. Well, a bunch of texts."

"Yes. I heard all about that."

I pause. "Maybe I could just show you on my phone. It would be a lot easier."

"No, Dr. Goldman. I do not want to see your phone." There is not an iota of patience left in his voice. "The warden and I have spoken at length about your texts."

"You have?"

"Yes, we have. More than enough." He puts the brain model down, though the temporal lobe is still a bit squished. "He's been talking with the detective on a daily basis as well."

"Okay, good. I knew they were communicating."

"And Warden Gardner told me that he has examined all of the cases mentioned, thoroughly, and found nothing untoward in any of them." The rubber brain is back in his hand. "Not a one. He even took Andre out of gen pop for his own protection. Gen pop, where he could be getting a lot of positive interaction instead of sitting in his cell all day." He thumps the brain down on his desk. "There is nothing, Dr. Goldman, nothing, that exculpates your recent behavior."

I stare at a coffee stain on the gray carpet.

"I don't understand you," he says, his voice almost plaintive. "I've been trying to protect you, I really have. Trying to make excuses for you, running interference for you. But I can't do it anymore. I just can't. It's impossible."

Hot tears prick my eyes, and I hold them back.

"You're treating Andre, not his father. I know the family unit is important, but this is different. It's almost as if you've got some vendetta against him."

"It's not a vendetta," I argue. "It's just that if he *is* involved in his wife's death and the texting, he could be planning to harm Andre as well. That's all I'm worried about."

He squeezes the brain again, his knuckles turning white. "Let me ask you something." He pauses, as if calming himself down. "Did it ever occur to you that you are the only one making these connections?"

My foot is tapping the carpet, like a motor, and I stop

it. "I'm the one being texted, so obviously it's more on my mind."

"Have you considered changing your number, then?"

Which is something Mike also suggested. "But that's not the point," I argue.

"Zoe," he says, almost sadly, "I don't even think you know what the point is anymore." I don't answer because I don't know what to say. He may even be right. My foot is thumping again, and this time I just let it go. "The warden wants you fired. I won't sugarcoat it. It's as simple as that. But I am giving you a reprieve. I'm putting you on probation."

"Okay." I take a breath of relief. Probation is better than suspension, at least. I can get off probation eventually. "Thank you."

"With the understanding," he says, raising his hand in warning, "that you are not to come within five feet of Andre Green. Or his father."

I nod. "Understood."

I sit in the car for a while.

The heater's buzzing is a comfort, and I turn off the radio, which was blaring some sports station Mike had on. The silence is oddly soothing.

In a sense, I can see how this would be an ideal way to go.

To turn on the engine with the garage shut, close your eyes to the sweet fumes, and let it all fade away. Everything.

Every problem. Evil texters, evil sisters. Probation. Patients who rely on you until you fail them. Apricots you don't even deserve.

All fading away in a twinkling, stuporous moment.

But I'm not in a garage.

I'm in the parking lot of the prison, and I should get going, or a guard might come out and check on me. But I can't move. My hand doesn't want to move the gear shift. I am stuck in this moment. The purr of the motor, the muted gray sky turning black, the snowflakes drifting down against the light. And Mike's late again tonight, so I have nothing to go home to anyway. Then I picture Arthur's face. His frizzy head, his pink tongue. Arthur is probably missing me, at least. Or if not me, at least the dog food provided by me.

The sound of my phone buzzing snaps me out of my reverie. I am searching for it in my satchel through all my crap, but by the time I get to it, the call has gone to voice mail. Looking at the number, I realize with a jolt that it's Zena, Andre's other aunt.

I hit the button to listen.

"Hi, Dr. Goldman. I'm happy to talk to you about Andre. His father says he's been too sick to visit, or I would have seen him. Do you want to meet sometime? Maybe for coffee? I was thinking..."

I dial the number back before the message even ends.

Chapter Thirty

I didn't have a name this time. I had something even better. Something that would get you back for sure, the real you. Something that would make you love me again.

A secret, I said.

You looked at me with doubt. What secret?

So I told you, and your eyes opened wide in delight, your lips spreading into a smile. You even held my hand. We never hold hands. I closed my eyes to imprint this moment on my mind, to remember it forever. For the late nights, when the girls are crying all around me. For the cold afternoons in the rec yard. I could turn to this moment.

You looked thrilled, enamored. You reached over and cradled my head with such tenderness, and you kissed me.

Then we made love. Slowly, luxuriously. Like we had all the time in the world. Not fierce or fast. Not fucking me, not hurting me like last time, just making love.

Then, as we lay there, on the hard floor, you asked if I wanted to hear a poem. I said yes, and you recited it, by heart.

"Alas, alas, who's injured by my love?"
Your voice was low, purring.
"Call us what you will, we are made such by love."
I could imagine the words, forming in front of me, dancing.
That's beautiful, *I said.* Who wrote it?
John Donne, *you said.* An old poet.

I wrote those words down when I got back to my cell that day. And I say them before I go to sleep every night, like a prayer. I will never forget those words, as long as I live.

And I realized then that it was fate that I was sent here. I never wanted to be in prison, of course. In this cursed, rat-infested, godforsaken place. I've been fighting, railing against it with my whole soul. But I now understand, it was meant to be. Everything that happened to me up until now was all leading up to that moment. That perfect moment in a musty utility closet, listening to my lover reading poetry to me.

This perfect man. My Professor.
You.

Chapter Thirty-One

Aubrey wasn't on my schedule, but asked to be seen "to get something off her chest."

But so far she hasn't spoken a word, just sits there fidgeting, her eyes darting around like a caged animal. Aubrey bites off a hangnail, and a spot of blood pops up.

"Aubrey, what's going on?" I ask, trying to project a calm demeanor. I'm trying to center myself with green tea, which isn't working very well.

She rubs her lime-green friendship bracelet back and forth on her wrist, where her skin is already blistered. "I need to talk about it."

I nod. "About that night?" I ask, in a soothing voice.

"No," she says, her voice tired. "Not that. About something else." She sucks on the remnant of her hangnail, then, her eyes still shifting around the room. "It's about what I did. Something terrible that I did." She wipes her nose with the back of her hand, like a child, and I hand her a tissue box from my drawer. "It's about my mom."

"Okay."

"Remember when I told you about her?"

"Yes, I do. You said she died of cancer."

"Yeah, that's right." She sighs. "But I didn't tell you everything." Now she stares at the floor, a tremor in her upper lip, as I wait her out. "I also told you that I used to get pain pills from her."

"Right." I do vaguely remember this.

"She had plenty of them when she was so sick. Ovarian cancer, it was." She pulls her knees to her chest then, just fitting in the chair and looking like a scared little girl. "She didn't even notice at first. She had so many. I just took one here or there. But then I met Todd." Her face sours. "And we starting doing more. And so I took a few more. And more. And then he wanted me to sell them."

I nod along in support.

"But then the cancer got bad. Real bad. End stage they called it. It was in her bones and all that."

"Oh, Aubrey. I'm sorry."

"No." She shakes her head, vehemently. "Don't feel sorry for me. You shouldn't feel sorry for me. Feel sorry for her." She glances up at me, her face in agony. "I'm the monster here. I'm the one who took her pills. Don't you get it? I took the one thing she needed right then to feel better." She starts crying, a high-pitched whine like a hurt animal. "She was in pain. My dad said he watched her suffer through it and held her hand. And the doctors wouldn't give her more. They thought she was just trying to kill herself. And my dad tried to explain but they said they couldn't, and she was in pain. Bad pain. And I had taken all her pills."

She doesn't say any more then, just keeps crying. And I put my hand on her arm. "Addiction is—" I try to say.

But she interrupts me with a fierce head shake, her eyes full of tears. "It was me, not addiction. Me. I'm the only one to blame."

"I understand how you feel. But Aubrey," I say, my hand still on her arm, "do you honestly think your mom would want this? That she would want you to keep hurting yourself in her name?"

She sniffles, then her eyes drift up toward me.

"It doesn't help anyone now," I say, "to do that. You may want to punish yourself, but you're not honoring her memory by doing that. She wouldn't want you to. She would want you to be happy, successful. She would want you to celebrate her memory, not feel guilty about it."

She sits, staring at me in a daze. "I never thought of it that way."

"You should. You should think of it. I know she would have forgiven you, Aubrey. She loved you. It wasn't your fault that she died."

"It's not, is it?"

"No," I say. "It's not." I let go of her arm, and after a few more minutes, she wipes her eyes and sits normally in the chair again with a loud inhalation.

"Wow. I guess that's what they mean by sharing, huh?"

I smile. "That's what I'm here for." She touches her bracelet but then lets it be. "I'm glad you called for me,

237

Aubrey, instead of hurting yourself. It's a step. A really positive step."

She looks at me with renewed hope. "You think?"

"Yes. You're facing your problems, not just trying to push them down. And that's a good thing, a really good thing."

"Dr. Goldman." She takes another breath and seems to relax into the chair. "Thank you."

A text jumps on my phone. It's Zena, confirming the time for our coffee this afternoon. I text her back a yes.

"How's Andre doing?" I ask, as Jason sits at the computer.

"Seeing him in a bit," he says airily, to avoid the awkward fact that he is seeing him now because of my probation.

I stare at the boring, blank wall, at a loss with my unfilled day. I've done all my notes and all my orders, and reviewed all my labs. My schedule looks like a slab of Swiss cheese with too many holes. "I could grab some of your patients," I offer.

"That's probably not a good idea for right now," Jason says diplomatically. He squeezes my shoulder as he gets up, which makes me feel pathetic instead of comforted, then goes into his clinic room to await his next patient. I'm literally twiddling my thumbs when Maloney comes by. Tyler Evans swaggers as best he can in his chains. "It says he's here for some study?"

"Yes," I say with cheer, actually happy to see a white supremacist, something I never thought I'd be in my entire life.

"Have a seat." Maloney doesn't take his eyes off him as he sits down, then goes to stand right by the door, just as Harry did.

"So," I say, pulling a notebook out of my desk, "this is our last session."

"Yup. And I think I learned a lot."

"Yes, I'm glad to hear that. Now we just have to repeat that one scale again. The Hare scale."

"Oh yeah. I told some of my friends about that scale. I had one of the highest scores."

"Uh-huh." Thus proving himself quite the accomplished sociopath. "Let's start with one again..." I retest him, and he scores even higher this time. As if he's studied to be a better narcissist. So far our pilot is failing miserably.

"Did I do good?" he asks, bouncing in his seat with antic- ipation.

"You did just fine," I say. "You'll just have to sign this form, and then we'll be all done."

Tyler takes the pen but looks at me without signing any- thing. "Do you use lotion or anything?"

"Lotion?" I touch my face. "No, not really."

"Any kind of makeup?"

"Why?" I ask, uncomfortable with this personal line of questioning.

"I was thinking about your freckles," he says, "wondering how they would look on a lampshade."

Sitting in the hall, I'm trying to figure out how to break it to Dr. Novaire that our CBT project is a bust when Janaya Jones walks by. "How are you?" I ask, more out of politeness than as a psychiatrist.

"At peace," she says. She does have a beatific smile upon saying this.

"Happy to hear that. Any reason for this turnaround?" I ask, as Harry leans against the wall, waiting for us to end our little exchange.

"I spoke with one of my sisters about my situation at length. And she reminded me. This is God's will. Everything is God's will."

"So you don't think people are after you anymore?" I'm wondering if she is back on her meds.

"God's will," she says with that unearthly smile. "That's what Sofia said."

I swallow. "Sofia told you that?"

"Yes, she did. She's a very centered soul." She glances up at Harry. "I'm ready."

"Library time?" he asks her.

"Library time," she answers, and they walk off, like an odd couple about to waltz. And I walk off because I'd like to know why Sofia is suddenly, coincidentally, talking to Janaya. When I go to her cell, though, she isn't there.

"She's in the kennels," Maloney says, seeing me checking the logbook.

"It says rec area."

"No, rec is closed. Fight broke out."

So I take the elevators up to the kennels. If the rec area

is downtrodden and depressing, the kennels are worse. The rec yard is cruise-ship luxury compared to the kennels, which are essentially oversize cages atop the building's roof. For a full hour, prisoners can tromp on the beaten-down snow in a cage, owning their two square feet of the world. Though it's actually a decent view of the Buffalo skyline.

Sofia's breath comes out in puffs. She jogs in place in her oversize green rubber boots and matching coat. I lean against the cage, shivering in my coat as well.

"Is it even worth coming out here?" I ask.

"You try hanging out in a cell twenty-four hours a day," she grouses. "It's not exactly enlivening."

"I guess not." The wind blows through the cage, dusting off some snow.

"So what brings you here today?" Sofia asks. "Or shouldn't I ask?"

"Janaya Jones," I answer.

Sofia squints, as if trying to remember the name. "Am I supposed to know her?"

"Ol' White Lady."

"Oh yes. What do you want to know about her?"

"She told me that she thinks people are after her."

"And that surprises you?" Her head bobs with her jogging. "I mean, I'm not a psychiatrist, Dr. Goldman. But the woman is a little..." She makes the universal sign for *cuckoo*.

"Yeah, I know all about that. I just wondered if there was any truth to her fears. Because, oddly enough, she's not so worried about them anymore. And the reason is you."

"Me?"

"Yes. She said you gave her advice. Something about God's will."

She shrugs. "I talked to her. It's not illegal. I tried to make her feel better."

"So you're saying you're not behind the threats at all?"

She stops jogging. "Listen, Tanya. I've done some evil shit in my life. I'm well aware of that. But I already told you. I'm being straight with you. I'm done with all that now." She starts jogging again, her breathing loud. "I know you've pegged me as some mastermind behind all the problems in your life. But did you ever think maybe that's just the easy way out?"

"I'm not trying to blame you for everything," I grumble.

"Oh yeah? Then why is my cell being searched ten times a day?" Her boot hits the cage with a bang, scattering snow. "Not that I mind. It does give me some street cred with these bitches."

"Okay, Sofia." I lean on the cage, making it squeak. "You want to be straight with me? Then be straight with me. Let's have an honest heart-to-heart here."

"All right," she says, her voice bouncing with her jogging.

"I have just one question for you."

"Go ahead."

I can hear that I'm breathing to the rhythmic thud of her feet. "Why did you do it?"

"Do what?" she asks.

But I know she knows. "It. The big it. That night. Why? Why did you do it?" I repeat.

Sofia lets out a slow breath, like smoke.

"Kill our mom. Try to kill me. You've never, ever said why you did it." My heart patters in my chest. "You want my forgiveness? Fine. But I can't give it to you when I don't even understand why you did it. And don't tell me it was PCP or some shit, because I won't believe you for a second."

Her jogging slows, then stops, bringing a sudden quiet to the rooftop.

"I've never told you why," she says, softly, "because I don't know why. I was full of hatred and anger. I still am, but I'm trying not to be. And that's the best I can tell you, Tanya. That's the honest truth." A rush of wind swoops down, snaking into my collar. She stares off into the distance then, and I do, too, both of us looking at the skyline. "I know it was asking a lot, for you to forgive me. But I'm not giving up on you yet."

"Okay, Sofia. Fine," I say, exhausted and resigned. I still have no idea why she did it. And maybe neither does she. I don't know if she's lying or not. But perhaps Jack is right, you don't ask the devil how to get to heaven.

So I leave her to her cage and go back to the clinic, where no patients await me. But I do have one task to complete before five o'clock rolls around and my coffee with Zena. I click the door shut, dial the number, and wait out the rings.

"Hello, this is Dr. Marchand's office. Can I help you?"

And this time I don't hang up, as I have the three times before.

"Hi," I say. "This is Zoe Goldman. I needed to make an appointment with the doctor. We had discussed some, um, different options regarding my pregnancy."

Chapter Thirty-Two

I feel a bit like a traitor at Starbucks instead of the Coffee Spot, but I needed to stay away from the prying eyes of a certain brother. So I sip my decaf tea and enjoy the branded but earnest music and have to admit the whole atmosphere is really quite pleasant.

A tallish (though not as tall as me, of course) woman with a cream-colored sweater, dark jeans, and black boots strides in, peeling off stylish sunglasses. She is a big woman, not obese, just the sort who takes up a lot of space. She peers around expectantly, and we meet each other's gaze.

"Zena?" I ask. She gives me a polite smile and comes over to shake hands. "Do you wanna grab something?" I ask. "I'll wait."

"You know, I think I will," she says, and I wait for her to get through the line. She comes back with a large something that smells like hazelnut, with "Xena" scribbled on the cup in black marker.

"Every time I tell them. Zena with a Z." She shakes her head. "It's not that difficult."

"Yeah," I say, but I can also see how she channels the warrior princess.

"So about Andre," she begins, which I appreciate, because I'm really not up for small talk. "How is he doing?"

I make the *so-so* motion with my hand. "He fluctuates. One day he's pretty good, then the next minute he's not so good. It's tough."

Her expression is hidden by her coffee cup as she drinks, though her eyes look sad. "That family has been through so much," she says. We both nod to this, drinking our drinks while an acoustic guitar song with a woman singing mournfully comes on.

"So how can I help you, then?" Zena turns to me. "You said you had some questions?"

"Yes. More about his father. Abraham Green."

"Okay," she says, her voice measured. "What about him?"

"I was talking to your sister Marion, and she seems to think that—"

"Abe killed her."

I sit back in my chair. "Yes." I hadn't expected her answer.

Zena waves me off with a knowing smile. "Here's the thing with Marion. She means well, she really does. But she's got a thing when it comes to Abe. She *hates* that man. And I mean hates him. Always has."

I stir the sugar crystals in my tea. "Why is that?"

"You know what?" she says in a tetchy tone. "I have no idea. I suppose to get to the bottom of all that, you'd have to ask her."

"Do you guys still talk?"

"Oh, sure. We talk. Just not about Abe." She crosses her legs. "I get where she's coming from. She thinks no one was ever good enough for our sister; she may be right. But honestly now, the man didn't go and give her a heart attack, rest her soul." She shakes her head, slowly and sadly. "None of us can choose when we're gonna go."

"That's true." I flick my finger against the paper cup, figuring out how to phrase the next question. "What would you say," I ask, "if I told you his first wife died under mysterious circumstances?"

She leans back in her chair. "And who told you that, Marion?"

"She started the line of inquiry," I admit. "But Mr. Green said his first wife died of a heart attack as well."

"Right, I heard that."

"It turns out...that's not true. She fell down the stairs, and Abe was the one who found her." Zena doesn't say anything but is hearing me out, warily. "And," I add, "he then collected a million dollars off her life insurance."

She looks down at the table. "That does seem kind of funny." She takes another drink of her coffee. "This all through Marion?"

"Various sources." In other words, my hacker-barista brother.

She shrugs again, in a cool way. "Truth is, I expect if there were *really* something to all this, it would have been found out back when it happened."

"You would think," I say. Again we sit through silence,

though it is a bit more uncomfortable this time. I can tell she doesn't fully trust me or know what to make of me. And I don't blame her. "Did you know he's got a new girlfriend?"

"No," she says, cradling her cup in her hands. "I didn't know that." She frowns. "Of course, the man is entitled. It's been over a year now." She gazes out the window at the snow-covered row of shrubs. "We haven't talked much lately. So it wouldn't be totally out there." She puts her drink down then with some finality. "I don't mean to be rude here, Dr. Goldman."

"Zoe."

"Zoe. But what does any of this have to do with you? Or Andre, for that matter?"

I pause, as I can't tell her about the texts or the burner phone, which I'm convinced is in his briefcase. "I'm not sure if it does. I just want to do right by Andre. And I'm trying to put all the pieces together to help him."

She nods but appears unconvinced. Then she finishes off her coffee and reaches down for her purse. "Anyway, I appreciate you helping Andre. And believe me, I'll be out there to visit him when he's well. And I really should be giving Abe a call, too," she says with a sigh. "I'll tell you, Dr. Goldman, I loved my sister. I still do. I think about her every day. But I don't think Abraham had anything to do with her death. He was always good to her." Zena pulls a black purse onto her lap. "And besides, he wouldn't have benefited from her will anyway."

"No?" I ask, trying not to be overeager, but desperate to grab this bit of information.

"No. She changed it." She stares out the window again.

"Come to think, it was a couple months before she died. She had a big policy, too, she said. But for whatever reason, she wanted to change it. Abe wasn't the primary beneficiary anymore." She loops her purse over her shoulder. "She decided to leave everything to Andre."

"Is that right," I say, as a lightbulb goes off.

Driving home, I'm trying to figure out a way to tell Detective Adams the news without mentioning that I might have met Abe's sister-in-law for a spot of tea. Then again, he didn't specifically ask me to stay away from Abraham Green's family members, just from him.

In the end I call Mike instead.

"Hey, what's up?" Mike asks. I can hear the hum of the ER in the background.

"Not much. Checking on dinner thoughts tonight?"

"Oh, I'm on tonight," he says with disappointment. "Three-'til-midnight shift. I put the schedule on the fridge, remember?"

"Yeah," I say with equal disappointment. "I guess I forgot to look." The noise of the background seems to grow over the phone, and I hear the muffled sound of Mike answering something. Then I hear another, more irksome, voice: "Mike, sweetie? Could you help me out here?" XO Serena. The voice has a plangent tone, soft and pitiful. Like fingernails on a chalkboard.

"Gotta go, hon," Mike says. "See you tonight?"

"I'll be there," I say with resignation.

When I get home, Arthur at least is happy to see me and announces this in the most explicit way by lustily humping my leg. "Arthur," I grumble, and shove him away. He trots around the kitchen, unoffended, in pure merriment that somebody is home, even if it isn't Mike.

I pour him some kibble and freshen his water, then sit down in the kitchen chair, watching the night fall to the sound of Arthur's munching. After pulling out my phone, I head over to my most visited website lately. "Congrats! You've hit the second trimester! Are you showing yet? Your very little one is now the size of a lemon!"

Cranberry bean to apricot to lemon. At some point a watermelon, I suppose.

I shut down pregnantbabes.com and feel Arthur appear under my hand for a head pet. The long night looms in front of me, and I pull out my phone again.

"What's up?"

"Hey, Scotty. Want to come over for dinner?" I ask, hoping I don't sound desperate. "I can order pizza."

He doesn't answer right away. "I don't know. I probably should—"

"Bocce," I add, to sweeten the deal with his favorite kind. "Invite Kristy if she's free."

He pauses. "I'll be there. Just me," he says with a sigh. "See you in an hour."

⌐

The pizza is cold by the time Scotty gets here. He mopes around a bit, then sits at the table, where I'm already eating. "So," he says. "She gave me back the ring."

"What?" I put my pizza down, utterly floored. "She gave you back the ring?"

"She did."

"Oh, Scotty." I reach over and touch his shoulder. "I'm sorry."

He shrugs, but his jaw is clenched from holding back emotion. He uncaps a bottle of beer.

"Did she give a reason?"

He takes a swig but doesn't answer.

"Oh no. You didn't sleep with—"

"No," he growls. "I didn't sleep with anyone, Zoe. But thanks for the vote of confidence."

"Sorry," I mumble. But it wouldn't have been the first time my brother lost one girl because he'd slept with another. In fact, however deplorable, it almost seemed to be his go-to breakup method in the past.

"And no, she didn't give a reason." He puts his beer down with a clunk. "Not a real one, anyway."

I drink my caffeine-free Diet Pepsi, though Scotty looked askance when I declined a beer from my own refrigerator. "What did she say?"

His laugh is doleful. "She said that she loves me, but it's

not enough. Our long-range goals aren't the same." I have no idea what to say to this, except that it sounds like something a financial planner might say. "She said she thinks we should spend some time apart."

"Time apart," I say, grabbing on to the phrase. "Not totally broken up, then?"

"Yeah, I asked her that," he says with a heavy sigh. "She said spending time apart was her way of saying breaking up."

Standing up to get more pizza, I put my hand on his shoulder again. I pull out a plate for him. "Here. Have some pizza."

"Thanks." He tears into a piece while Arthur drools next to him. "Kristy didn't like me eating pizza," he says, his mouth full of food.

"Uh-huh."

"Said some stupid fucking shit about a calorie bank account."

"Yeah, I remember that." I'm holding back from wholeheartedly agreeing with him, just in case they get back together next week.

Scotty rips a piece of paper from the sweaty neck of the beer bottle. "Just because I didn't want to go back to school," he goes on, as if we were debating this point. And I'm sure it's been a soundtrack in his head. "So what? I could teach fucking coding to those professors." He feeds Arthur a slice of pepperoni, thinking I don't see, which I do. I grab yet another slice of pizza for the lemon (though pregnantbabes.com chided me, "Don't forget, you only need 300 calories extra per day right now!" I mean, seriously, who shames a pregnant girl for eating?)

Sandra Block

"So I've got this patient," I say, to change the subject. "And his father—"

"Zoe," he says, spinning his bottle, "not to be an asshole, but I really don't want to hear about your patients right now."

I nod. "No, that's fair." We sit in silence as Arthur softly whines for pizza.

"What's up with Mike?" he asks. "Anything new with him?"

"Not too much. Some girl has a crush on him," I say. "Hopefully that's all it is."

"Why do you say that?"

"Because I know. Another ER doc. Serena is her name." I drink from my pop. "She's absolutely stunning and vapid as fuck."

"Are you sure?" He sounds unconvinced. "Because sometimes you get a little jealous. I remember that Frog boy and Melanie."

He's talking about Jean Luc, my ex. "Yeah, well, he ended up marrying her, so my suspicions were sort of borne out on that one." It strikes me then that they look similar, in fact. Serena and my first love's girlfriend, now-wife, Melanie. Both thin, glowing, nymphlike creatures with dreamy blond hair and dreamy blue eyes. Maybe that's all this is. Me reacting to a Melanie doppelgänger. "She signs her texts 'XO.'"

"You looked through his texts?"

"By accident."

Scotty shakes his head. "What did Mike say?"

"That they're just friends. And that's just how she signs things."

252

We both stare into space a moment, thinking our own sad thoughts, then Scotty stands up abruptly. "He's a good guy, Zoe. Don't fuck this up. If he's says they're just friends, they're just friends." He grabs his black wool coat off the chair.

"You leaving already?" I feel a beat of panic thinking about the maw of the evening opening up before me until Mike gets home. At which time I tell him about the lemon, or I don't. If I'm even still awake at that point.

"Yeah, I have to open tomorrow. Eddie's got something going on."

"Still." I look at my watch. "It's early yet." Then I figure it out. "You're not going to go see her, are you?"

"No," he protests, but he looks guilty.

"Don't, Scotty."

"I'm not," he answers, annoyed, then tromps out the door, either to plead his case to Kristy or not.

An hour later I have read hundreds of words out of my forensic psychiatry text and absorbed none of them. I turn on the television to a show about weight loss in which morbidly obese people are paraded on camera to be shamed for their adiposity. Arthur plays a game of I Just Came in So Now I Want to Go Out, and I open my psychiatry book again but it's hopeless. My mind is skittish when I'm off my medicine, and I can barely concentrate on the reality TV show, let alone my psychiatry book.

And my mind keeps returning to Zena's words: *She decided to leave everything to Andre.*

Which equals motive. If Abraham Green is behind the texts, then Andre is in danger, and despite my assurances to the detective and Dr. Novaire, I can't just sit here and do nothing.

I have to do something.

A quick peek in the white pages gives me Abraham Green's address, and I throw Arthur a treat and head out. I have no idea what I will do when I get there, and he probably won't even be home, but I can at least investigate.

As I get ready, which means practically dressing for a trip to the Antarctic on this blistery, zero-degree night, a text sounds on my phone.

Just so you know, Puff Diddy is feeling better! See ya soon... XO Serena.

There is a black cat emoji on there, which leads me to believe Puff Diddy is her cat, and she probably believes the name to be hilarious and not at all racist, and I'm trying to quell my rage when another text pops up two seconds later.

Oops! Sorry. Meant to text Mike! Hahahaha

Right, I think. *Oops! I didn't mean to plant a seed of doubt in your head! Hahahaha!*

How transparent could this woman be? And how the hell did she get my number, from Mike's phone? I don't bother to answer the text or consider the implications of that possibility, just shove the phone in my pocket. Heading out to the curb, I grab the scraper from the floor of my car and start stabbing at the ice on the windshield, getting out some aggression while simultaneously clearing my window and flicking pulverized ice onto the ground. Throwing the scraper in the back, I sit down on the stiff leather and turn on the engine. Cold air blows through the vents.

"Okay, Google Maps, let's go."

In about fifteen minutes I'm there, in an outer ring of the suburb of Snyder, near the Italian restaurant. The place is a medium-size, older brick house with a For Sale sign in front of it. I leave the engine running, squinting to see if anyone is inside. When I peer through the windows, the house is dark and empty looking. It might not even be occupied. I'm about to cut my losses and head back home in time for *The Bachelor* when I hear the garage door open and his dark-gray sedan snakes out of the driveway. I duck down and wait for Mr. Green to pass me, then I start trailing him. Mike has the radio on "new country" (whatever that is) from the last time he was in the car. I scan through a couple of ads, then just turn it off, preferring to sit in silence. We drive a ways out of Mr. Green's neighborhood and into Kenmore. He parks on the street, then goes into a house without ringing the doorbell. About ten excruciating minutes later, he emerges with a shovel.

He is shoveling the driveway now, hefting snow in heavy throws. I'm wondering if this is his mother's house maybe, but then a woman comes out and yells something to him. It's hard to see in the dark, but from the bit of porch light, she looks young. I'm fairly certain it's the woman from the restaurant.

Which doesn't tell me much. As the detective said, they

could very well be dating. He could in fact be moving in with her and selling his house. And good for him to find love again. Not exactly a crime.

I yawn, the car heater having a stultifying effect on me, as a light snow falls and Abraham keeps up a hypnotic rhythm with his shoveling. Suddenly a little boy runs out in snow boots and no coat, barreling toward the mailbox. The woman comes out on the doorstep again.

"Put your coat on! You'll catch your death," she cries out to him. So she has a child. I take a quick picture of him with my phone, sensing that he looks familiar somehow.

"I'm just getting the mail," he complains, trudging back over the snowy lawn.

"Listen to your mother, Jermaine," Abraham calls, out of breath from his shoveling.

"Okay, Dad," the boy says with apology in his voice. He races up the steps and in the front door.

As Mr. Green returns to shoveling, I remember Andre's words and am invaded by a deep chill despite the warmth of the car.

The double. They sent him to replace me.

Chapter Thirty-Three

Timothy Gordon, *I said.*

What about him? *you asked.*

I told you that I didn't really know. I heard her talking to the old doctor about him in the hall. They were saying something about him not liking his arm.

Not liking his arm? *You sounded unconvinced.*

I said I knew it sounded weird, but it was just what I heard. You nodded with that faraway look again, thinking.

But I can't get to a man, *I insisted, before you could try to convince me otherwise. You said you would take care of him, but that I had to take care of Janaya Jones. I swallowed, my throat dry. We had talked about it, how to get her up there, just her and me. Then it would only take a second, and it would be over. But I still wasn't sure I could do it.*

You told me that I was your soldier, that I had to do it. But I don't want to be your soldier. I just want to be your lover. I didn't say that, though, because I know you don't want to hear it.

You could tell I was getting upset so you grabbed me by the hips, pulling me on your lap. I wrapped my legs around you immediately, though we still had our clothes on. I could feel you getting hard and started rocking on you, but you stopped me, your grip bruisingly tight around my waist.

Don't, you scolded me. Just sit there.

So I did. You wanted to play more games, fine. We stared at each other. Then you pulled my hips toward you again but would stop if I started grinding. You did it again and laughed. Teasing me, but not nice teasing. You're too easy, you said with something of a smirk.

And I started to crawl off you because I was mad and knew I didn't deserve this but you kept me on top of your lap, your hands strong on my hips again.

Go ahead, you said, I'm sorry.

And when I started writhing on your lap, you let me this time. I leaned over and put my arms around your neck, and your hands loosened, gentle around my waist.

We're almost at the final act, you said, grinding against me, too, now.

What's going to happen? I asked, into your ear.

You'll find out soon, *you whispered back, your breath hot against my skin.* Very, very soon.

Chapter Thirty-Four

The next morning is a Saturday, and I am sitting in the chair, watching round women get weighed and waddle into rooms. I've been fasting, even though the procedure is not truly a surgery, just on the remote chance that it should be necessary. So now I am ravenous, with a blinding headache, and close to tears.

A hormonal trifecta.

The woman next to me is very pregnant, with bright-red lipstick. Her stomach protrudes between buttons on her top, and I look down at my own. Nary a bump. The lemon is still invisible. And will remain that way.

It was selfish of me to go this long, I finally realized, just because I don't want to make a decision. Not making a decision equals having a baby, and I'm not ready for that. Seeing as I unknowingly dumped medication into the poor thing for months, drank wine who knows how many times, am close to losing my job, and can't even seem to tell Mike the truth.

I've been waiting almost an hour now, light-headed and hungry. I've looked through my e-mail and Facebook a hundred times but barely have the mental capacity to concentrate on even the simplest of Internet tasks.

The red-lipsticked woman is flipping through *Parenting* magazine and chatting with an older woman I assume is her mother. "I don't know what's taking so long," she mutters, and a couple of other women around her nod in sympathy.

"Did I tell you about the birthing plan?" she asks her mother. "Dustin told me to make sure I have it in writing, every detail."

"Uh-huh," the mother answers, not sounding all that excited about the birthing plan.

Red Lipstick tucks the magazine back in the basket and pulls a printed list from her purse. "Let me just go through it with you. Okay"—she clears her throat—"number one: natural. Of course. I'm going to make that totally clear. Absolutely no chemicals whatsoever."

"Uh-huh." The mother turns her own magazine page.

"I read on one of my blogs that an epidural might cause autism," she says. "I guess there are a lot of studies."

I actually have to bite my tongue, not figuratively, so as not to start screaming at her.

"Number two: soothing music. Dustin's bringing that in. He got a natural birthing CD off Amazon. It's very important for the baby to emerge into a relaxing atmosphere. Or they might have issues bonding."

"Zoe?" the receptionist calls out, interrupting the idiocy spewing from Red Lipstick. The receptionist looks around the room. It's a new woman, who doesn't recognize me. "Zoe? Zoe Goldman?" Everyone looks up from their magazines or cell phones, then back down. "Huh," the receptionist says, baffled. "She must be in the bathroom." And when she returns to the back office for a second, I grab my purse without any idea why. I stand up and I leave.

On the way home, I send off a quick text to Detective Adams, too chicken to call him after he told me in no uncertain terms to stay away from Mr. Green and I completely ignored his advice. But I also can't let Andre get hurt without doing anything. I already asked Jason to throw a tox screen in his labs, which he did. Just in case Mr. Green is getting a prisoner to slip him something. Like Elavil.

What's up? Any more texts?

Not that. More news on Mr. Green. I can almost hear him yelling over the satellite. Getting to the red light, I keep typing. Charmayne changed her will a few months before she died. Andre is full beneficiary.

How do you know that? pops right up.

Can't say.

???

And he lied to me about Jermaine. Said he was his nephew. Actually his stepson.

The phone rings then, so I have no choice but to answer it and take my lumps. The car behind me honks as the light turns green. "What do you mean, he lied about his nephew?" His gruff voice comes over the phone. "And how do you even know about a nephew?"

"I saw the picture of this kid in Abraham's wallet during a family visit with Andre."

"Okay?"

"I asked him point-blank who it was, and he said his nephew Jermaine. But it's not. It's his stepson. Or his sort-of stepson, at least. The boy called him Dad."

A sports car with a spoiler zooms by. "And can I ask how you know all of this?"

I pause. "I really don't want to get it into it."

"Fine." He takes a deep, frustrated breath. "Then let me explain something. Both of these things may be odd, Zoe, but neither is illegal."

"But why would he do that? Lie about this boy?"

"I don't know. Who knows why people do anything they do? That's your job, right? Maybe he was too embarrassed to tell Andre."

"Embarrassed? I don't believe it. How do you hide that from your own son?" The detective doesn't have an answer. "And if she did put everything in Andre's name, it sure seems like good motive to kill the boy with the bright-red gloves."

Again the detective doesn't answer right away. "Zoe, I'll look into the will. Since apparently you won't reveal your source."

I smile into the phone.

"If it's valid, then I'll run it by the DA, at least. I can't promise anything, but it's worth a discussion."

"Thanks."

"But listen to me," he says with a warning tone again. "And I mean it this time. Stay away from Abraham Green."

"Okay," I agree. "I'll try." Then I hang up before he can protest. Turning onto our street, I see Mike's car in the driveway, which is a surprise. The refrigerator schedule definitely said he was on today. Which makes me doubly happy I didn't go through with the procedure.

Not today, at least.

I walk into the house, and Mike and Arthur are watching me expectantly. "What is it?"

Mike gives me a Cheshire grin. "I got a surprise for you."

The gun feels surprisingly good in my hand. Compact, well fitting.

"Elbow straight," he corrects.

I can barely hear him with the headphones on and the ceaseless Jiffy Pop going on all around me. I sneak a look over at Mike, who has ringed the heart of his target. I think I might have hit the knee once (which would still be painful, I suppose). I'm not sure what the lemon is making of the commotion, but it doesn't seem to notice one way or the other.

Mike reloads. "Fun, huh?" he yells.

"Sure. In a primal kind of way," I yell back. I shut one eye, arm ramrod straight, and hit a shoulder. "Look!" I yell, like a kid who almost popped the balloon throwing darts at a fair.

"Good job," Mike answers, trying not to sound patronizing, and not succeeding. He goes for the head shot this time, leaving a hole in the target's forehead. He could probably shoot the apple off William Tell's son.

After a while my arm is getting tired, and, having taken out the poor guy's other knee, we decide to go. We hand in all our gear and head out to the car. A light snow dots the air. "Before you even ask," I start.

"I'm not," he says. "Just want you to keep an open mind." We climb into his Jeep, and he turns on the heat.

"That was pretty fun," I admit.

"Only thing my dad and I ever really liked doing together." His smile is bittersweet.

"That's sad."

"It is. My life has been one long sob story after another."

Chuckling, I fondle the adorable scruff on the back of his neck. "Is that your way of asking me not to overanalyze it?"

"Uh-huh," he says with a grin, and turns the steering wheel.

"So, what's new with you?" I ask. "It feels like I haven't seen you in forever."

"Yup. Busy me, out there saving lives. And treating colds."

I laugh. "And I get to have you to myself, all day."

"Until six, at least. I had to switch with Damien, so I'm covering second shift." He taps the steering wheel, waiting out a light. "Any more texts?"

"No. But after what Zena said, I'm really convinced it's Andre's father." I can't explain the newer discovery about Jermaine without revealing that I stalked his father, so I don't. "Anyway, Detective Adams is looking into it."

We drive in silence a bit until Mike turns on "new country" again. The silence was heavy, for me at a least, suffused with all the things I haven't told him. Probation. The lemon. Dr. Marchand's office. Tapping my foot to a song despite myself, I spy Anderson's up ahead. "Hey, you want to do a late lunch?"

"Sure," he says, crinkling his eyes. "But are you even hungry? You had two peanut butter sandwiches before we left."

"Oh yeah. That was just a late breakfast. And since you won't be home for dinner." As he turns into Anderson's, my phone rings. It's Jason.

"I hate to ask you this, but could you cover my call tonight?" His voice is hoarse.

"Sure," I answer without hesitation. "No problem."

"Thanks. I feel like crap. Fevers, the shits. I think I'm dying."

"So a man-flu," I say.

"Fuck you."

"Hey, I'm taking your call."

He pauses. "Okay, then fuck you *and* thank you." Jason hacks into the phone before hanging up. Putting the phone in my purse, I feel an unexpected sense of relief. I hate call as much as the next guy, but at least it will take my mind off things. Mike's on tonight, so it would be just Arthur and I alone again. And I could have Scotty over, but that means listening to all the various and sundry ways Kristy sucks.

Taking call might not be the definition of fun, but at least it's a distraction from the ongoing disaster otherwise known as my life.

Chapter Thirty-Five

Watch what you wish for.

Call was brutal. I made the mistake of not checking the lunar calendar before agreeing to cover for Jason. Sure enough, full moon.

Saturday night was light, but Jason was still sick so I took the next day and got hammered. All Sunday I ping-pong between prison and Buffalo Psych Center for a baker's dozen of psychoses NOS (not otherwise specified, in this case mainly due to street-drug cocktails that didn't mix). I spend the night in the suburban ER (not Mike's) with consults for various nonpsychiatric disorders (one patient hallucinating due to kidney failure, one hallucinating due to d.t.'s, and one with an "acute personality change" due to a frontal lobe stroke). Finally, at one in the morning, I am climbing into bed, praying for no more calls.

Mike is dead asleep already, and Arthur sticks his head up to give me a sleepy-eyed smile and lies back down to dream of squirrel adventures again. I don't bother brushing my teeth or taking off my scrubs, just climb straight into bed. Mike reaches over for a semiconscious snuggle, and I'm asleep within seconds.

When the phone blares me awake, it feels as if five minutes have passed. Checking the clock, I'm amazed that three hours have slipped by. I pull the phone to my ear, tucking my arm back under the covers, unwilling to relinquish the delightful warmth of my bed and the perfect heft of Mike's arm lying over me. "Hello?" I mumble.

"Hi, Dr. Goldman, it's Larissa." My not-favorite nurse. Just my luck. "I'm sorry to bother you. I'm calling about Andre Green."

"Okay?" My voice is husky with sleep.

"We brought him down to Medical because he's been pretty lethargic."

I yawn, and Arthur puts his head on my hip again, burrowing in. "Jason told me he increased his meds on Friday. Is he worse?"

"I don't know. I didn't see him Friday."

Ask a stupid question, get a stupid answer. "Did the internist see him yet?"

"Yes, Dr. Kohlman. But he suggested psych since you know him best. And the meds."

I sit up, and Mike opens one eye. "Larissa?" he guesses, and I nod. "Might as well just go in. There's no getting out of it."

He's right, of course.

"Fine," I mutter. "Be there in ten." As I leave the bed,

Arthur takes the unexpected opportunity to crawl into my warm, vacated spot. Then, to add insult to injury, Mike throws his arm around him. I shove on my comfiest UGGs, ruined by stiff salt stains all around them, and get into the car.

The streets are empty, the landscape all white, with snow-banks sculpted like dunes by the wind under a brown-orange sky. Unearthly, like another planet. My car is almost warmed up by the time I hit the parking lot of the prison. After flashing my badge, clomping off my boots, and nearly slipping on the floor into the elevator, I finally get up to Medical to see Andre.

He is lying on the cot with one red-gloved hand chained to the bed rail, pale, sweaty, and mumbling. "Nuke...gonna... Nuke...no, no, no..." Andre weakly swats away something with the other hand.

"Jesus." I grab the stethoscope from the wall to listen to his heart and lungs. "He looks terrible. Do we have any labs on him?"

"Yes." Larissa pulls up his chart on the computer. "UA was negative, so was CBC."

"How about his chemistry?"

"Pretty good. His BUN and creatinine were up a little. We were gonna run an IV in case he's dehydrated."

"Or on his way to renal failure," I say. "Unless we're looking at neuroleptic malignant syndrome." Then I remember the full tox screen I asked Jason to run and ask her about it.

"Negative. I printed it out for you."

"Anyone order a chest X-ray?" Larissa offers only a blank look in response. "Either way, he needs to go to the County. He's definitely too sick to stay here."

"Jermaine!" Andre yells out clearly, then starts mumbling again.

"You sure about the County?"

"Yes, I'm sure." And I'm also sure that Larissa does not want to fill out the paperwork involved in transferring him.

"So you really don't think he's malingering?" she asks.

The idiocy of the question catches me off guard. "Malingering?"

She puts a hand on her hip. "I spoke with Dr. Novaire earlier, and that's what he thought might be happening. Pretending to be sick to get out of going to school."

"No," I say, as calmly as possible. "If Dr. Novaire knew anything about this patient, he would know he loves school. And if he had actually examined him, he would know he is not malingering. He is very ill. I will put in the orders. Please call for a transfer. Now. As in right now. Not in a couple minutes. Not in an hour. Right goddamn now."

Larissa huffs, and I know I'm in for a write-up, which could be all Warden Gardner needs to terminate me, but right now I don't even care. My watch tells me it's five in the morning, which means two hours to sleep until rounds.

Grumbling, I trudge off to find the call room.

The devil flies in like a hawk, almost grabbing the baby.

"No!" I hold on to it, tight, bending my whole body to protect it. A demon swoops in again, and a flash of fire singes my hair,

leaving a sulfurous smell in his wake. "Please, no!" I am running away. But it's an endless prison hall.

"Bitch, you gonna fuck me now?"

"I always like you tall girls. I'll bend you over good, don't worry."

Piss is being thrown at me, shit, gobs of spit, semen, splatting against the wall.

"Mike!" I'm screaming, covering the baby. The hallway keeps going. "Mike!"

My voice echoes down the hall until finally I get to a door. I'm afraid to open it, but I can't stay where I am. I feel a lick of heat on the back of my neck from the devil's flaming breath. Leaning forward, I try the handle, but it's locked. I start knocking, shifting the baby on my hip. Knocking so hard my knuckles sting. "Please, let me in. Help me!"

I look backward and see the devil smiling. His split tongue moving up and down. Finally I body-slam the door with my shoulder, and it opens. Shutting it behind me, I am left in a sudden, deathly silence. I stand there, breathless, listening. Then, on the other side of the door, I hear the patter of the devil's feet, running away.

"It's okay now," I say to the baby snuggling against my chest. She smells like baby powder. "It's okay," I murmur, my body finally relaxing, but then a peal of laughter rings out in the corner of the room, and I look over to see.

It's Sofia with her nebulous smile.

"Do you forgive me?" she asks, and a nail file flashes in her hand.

I wake up to myself gasping and my cell phone ringing.

My scrub neck is damp with sweat. I have no idea where I am, but realize after a few disoriented seconds that I'm in the call room in the prison. Rubbing my eyes, I grab my phone, which tells me it's seven in the morning. The screen casts a hazy gray box-shaped shadow on the wall. The caller ID says Dr. Koneru, and I wonder momentarily if she's calling about the baby, then remember this makes no sense. Scrambling up in the cot, I push the answer button. "Hello?"

"Did I wake you?"

"No, no, I'm fine. What is it?"

"I finally got to review my file on Charmayne Green. And I came across something funny." I hear rustling over the phone. "It may not be anything, but it's worth a look."

"What is it?"

"It's about her fingernails. I'm just going to send you a picture. And I think you'll see what I mean." The picture lights up my phone, shocking my eyes, and I stare at it for ten straight seconds.

It can't be.

"Did you get it?" she asks.

"Yes," I answer, feeling sick with shame. All this time he's been so sick, and I couldn't see it through his red gloves. Planting seeds in his fingernails, it was so obvious.

"I'm sorry it took me so long to get back to you, Zoe. There's been a lot going on here. But I'll do some testing if the lab saved any of her blood work."

"Good," I say, in a daze.

"And I'll call Detective Adams. We really should reopen the case."

"Of course. Thanks for calling." I throw on my lab coat, ready to race over to the county hospital. Right now it's not even about Charmayne.

We have to save Andre.

⟁

"No!" Andre is screaming, all his lethargy burned away. "Stop!"

"Why isn't he at the County yet?" I ask.

"Don't shoot the messenger," Jason says. "I just happened to be rounding in Medical and saw him still in here. That's why I called you."

"Yeah, but..." I trot over to the head of the bed. "He was supposed to be transferred last night. Fucking Larissa. I told her."

"Then yell at her, not me. I put your orders through again, and EMT is on the way." He rubs his head. "And yes, I still have a fever, thanks for asking."

"At least we can take at look at his hands while we're waiting." I notice he is not handcuffed to the bed for the moment.

"His hands?" Jason asks. "Why would we want to do that?"

Andre is mumbling. His eyes are half-closed, bloodshot. Strands of hair are sprinkled all over his undershirt. But trying to remove one of the red gloves wakes up a demon.

"No!" Andre screams.

"I'm not trying to hurt you, Andre," I assure him. "I just

need to look at your fingernails." But he buries his hands underneath him while I try to tug out an arm.

"What the hell is going on?" Jason asks. "What do you need his fingernails for?"

"He's planted seeds in there," Andre screeches. "You can't take my gloves. I need my gloves." He is squirming away from me.

"I just wanted to check something. Lift his shoulder, would you?"

Begrudgingly Jason obliges, and I manage to yank off one dirt-spattered red glove, but Andre quickly shoves the hand directly under his body. "Zoe, seriously, tell me," Jason says, huffing. "What exactly are you looking for?"

"Lines," I say, grunting with the effort of holding him up.

"Lines?" Jason asks. One of the guards, a blond kid with peach fuzz, walks into the medical room. "Need some help there?"

"We just need to see his fingers," I explain.

"Okay." The guard puts on a no-nonsense voice. "You're not in trouble here, Green. We just need to see those hands." Finally the guard and I are able to rock him onto his back, but Andre pulls his balled fists up to his mouth.

"Can't get them," Andre is gasping out. "The roots. The roots." The guard manages to splay out two fingers of the ungloved hand, with Andre still braying and fighting. I hold up Dr. Koneru's texted picture to his hand, and there's no doubt.

"Damn it," I say.

"What?" Jason asks, peering over my shoulder. "What are you seeing?"

"Lines," I say. "Mees' lines." I turn to the guard. "Okay, you can let him go now."

"Thanks be to Jesus." The guard releases his hand. "Son of a bitch is strong."

"Here's your glove, Andre," I say, putting it back on. The gesture seems to placate him, and his breathing slows down again.

"Mees' lines?" Jason says with astonishment. He grabs the phone to look at the picture again. "Holy shit. Nice catch, Zoe."

"Not really. We did a tox screen. But the wrong one. I never looked for heavy metals."

"Mees' whats?" The guard surveys us with confusion.

"Mees' lines," I say, "from arsenic poisoning. I just can't believe I didn't think of it sooner." The EMTs are jogging into the room with a gurney. "His father is poisoning him," I explain. "Just like he did his mother."

Chapter Thirty-Six

I'm about to grab a quick lunch when the detective calls.

"Hi, Zoe. Got some news."

"Okay?"

"We don't have enough to arrest him yet, but we're getting there. And you'll be happy to know they're reopening the case in Atlanta, too."

I rub my eyes, which sting from lack of sleep. "Do we have any idea how he was doing it?"

"Not for certain, but we're assuming he was putting the arsenic in Andre's drinks during their visits. Unfortunately, the trash is emptied daily. So we might not be able to get that evidence."

"You could go to the dumpster," I suggest.

"Already being done, Zoe," he says, a smile in his voice. "Don't worry. We're doing everything we can to nail this guy."

A guard walks by the room, whistling "Whistle While

You Work," which strikes me as overly self-referential. "What about his other phone?"

"Getting a warrant for both phones," he says. "That should be in place by end of day. We'll know if he was the one sending the texts or not."

"Good." For the first time in a long while, I feel as if things are falling into place. As if there is some semblance of order in my chaotic world. "Do you know anything about his girlfriend?"

"Her name is Ms. Shonda Lee," the detective says. "She didn't think she was his girlfriend, though. She's been his fiancée for years. She thought they were getting married this summer. They had Jermaine while he was still married to Charmayne."

"So she didn't know about—"

"No idea," he says. "She didn't even know Charmayne existed, let alone died. And she certainly didn't know about Andre."

"Wow." The whistling guard is heading toward me down the hall. "Speaking of which, did you get a chance to see Andre yet?"

"Yes. He's at the County."

"How's he doing?"

The detective doesn't answer right away. "I don't know, Zoe. It's not my expertise, obviously, but he didn't look good. He's in the ICU. The nurse said he's on dialysis."

"Oh." The word is inadequate. I am engulfed by shame. I should have known. It was right in front of me the whole time. Hair loss, pale skin, hallucinations. Not schizophrenia.

Arsenic poisoning. I just couldn't see it through his gloves. "I'm going to see him as soon as I'm done here."

"Good." The detective clears his throat then. "Zoe, I owe you an apology."

"No, no," I break in. "You absolutely don't. I know I haven't seemed all that stable lately."

"I absolutely do. After all we've been through...I should have trusted you. And I'm sorry about that."

"Well," I say with a sense of vindication, "I was a little beyond the pale there for a bit. But anyway, apology accepted."

"And if there's anything I can do," the detective continues.

Then I think about it. "Actually, there is one thing."

"Name it."

"Talk to the warden for me," I say. "Tell him I'm not crazy."

"Oh, hey, you guys," Logan says with cheer as, uninvited, he pulls up a chair next to me and Jason in the cafeteria. I don't have time to linger, and he's not a welcome sight. I just want to eat before racing over to the County to see Andre and then home to sleep. I'm running on fumes right now.

"Heard some rumors," Logan says. Neither of us answers, but I notice Jason preening his hair a bit. "They're saying something about a poisoning?"

"Probably best to talk to the warden," I say.

"I'm going to," he assures me. "But from what I heard, you guys were the ones to discover it."

"Zoe was," Jason says, and I shoot him a look, as he just fell for the oldest trick in the book.

"So there *was* a poisoning," Logan confirms, pulling out his notebook.

Jason offers me a sheepish, apologetic smile. "We are suspecting poisoning," I say, twirling my French fry in a pile of ketchup. "But it's not been confirmed."

Logan leans back with a look of approbation. "So that seems like a feather in the cap of the forensic psych team, huh? Which would work nicely in the feature."

"I guess," I allow, thinking of my own win-loss column. I can't put Andre in the win column yet, though. Not until I see how he's doing. Which sounds as if it's not very good.

"Don't sell yourself short," Logan says. "I hear they're calling you Dr. House around here." I try not to smile, well aware that he's using flattery to butter me up.

"Girl's got some mad diagnostic skills," Jason says.

"No pun intended," Logan says, and Jason laughs, too hard. There is silence then, as I finish off more than enough French fries for me and the lemon. I notice Logan stealing a glance at Jason, who fixes his eyebrow as if he's in a Ralph Lauren ad while pretending not to notice.

"Anyway," Logan says, turning to me, "let's get that interview done. We definitely have a positive slant at this point."

I half nod in answer, which I hope is enough to put him

off for now. He pats both of our shoulders in a farewell gesture and walks off.

"You know," I say, "I think he *might* actually be into you."

"I know, right? I've been telling you." Jason stands up with his tray. "I might ask him out, but not until after the article is done."

"Quite the restraint, Jason."

"Go to hell," he says pleasantly, and goes to return his tray.

After finishing every morsel on my plate, I return my tray a few minutes later, and leave the cafeteria. I'm heading to the clinic to grab my stuff when the overhead speaker comes on.

Alert Delta A wing. Code 327. Alert Delta A wing. Code 327.

No. Not again. Oh God, not again.

A guard is running by me. "Where's the code?" I ask him.

"The kennels," he calls back to me.

The wind is ferocious, whipping so hard it pushes me back.

"Did she fall?" Maloney is asking Harry, the guard who was stationed there for the day.

"I wasn't even here," he says breathlessly. "No one was scheduled for rec time right now. I just came up with the announcement." We gaze around at the empty kennels. "She must have jumped."

"How did she even get up here?" Maloney peers over the

rooftop edge and winces. I look over, too, and he pushes me back. "Be careful, Dr. Goldman."

"Who was it?" I ask, seeing only a body dressed in orange, in odd angles on the ground.

"We have to get verification still," he says. "But word is, Janaya Jones."

"Ol' White Lady?" I gasp.

Harry looks puzzled. "I'm pretty sure she's black."

"No, I know. I just—" The wind swoops in again, knocking my breath away for a minute. "She said someone was after her. That someone wanted to kill her. But then she said she was okay again. That she was at peace. I just figured..." We look around at the scene. There's snowy footprints everywhere from the prison-issued boots. "No one else was up here with her?" I ask.

"Like I told him," Harry says, "I wasn't here. But there's no one signed in on the logbook. I just checked."

"Did you tell anyone?" Maloney asks me. "That she said she was in danger?"

"Yes." I have to almost yell above the wind. "I told you, remember? I told a couple of the guards that very night. And I was going to tell the warden, but..." I don't bother finishing the sentence. *He wouldn't have believed me.*

Then the inevitable text interrupts our conversation. And I know whom it will be from, and what it will say.

Warden's office. Right now.

From Dr. Novaire.

"You," the warden says, pointing a finger at me to clarify as I walk into the room.

"I just saw her," I say.

"That's right. Which is even more troubling."

"But she wasn't suicidal. She was at peace, she said. She just told me that."

"I've heard it before from you, Dr. Goldman. Again and again."

"But really." I turn for support to Dr. Novaire, who is looking away. He looks just plain worn out and ready to retire already. "She said someone was after her."

"Who?" the warden asks.

I pause. "She wasn't sure. She said that was the rumor, though. Someone wanted to kill her."

"And did you tell someone about this?"

"I-I...told the guard on duty that night. A couple of guards," I say, realizing how lame this sounds. "Honestly, I thought she was just paranoid from her disorder."

"Which she may very well have been," Dr. Novaire says, happy to be able to contribute to the conversation.

The warden strides toward me. "Did it ever occur to you that this paranoia may have been what sent her over the edge? That she may have jumped because she was so frightened of whatever she thought was after her?"

I consider this for a second.

"And that she may, in fact, have required stronger medication for her disorder?"

"That's possible," I say. "But she was being treated. Very appropriately. I mean, she didn't always take her medications, but..."

"Did we have a recent level?" Dr. Novaire asks.

"Her last one was low. But she had just started taking it again." Both Dr. Novaire and the warden look away in disgust. "But don't you see a pattern here?" I ask. "The Elavil, which my patient wasn't taking. Andre Green getting poisoned. And now this? A suspicious death?"

"Suspicious?" The warden echoes with incredulity. "This is hardly suspicious, Dr. Goldman. The only thing that's suspicious is that another one of your patients is dead."

Dr. Novaire rubs his hands together. "Until we can figure out what is happening, perhaps Dr. Goldman's probation should be extended."

Warden Gardner lets out a stupefied laugh. "We're way past probation here, Dr. Novaire."

"But what if someone pushed her?" I ask.

"Dr. Goldman," the warden says, his face serious, fully professional, "you are being placed on an unpaid leave of absence pending further investigation."

"I'm not sure... That might actually be a university decision," Dr. Novaire protests, feebly.

"The texts," I say, grabbing for a life raft. "Detective Adams is still looking at them. We think they might be coming from Mr. Green. Did he talk to you about that?"

The warden shakes his head in dismissal. "We've looked

high and low to find out the origin of those texts," he says. "And in the end, after too many man-hours, we have found absolutely no credible evidence that these are coming from within the prison."

"But maybe they're not coming from within the prison," I counter.

"Do you want to know what conclusion I've reached?" the warden asks.

"What?" I would honestly like to know.

"My conclusion," he says, pointing his finger at me again, "is that *you* have been the one sending the texts." He pauses for effect. "For whatever sick reason or whatever weird thrill it might give you, Dr. Goldman, I believe that you, and only you, are sending them. Quite possibly trying to deflect attention from yourself."

"*Me* sending them?" My voice has risen an octave. "But what about Andre? His father's been poisoning his own kid. Don't you think maybe *he* could be related to all this?"

"Interesting you should mention Andre Green," the warden says. "I'm talking to Detective Adams about widening his search. And getting a warrant on the other person with complete access to him."

"Who?" I ask, then it hits me like a hammer. "Me?" He doesn't bother to answer. "I didn't have anything to do with hurting Andre..." I stammer. "I'm the one who figured it out!"

A cell phone ringing interrupts my defense, and Warden Gardner grabs his phone out of his breast pocket and brings it to his ear. "Yeah, what is it?" He waits a second, then shakes his head in disbelief. "Jesus."

My knees are trembling.

"What?" Dr. Novaire asks.

"Another one of your patients, Dr. Goldman," he says. "Timothy Gordon, remember him?"

I flash back to Timothy Gordon, his freckly arm out of his cast. Body integrity identity disorder and the "healing tattoo" encircling his biceps. "Yes. I remember him."

"He's at the County, barely alive. Just cut his own god-damn arm off."

"Mike," I say into the cell phone, though it's just his voice mail, "I don't know if you'll be late tonight or what." The evening darkens around me in the parking lot, snow sliding in wafts across the pavement. "I'm going to the County to visit Andre, but we need to talk." I pause then, too long, and realize the voice mail might run out. "I don't know what to say, Mike. I'm in trouble here. I need to talk to you."

I am saying, "I love you" into the phone just as I get into the lobby. I go up to see Timothy Gordon first, but find out he's still in surgery, so I make my way to Andre's room.

He is barely recognizable. His face is bloated and patches of his hair are missing, showing dry, scaly scalp underneath. His face has a yellowish hue, which means he's probably in liver failure by now. His chest puffs out rhythmically with the ventilator while five different IV bags hang from ma-chines.

I walk over and put my hand on his forehead, which is sweating.

"I'm sorry," I say, and as the words come out, I am overtaken by sobs. My body is heaving as I cry soundlessly, surprised by my own tears. I sit down, and a nurse walks by and glances at us, likely assuming I'm a family member or friend. Efficiently she changes the IV bag and straightens his ventilator tube, then touches my arm with a sympathetic smile on her way out.

Sitting in the chair next to him, I watch Andre for I don't know how long. Television shows blare in the next room. Patients are carted in and out beside me for testing. Doctors round, nurses fix up medications. And I just watch, until a shadow falls over the bed, and I look up.

It's Mike.

He drags a chair up next to me and sits down, his warm fingers lacing through mine. "It's not your fault, Zoe," he says, his voice low and quiet.

I nod, with new tears now, my nose running. "I should have looked at his nails."

"Nobody knew, Zoe. Who could have thought of that?"

"I could have. I should have. I did the wrong tox screen. I should have checked for heavy metals." He puts his arm around me, and I lean into him, still looking at the floor. "And did you hear the other big news?" I ask.

"No, what is it?" The IV pole starts beeping.

"I got fired."

He pulls away to look at me. "For what?" he asks with dismay. "For this? You were the one who diagnosed him."

"No, it wasn't that. Another one of my patients jumped off the roof at the prison." I wipe my nose with a soggy tissue. "But she might have been pushed. I swear she was pushed."

He stares at the blank wall, stroking my hand. "I can't believe they didn't even put you on probation, though."

"No," I say with a sigh. "That was last week."

He turns to look at me again. "They did?"

I slump over, putting my face in my hands. "I was going to tell you, Mike. But I was too... embarrassed. That's the truth. I was too goddamn humiliated to tell you."

Again he puts his arm around me, handing me a tissue box. "We'll get through this, Zoe. It's okay. It'll be all right." We sit there watching Andre for a while then, the machines whirring and beeping around us.

Finally I work up the courage and lean my head against his shoulder. "Mike, there's something else I have to tell you."

287

Chapter Thirty-Seven

You finally told me. The last part of your grand plan, the final act.

But I told you I couldn't do it.

No way, never. I offered to get you another name but you got annoyed and said we were done with all that. It was time for the next stage. But I couldn't do it. I killed Janaya Jones for you, just like I promised. But I couldn't do that. I begged you not to make me do that.

You're no use to me, then, you said, turning away from me like a cloud blocking the sun.

I was sick with the thought of losing you. But I couldn't do that. She never hurt me. She helped me. Even when she knew everything, she still helped me. I wanted to cry, but you hate it when I cry, so I tugged on your arm, and you flicked me off. You whined at me, that I was supposed to be your soldier, that I was supposed to help you. Your expression was puppy-dog hurt. I said that I would help you, but I couldn't do that. Anything else, just *not that. You were chewing on your lip, looking like you might ex-plode.*

I love you, *I said, realizing that I had never said it before.*

But you shook your head. If you loved me, you would do this for me.

I didn't have an answer, just a churning in my stomach. So I lay down on the floor, in an obvious, pathetic invitation to sex, trying to make things better with you in the only way I knew how. But you just snickered and stood up. Then you opened the door, and I had no choice but to follow you.

One week, *you said.* You have one week to decide.

But what if I can't? *I asked, my voice shaking because I knew the answer already.* No more poetry. No more hours making love in our ugly, beautiful room. *The thought was unbearable.*

Maybe you can find some guard who'll fuck you, *you said with a shrug.*

Chapter Thirty-Eight

I didn't end up telling Mike about the lemon.

I couldn't. I don't know why. I tried to, but I couldn't.

So the secret is still out there, taking up air between us. When it was bedtime, I pretended I was okay but didn't sleep for a second. I went downstairs and watched infomercials for trimming your waist, kitchen splicers, and, ironically, miracle cures for insomnia while Arthur rested his head on my lap, every once in a while raising his head to lick my face.

Checking with the receptionist, I find Sam is running behind, so I walk into the cold, maroon-walled vestibule and call the detective. "Any news?"

"Yes," he answers. "But I'm afraid it's not exactly good news."

"What?"

"It's not Abraham."

"What isn't?"

"He poisoned Andre, but he's not the one texting you."

290

Someone tromps in, pulling off a winter hat and stomping boots before entering to check in. "What do you mean, it's not him? It has to be him."

"It's not his phone, Zoe. It's possible he has another burner phone out there somewhere, but this one has nothing on there about any patients. And no texts to your number."

"Then what was the phone for?"

"Apparently he used it for his second family. One had been for Charmayne, and one for Jermaine and Shonda."

I start pacing the little vestibule. "Then who's texting me? We have to figure that out."

"I know, we're trying."

"The warden thinks *I'm* behind all this now."

"What?" His voice betrays definite surprise, which means that at least for now the warden hasn't shared his pet theory with him.

"Yeah. He thinks I'm sending the texts myself out of some sick need for attention. Like he thinks he's a psychiatrist or something. He wants to search my house."

The detective actually laughs. "We're still combing through evidence from Abraham Green's house. I've got about a billion better things to do than go search yours. Don't worry. The warden's got his head up his ass."

"That was my professional opinion as well," I grumble. "But he doesn't seem to want my professional opinion." A sad silence follows this statement. "So what the hell am I supposed to do? Just sit at home baking cookies and waiting for my name to be cleared?"

"Zoe—"

"Someone is out there killing my patients!"

"Listen, I get that you're under a lot of stress right now."

"With good reason," I exclaim. "I'm being set up while my patients get picked off, one by one. I'd say that's a fairly stressful state of affairs."

"*If* that's what's happening, Zoe," he says. "Obviously, I agree with you on Abraham Green. But the other patients are just theories right now. And I must point out, the concept of these patients killing themselves is far more likely than the idea that someone else is orchestrating it."

"But what about the texts?"

"A disgruntled patient, maybe, or coworker. Someone trying to hurt you."

"Like Sofia."

"Maybe. We're on it, Zoe. We're looking."

"But Janaya Jones. I'm telling you. She wouldn't have jumped. She just wouldn't have. Detective," I say, my voice growing desperate, "you said you would trust me on this. You promised me."

"And I do trust you, Zoe. A hundred percent. We're doing our best here. I've got everybody I can spare out there on this." He sighs, and there is a long pause on the phone. "But Zoe, I hope you don't take this the wrong way. You seem really, really stressed right now. It sounds like you could absolutely use a break. Maybe think of this suspension as a good thing. A blessing in disguise."

Another patient comes in, blasting the vestibule with cold air. "I do have a lot going on right now."

"This will all work itself out eventually. They gave you

292

some time off. Pretend you're on vacation or something. Take advantage of it."

I'm sitting on the couch, my head cottony and disconnected.

Whether it's the lemon, my lack of sleep, or the lack of meds in my system, I'm not sure. But I can barely string a whole thought together.

"I'm worried about you, Zoe," Sam says.

No shit, Sherlock, I think, then stand up from the couch and start pacing. I can't sit on the couch another second. And I can't play with his ridiculous water toy. Sam stares at me pacing the room.

"We need to discuss whether this fellowship is the best thing for you right now."

"Actually," I say, sitting down, then standing up again, like a jack-in-the-box, "I think that's been taken care of."

"What do you mean?"

"They booted me."

"From the fellowship?"

"The very one." I try sitting again, picking up the toy and madly twisting the knobs.

"Because of your condition or because of the patient deaths?"

I stop twisting. "My condition?"

"Yes."

"What condition?" I ask. "The anxiety-ADHD-depression thing?"

293

"Yes." He adjusts the temples of his fashionable new rec-
tangular glasses. (Seriously? It's been less than three months.
What the hell is his eyewear budget?) "I'd say it's become
quite a bit worse lately, Zoe. And you were doing very well
on all the medications, so I'm not sure why, but that happens
sometimes."

I know why! I'm not on any medications. I'm pregnant!
Tell him, tell him, tell him.

He must see something in my face. "You are taking your
medications, right?"

I should grab my chance. It's confidential. He can't tell
anyone. He could help me. I could just tell him, but I mutter,
"Right, of course."

"Would you like me to talk with Dr. Novaire? Would it
help?"

"I doubt it. He's pretty useless. And it's more the warden
who's after me."

"Really?" He taps the keyboard. "Why do you say that?"

I spring up again and start moving. "I told you about the
texts."

"Yes, and they thought Andre's father was behind them."

"Yeah, that's the problem. It turns out he's not. And
now the warden thinks *I'm* the one behind them. He even
thinks I'm poisoning Andre!" My boots scrape a rhythm
against the carpet. "But someone else is doing this. Someone is killing all my patients. And I just don't know how to
prove it."

"Uh-huh," he says, calmly, though I read alarm in his eyes.

"Someone is setting me up. Maybe Sofia. Obviously that

would make the most sense. But I don't know that for sure. They've searched her cell quite a bit, supposedly."

He pauses, his hands in a prayer position at his chin. "Let me see if I understand what you're saying. You think someone is killing your patients?"

"Yes."

"And you think they're blaming you?"

"Yes."

"But you believe Sofia is behind all this?"

"Stop with the reflective statements, Sam. Yes, yes, yes."

Another pause. "Do you mind if I contact Detective Adams?"

"Of course. That's a great idea." Sitting down again, I grab the toy. But there's something about the way he is looking at me. "Wait a second. You don't believe me?"

"It's not that, Zoe."

I put the toy down, indignant. "You think I'm making all this up?"

"Not exactly."

"Oh no. That I'm just paranoid? Is that what you think?"

He sighs, pulling his chair away from his desk and toward me. "You've been under an inordinate amount of stress lately, Zoe. I'm just trying to help you. We're both on the same team here."

And I do something I've never done to Sam before. Which is to pack up my stuff and leave.

⤶

Are you ok? It's Mike, checking on me.

Fine. Walking Arthur, I text back. It's a clear, dark night, and Scotty brought over pizza again so we could both mope around together. Misery loving company and all that. All night it was Kristy said this and Kristy said that, and no, she won't take back the ring. After he left, the house was morbidly quiet, so I decided to take Arthur, who couldn't believe his luck, on a second walk.

Be home around midnight, Mike texts. Earlier if I can. Love you.

Love you too.

I'm musing that we don't use XO anymore when my arm nearly detaches from its socket as Arthur zooms after a rabbit. "Arthur!" As I yank him back, I skid on a black ice patch and nearly wipe out. Arthur gives me a disdainful glance as I right myself. "Don't look at me like that. If I break my hip, it's your fault."

He doesn't answer. Not verbally, anyway.

A car whizzes by us, too fast, and I hold his leash tight. After the car fades down the road, the night turns deathly quiet again, the cold silencing everything all around us. I can hear my breathing, the crisp crunch of the snow. The stars are glittering dots in the frigid night.

I called Dr. Marchand's office for a new date, and I've given myself a deadline.

Two weeks. Two weeks to decide.

"So," I say, to hear myself speak, "it looks like it's gonna be just you and me for a while tonight." He darts around the base of a tree and sniffs around. "And the lemon. But I'm not so sure about the lemon." Arthur lifts his head, having gathered all possible scented information from the snow around the tree.

We walk on then, the wind biting into my cheeks as my brain scurries back to my patients. The patients in the loss column.

Dennis Johnson—hanged himself in my first week on the job. Carrie Cooke—heroin overdose, probably from a hot shot after not having used for so long. Barb Donalds—strongly denied suicidal ideation but overdosed on Elavil, which she had not been prescribed. Janaya Jones—jumped off the roof.

Pushed?

"So who is connected to all these patients, besides me?" I ask Arthur, who manages to get his front paws stuck in a snowbank, then awkwardly retracts them. Dr. Novaire? He might be clueless and way past his prime, but I couldn't imagine him killing off my patients. The warden? Not unless he's scheming to lose his own job. Jason? Not. Abraham Green? Apparently not.

Sofia? Sofia? Sofia?

Arthur lunges at his shadow (yes, he is that stupid), nearly toppling me again. "Arthur, quit it." I yank him back. He jumps out at an invisible squirrel, and I yank him again. "It's freezing, buddy. Let's go home already."

My phone text sound goes off again, and I reach into my pocket, peeling off my mitten. I find a smile on my face, thinking of Mike texting to check up on me again. But the message isn't from Mike.

Did you miss me, Angel of Death?

My eyes glaze, staring at the message in my hand.

So sorry about Andre. Looks like another patient you couldn't save.

WHO ARE YOU? I text back, furiously.

That's for me to know and you to find out. If you can. Are you ready for another riddle?

I don't respond, but the next text comes up anyway.

What do you get when you mix the Angel of Death with the seed of the devil?

Arthur is tugging on my leash as I stand there, frozen to the spot.

Give up?

I watch the screen, waiting, as wind chimes gong out in the distance.

You get a tainted, rotten fetus. That will die inside of you.

Chapter Thirty-Nine

I didn't think you'd still be up," Mike says, shaking snow off his boots onto the rug. A waft of cold comes in with him.

"We have to talk," I say. I'm holding a mug of chamomile tea, having read somewhere about its calming effects. With no wine or Klonopin at my disposal, I'll take anything I can get.

"What about?" He hangs up his coat, his usually imperturbable demeanor etched with worry. Arthur lifts his head in greeting, then drops it again on my foot.

Mike sits next to me on the couch, and I can feel the cold off his body. "Is this about Serena?"

"Um...well..." It isn't, of course, but I decide to hear him out nonetheless.

"Listen." He wrings his hands. "I told her point-blank that I'm with someone else. From the very beginning. I'll admit, I didn't mind the attention at first. But now it's gotten out of hand. I've started finding shifts she's not on." Frowning, he shakes his head. "I thought about telling the head of the department, but that seemed a bit much. And I wanted to tell you, but you've had so much going on with you lately. I didn't know how to bring it up."

I don't answer.

"Is it about the pen?" he asks.

"Don't, no...It isn't that. It isn't even about Serena at all."

"Oh." He looks perplexed. "Then what is it?"

"I got another text." I pull out my phone and show him.

He leans over me, his lips moving while he reads it. "I don't get it. Do you?"

I take a fortifying sip of tea, then try to talk, but the words won't come out.

"This is getting crazy," he says, determination in his voice. "We should call the detective right now." But I shake my head and take another sip. "What, what is it?"

I nod but still can't speak.

"What's wrong, Zoe?" He puts his hand on my knee. "Tell me, please. You're scaring me."

"I'm..." I take another swallow of tea while he watches me intently. "I'm pregnant."

Mike looks at me, his jaw actually fallen open so that I can see his uvula. "Pregnant?"

"Yes, pregnant. We're pregnant, I guess is the vernacular these days."

"Pregnant?"

I don't answer the now-rhetorical question, and it seems to dawn on him. "So the riddle is about the baby?"

"It must be."

"I'm...I can't even...Who else knows about this?"

"Two people," I say, trying to ignore his look of hurt. "Jack. And it was kind of a mistake. I was asking about our family history, and he guessed it."

"Okay, Jack. And who else?"

"Jason...I...I don't know. We were eating lunch, and I just started crying, and it just came out. I didn't mean to tell him either."

It's utterly silent then as Mike scratches his head, awkwardly. "How long have you known?"

"A couple weeks."

He nods, still looking shocked. "How far along?"

"Twelve weeks. I think it's thirteen weeks now."

He looks down at his lap. "And have you seen your..."

"Yes. I saw Dr. Marchand."

"And?" He swallows. I don't answer, fixing my gaze on Arthur, who has settled back to sleep at my feet. "Are we keeping it, Zoe?"

I put the tea down. "I don't know. That's the best answer I can give you right now. I was giving myself two more weeks to decide. Giving us two weeks, I should say. I...I just don't know."

"Two weeks," he repeats softly. He is quiet again when his forehead wrinkles up. "Are you still on your meds?"

"No," I answer, right away. "I mean, I was up until I found out. But I'm off them now." I watch him watching me. "Why, can you tell?"

He bites his lip. "I think I'll plead the Fifth on that one."

I smile, but it turns shaky, threatening to become a smile-cry, so I lean back on the couch, and he puts his arm around me. "I'm here," he says. I lay my head on his thick, warm chest. "I'm here, Zoe. No matter what. No matter what we decide to do."

"What about you?" I pick my head up and look squarely at him. "Do *you* want to keep it?"

He doesn't answer immediately, seeming to weigh his words. "I want to do whatever you want to do. If it were only up to me, yes, I would keep it. But it's your decision. And if you need two weeks to decide, I can handle that. We're in this together, either way." We don't speak for a moment, and I stand up from the couch. "But what are you going to do about the text?" he asks.

"I already called Detective Adams. He didn't answer yet."

"Jack and Jason are the only ones who know?"

"Yes. I mean, my ob-gyn. But she wouldn't have any reason to do this, and I can't believe Jason would be involved." I rub my temples to ward off a headache. "You think Jack is the one texting me?"

He shrugs. "How well do we really know him?"

"Well enough. He's my brother."

Mike raps his fingers on the coffee table. "Sort of."

Then I have a sick feeling. "Unless he told..." I'm already dialing his number, but I get his voice mail. "Call me as soon as you get this, Jack. Please. It's important." Then I add, "It's about Sofia."

Chapter Forty

This was my life before you. Eat, kill time, sleep, repeat. This would be my life, day after day, year after year. Then I met you, and everything changed.

I can't lose you. I can't go back to what I was before you.

So I made the decision. I would do it.

If I didn't, you would leave me. Just like my mother left me, and my sister. And I couldn't take that. I pretended that I had a choice. But I had no choice. This was a test, my final test. I said I would do anything for you, and I meant that. Anything.

When I told you, your sullen look vanished. Your face lit up. You will?

But I'm afraid, I said.

It'll be fine, you said, smiling now, reaching over to caress me.

I told you how the warden's been talking, and that I didn't want to get caught. You told me I wouldn't get caught, and pulled me in close, so close, in that aching, smothering way. So close that I forget everything else. Enveloped by you. Lost, even to myself.

You promised it would be over quick, just like Janaya. But I know it won't be quick. I can't lie to myself. You said you would be there for me when it was done. You promised me. Then you lifted up my shirt, and your lips were running over my skin, sending chills through me.

And that's what I try to think of now. Your lips, your hands, your voice, you.

As I sit here, wanting to retch, trembling on the cot, my hands slick with sweat. My head screaming against what I'm about to do.

The cold, sharp metal in my hands.

Waiting.

Chapter Forty-One

Detective Adams stares at the phone in puzzlement. "I don't get the baby part."

"Who knows?" I shrug. "Maybe he thinks I'm pregnant or something."

"Right," he says, and doesn't ask. "You sent me the snapshot, right?"

"I did," I say. "You think it's a burner phone again?"

"Most likely, but we'll look into it." He furrows his brows, thinking. "It's very unsettling. But we've still got no direct threat to you. It would be hard to arrest based on this."

"But the patients," I argue.

"I know." His purses his lips in a frown. Someone in dirty jeans and a T-shirt passes us, being led into an interview room. "And you don't think your brother could be involved?"

"I'm going to call him, but I don't think so. It keeps coming back to Sofia."

"Maybe. But we've searched that cell up and down. She's

got a ton of religious stuff but nothing that ties her to any of this."

"And we're still sure it's not Abraham," I confirm.

"Nothing that's come up so far." As he folds his arms, horizontal wrinkles stretch across his suit. "Oh, I almost forgot. We did get some good news. I was going to call you if you hadn't come in."

"What is it?"

"Abraham was arrested. We finally found the smoking gun. He bought the arsenic over the Web from a foreign supplier. We got the transaction."

"So he's…"

"In jail. A quarter-million bond," he says with deep satisfaction.

"At least he can't get to Andre now," I say.

"That's for sure." He nods at a detective who walks by. "How is Andre doing, by the way?"

"I saw him the other night. Not great."

"Yeah, that's what the nurses said."

Standing there, I notice a pseudo-line snaking around us, of people waiting to talk with the detective. "I guess I'd better be on my way."

The detective tucks his notebook into his pocket. "I'll get back to you as soon as I can. And I'll have a word with the warden about Sofia again. But you take care of yourself, Zoe. Okay?"

And by his look, I understand what he's trying to say without saying it.

"I didn't tell her a goddamn thing!" Jack's voice booms into the phone.

"Maybe just hinted at it, by accident?"

"No. Not a chance, Zoe. I swear. I haven't talked to her once since she's been in prison."

"I wouldn't blame you, Jack. If you did. She can be very manipulative."

"Yes, she can. I agree with you there. But I promise, I didn't tell her."

"Okay." I am straightening up Mike's DVD collection. Which basically means alphabetizing a bunch of horror movies. Since being off work, I've become unmoored and taken to creating activities for myself. I put *Re-Animator* in front of *Rosemary's Baby*. "I'll just have to talk to her myself."

"You think that's safe?" Jack asks.

"I'm not worried. She's had plenty of shots at me already."

"Maybe I should talk with the warden," he offers. "Before she kills someone else."

"It's not a bad idea." I agree. "Just don't tell him about the...baby thing...you know..."

"Don't worry," he says. "I wouldn't." Banging and yelling comes over the phone. "Oh, damn it."

"What?"

"Nothing. The guys just dropped something. I have to go. I'll call you after I've spoken with the warden."

Sandra Block

As I hang up, Arthur takes the opportunity to snatch the next case from my grip. "Arthur, no," I say, and am chasing *Hellraiser*—the dog and the movie—around the room when the front door opens.

"Just me," Mike says, taking off his winter hat.

I glance up at the clock. "You're home early."

"Yeah, I got a certain female doctor to cover for me."

"Working those masculine charms again?" I fit another DVD in a blank slot.

"Desperate measures." He comes over, his white socks immediately covered in hair from our dog who's not supposed to shed.

"It's sweet that you're here, Mike. But you don't have to check up on me. I'm not an invalid, you know."

"I know." He wanders to my side. "What are you doing with the DVDs?"

"Oh," I say, brightly, "arranging them. Alphabetically."

"Hmm." He sits down on the couch, and Arthur bounds over for a pet.

"Why? Did you not want me to?"

"No, that's okay. It's just, I had them arranged by year already."

Says one anal-retentive person to another. "Oh."

"No, it's good. Alphabetical is good. It's better," he assures me. But as I continue sorting, I notice that he is quiet, just staring at the wall.

"Is everything okay?" I ask.

He turns to me. "I need to know something." His hand is rubbing Arthur behind the ears in an automatic motion.

308

"Like I said, I'm okay with what we do, either way. But I just need to know. Were you going to tell me? If you didn't get the text, I mean. Were you still going to tell me?"

I sit down next to him. "Yes, I was," I say. "I tried to a few times, but I just couldn't. But I promise you that I would have told you. Eventually."

He breathes in deeply. "Okay," he says, nodding, possibly to convince himself. "I'm okay with that. I can be okay with that." And we are sitting together on the couch, both petting Arthur, who is in absolute heaven, when the doorbell rings. We turn to each other with the mutual question of who it might be, and I get up to solve the mystery.

I peer through the window. "Oh, Christ."

"Who is it?" Mike asks.

Standing on the doorstep is quite literally the last person I want to see: Newsboy.

Logan extends his leather-gloved hand as if he's campaigning for mayor. "I don't know if Zoe has told you about me? I'm Logan, the pain-in-the-ass reporter guy." He adjusts his hat, which is covering one eyebrow, and gives an apologetic but winning smile, and I can tell that Mike isn't buying any of it.

"Yeah, she told me all about you." Mike and I hover at the doorstep above Logan on the freezing porch, and he's smart enough not to hint at an invitation inside.

"I don't mean to be stalking you, Zoe," he says, focusing

on me now. "But you won't answer my calls, and there's a lot going on."

"Yes, there is a lot going on. Which is *why* I haven't answered your calls. So I'm sorry about that."

"That's okay," he says, as if I were actually apologizing. "I had another interview with the warden. It's all over the papers, of course, the jumper."

"Of course," I say, thinking, *Janaya Jones*. She had a name.

"The warden said you were taking some time off for now, and the story's coming out next week." He stamps a cold foot on the porch. "I'll put it to you this way. Like I said before, I want you to be able to give your side of the story."

"The story is over," I say. "I won't be giving an interview."

"See, that might not be the wisest way to play this."

"No comment," I say.

Logan turns to Mike, apparently seeking a bro-to-bro intervention. "Can you talk to her, Mike? Honest to God, it's *her* future that I'm worried about."

Mike turns to me with a straight face. "Zoe, he's very worried about your future."

"Thanks for sharing that with me, Mike. I'm still going to go with no comment, however." But before reaching for the door handle, I pause. "As a matter of fact, I do have some gossip."

Logan leaps at this. "Oh yeah?" He is reaching into his satchel.

"Yeah. I think Jason has a crush on you." And the last I see of Newsboy is a look of utter confusion as I shut the door on him.

Chapter Forty-Two

As I go to the clinic to clean out my stuff, just the person I wanted to see is standing in the hallway. After some finagling from Jason, we are in his clinic room, which is the spitting image of my clinic room, a bare white box with a big red alarm button.

Sofia yawns, extravagantly. I find myself gripping the edge of the desk. "So this is it?" she asks. "The final hurrah?" She leans back and stretches her arms in a way that's almost feline.

"What makes you say that?" I ask, testing her.

She shrugs, carelessly. "I've heard rumors."

"Yeah, I'm sure you've heard lots of rumors."

She gives me a bemused look. "Such as?"

"Don't insult my intelligence, Sofia."

She backs up in her chair, which screeches against the tile. "Okay."

"What are you trying to prove?" I demand.

"Maybe if you could let me know what I'm supposed to have done, I could explain it to you."

"Texting your little riddles."

"Oh God," she groans. "We're back to those texts? I told you I have nothing to do with any of that."

"Sofia." I put both palms on the table, calming myself. "Whatever you're trying to achieve here, friendship, a relationship, forgiveness." I peer into those blue, blue eyes. "It's not going to happen like this. Whether you are truly trying to find God, I don't know. If so, good for you. You say you want a family again, I say that you destroyed that family."

She doesn't answer.

"Whatever the hell went on that night, I don't know. But I know this. It isn't going to happen. Not like this."

We stare at each other for some time.

"I spoke to the warden today," she says, finally. "Seems he has a lot of crazy ideas, too. Rumors of what I'm supposed to be involved in." She combs out her glossy hair with her fingers. "Even big brother Jack is in on it. Telling him all the horrible things I've done. Unfortunately, none of them are true."

"It won't work," I say. "What you want. It's never going to happen."

"The rabbi says—"

"Never."

Sofia moves in toward me then, her look questioning. "I could help you, you know. If you told me what's going on. But otherwise, I don't know what you want me to do."

I lower my voice, leaning in toward her as well. "Here's what I want you to do, Sofia. Leave me the fuck alone." I enunciate every word. "It's over. Done. Don't send your little messengers. Don't text me."

Sofia shakes her head, like a teacher disappointed with her pupil.

"Talk to the news, or don't. It doesn't matter now. I'll leave that up to you. And your God."

"You know what, Tanya?" She stands up then, motioning to a guard outside the door. "You're running out of chances here. Pretty soon I *will* give up on you. And believe me," she says, right before the guard gets there, "then you'll be sorry."

Jason helps me load up my box. I don't have a ton of stuff: some pictures, some diplomas, some files. And about a hundred mugs.

"Don't worry," Jason says. "You'll be back."

I drop a couple drug pens in a mug. "We'll see about that."

"I'm not planning on dealing with Novaire without you, so you better be."

I pause then, surveying the office. Gray industrial tile. White industrial walls. Laminated desks and outdated computers. Yup, I'm going to miss this place. "I better get going. Mike's waiting in the parking lot."

"Yeah, I should go, too. I have to decide whether my newest patient is fit to stand trial."

"What did he do?"

"Let his king cobra loose on his neighbor."

"Yikes. Did the neighbor survive?"

"Yeah, sans a foot, though."

"And how's the patient?" I ask with some jealousy. Because I won't be seeing him. Because I'll never be asking those questions again. "Competent?"

"I don't know. Supposedly he's speaking in tongues right now." Just then Officer Maloney knocks on the door.

"I'm almost ready," I say. "I'll be out in just a minute."

"No, no. It's not that." He looks embarrassed. "One more patient wanted to see you before you go. Can you do that?"

I toy with the corner of the box. "If it's Sofia, the answer is no."

"No, it's the redhead who's always cutting herself. She wanted to give you a gift or something. She's pretty upset."

I text Mike. Be out in 10.

As soon as I walk in, I can see she's been crying.

"It isn't fair that they're making you leave," Aubrey complains as Officer Maloney walks out.

"It's okay." I must admit I'm touched. As Sam says, you can't forget the good ones. "It's just for a little bit. While they do an investigation."

She sniffles with a weak smile. "The warden is such an asshole."

I cup my hand and say in a stage whisper, "I don't entirely disagree."

We pause, sharing a bittersweet moment, then she taps her fingers on her knees. Her polish is chipped and chewed. "Well, you helped me so much, I wanted to give you something back."

"You don't need to do that." I pull out the bracelet from under my sleeve, now stained and ratty. "See, I'm still wearing this one."

"No, it's something else." She lifts up an orange cuff of her own sleeve, and I see a sore, red mark on her skin. I figure it's a cutting mark, but then I see it's got blue ink embedded in it. A new prison tattoo, in a flowery cursive.

"You have a new tattoo?"

She stops reaching, confused a second. "Oh, that. It's nothing. Just a private joke." She lifts her arm to show me. "The Professor," it reads.

"Odd joke."

"Not really," she says, finally finding what she was reaching for, which is a shiny, metal tool with a sharpened end, like a homemade knife. It takes me a second to realize it's a shank. "I'm sorry, Dr. Goldman."

"Aubrey." I back away, but not quickly enough. She leaps on me, pushing me over with the chair. The red button is tantalizingly in view but unreachable. Squirming from her grasp, I feel a sudden, searing pain above my hip bone. I glance down in shock to see blood bubbling up. She lifts her arm again for another go, and I am pushing her wrist away with all my might.

"What are you doing, Aubrey?" My hip is pulsing. I can feel blood spreading on my shirt.

"I'm sorry," she repeats, more forcefully.

I shove against her wrist, but my arm is shaking with fatigue. In a last-ditch effort, I swat at the button with my other arm but don't get anywhere near it. "Aubrey, let's talk," I say, breathlessly. I'm still pushing but the knife is winning, descending. The blade grazes my abdomen in a flash of pain. My arm is giving out as she lays all her weight on me. "Why? Why are you doing this?" I grunt out.

"The baby first. That's what he said." Her voice is flat and emotionless, like a robot's. "Get the baby first."

"Who said that?" The tip of the blade sinks down a half inch, and my arm is burning. I can't hold her off much longer. "Aubrey, don't do this." The blade burrows deeper. "Help me," I yell out, more a groan than a yell. My arm is barely pushing now, the blood is coming out in pulses. "Help me," I say again, this time in a whisper.

And the door whooshes open.

A light of hope wells up in me.

Someone is coming to help me. A shadow lurches up on the wall behind us, and as I look up to see, Aubrey turns her head, too. Then Aubrey's face contorts in shock and pain. She yelps, comically almost, clutching her chest. And in slow motion crumples on top of me, a blade sticking out at an odd angle from her chest.

Not Aubrey's shank, another shank. A different shank.

Aubrey's weapon is lying beside me now, glazed with my blood, and someone else's dagger is protruding from her chest. I shove her off me with revulsion.

"You don't get to kill her," the voice says. Her voice is cool and smooth, with a hint of a sneer. "You don't get to do that. Not before my little niece meets her Auntie Sofia."

Sofia hovers over me then, her smile not mysterious, not small. Her smile is one of pure victory. The guards pile into the room then, and I'm holding my side, trying to stanch the gushing. They swoop down on Sofia and Aubrey. Voices are barking out, a hand is holding mine. Cloth is held against my stomach.

"My baby," I say, realizing right then that I do want this baby, more than anything. I've always wanted this baby. My cranberry bean. My apricot. My lemon. My baby.

"It's okay, Dr. Goldman. We got you. You're going to be okay."

"My baby."

"She's delirious in here. Somebody call Medical!"

"Wait!" I say, remembering it right then, what I have to do. Before there isn't time. In case I don't make it. In case I die, before there's time. I try to sit up, but my hip clenches in pain. "Sofia!"

"Don't worry about her." Officer Maloney says, his bristled, sweaty head right above mine. "She can't hurt you now." There is a gurney suddenly, and I'm being lifted.

"Sofia!" I call out.

"I'm here, Tanya, I'm here." Sofia turns around, fighting against the guards to see me.

I can barely lift my head up, but I make them stop as I'm passing by her. I grip on to her shirt to stop them. "I forgive you," I say. Then my head falls back, and they take me away.

317

Chapter Forty-Three

When the next morning comes, I am still alive.

I feel like hell, but all things considered, it could have been worse. No vital organs were punctured. No essential arteries nicked. The baby is alive and kicking (well, not literally kicking, but awfully cute, for a lemon). A little blood loss, but not enough to warrant a transfusion.

But there is pain.

A lot of pain. Shooting, throbbing, and constant pain.

Warden Gardner glances nervously about the room, out of his element. When I shift in the hospital bed, another round of pain blasts up from my hip. "Did Aubrey have anything to do with the texts?"

"We're still trying to work that out," Detective Adams says, standing at the bed rail next to the warden. "It may be something totally separate." A nurse comes by and, seeing the warden, adds a flounce to her step with a flirtatious smile, and the warden gives an uncomfortable smile back, twisting his wedding ring. She bends over to adjust something that probably doesn't need adjusting on my IV pole, then leaves. "No concept as to why she did this?" the detective asks.

"None whatsoever." I scratch my head, my greasy hair. I need a shower, though the idea of the pain involved terrifies me. "In fact, I thought she liked me."

"Maybe too much," the warden says. "She's had a few female affairs in the prison. We're looking into that, too." His typical strident demeanor is more cowed today. As if ignoring Detective Adams has finally caught up with him. As if someone else is worried about losing his job now.

"It doesn't make sense, though," I say. "Out of nowhere, Aubrey attacks me?" I take a sip of my coldish water from a straw. "She knows about my pregnancy, obviously. So she must be involved in the texting. Which means she must be involved in the prison deaths. But why?" I stop talking because my stomach is pounding in time with my hip, and I'm running out of breath.

"Or the attack may have been motivated by something else entirely. Money. Street cred. Another inmate," the warden lists off.

"Sofia," Adams says.

The name makes me sit up, wincing. "She saved me. She had nothing to do with this."

"Hard to know, Zoe." Adams puts his big paw of a hand on my shoulder. "Setting you up to save you? If she wanted to earn your trust, that would be a damn good way to do it."

"The oldest one in the book," the warden says.

I shake my head. "Not possible."

They exchange a look, and I yawn, in an unsubtle attempt to remind them that I'm the patient, and it's time to leave. "Well…" The detective looks at his watch. "I guess we better be—"

"Anyone here to help you?" Warden Gardner looks around because it sure as hell isn't going to be him.

"My boyfriend, Mike. He had to cover for a few hours, but he'll be back."

"Good," he says, and the detective pats my shoulder again.

Now I yawn for real. The pain medication is hitting. The doctors gave me the lightest pain pill possible with the baby in mind, but my body's been without medication for four months now, and it wallops me.

"Before we go," the warden leans down toward me and whispers, "I just wanted to apologize. I didn't realize your…condition, and we're going to get to the bottom of those texts, you can be sure."

I manage a nod.

"If you think of anything, you call, okay?" Adams adds.

I nod again.

And I do think of something before I drift off. Barely. The smudged, blue, flowery word. On her arm. "The professor," I mumble, before my eyes close.

"The professor?" I hear Adams repeat, and then I fall asleep.

I awake to a most unwelcome face. "Newsboy," I say, my tongue dry and furry.

Logan laughs. "Never been called that one before."

"Why did they let you in?" I ask, abandoning all politeness.

He shrugs, pulling out his press badge. "Membership has its perks." Then he holds out a box, abashed. "I come bearing chocolate, at least." He places the box on the table and pulls up a chair to sit down beside the bed. "How are you doing?"

"On the record?" I query.

"Off the record. I just want to know. As a human, Zoe." He tugs at his tie, and it strikes me that I've never seen him in a tie before.

"As a human, I've been better." I think back to my last hospital stay, when I almost died after Sofia slashed my neck. "On the other hand, I've been worse."

Nodding, he gazes around the bare room. A few bouquets, an IV pole, a TV, a clock. Your basic non-ICU setup. He sighs. "I hate to bother you right now, but you gotta admit, it's a great story."

"I could see that, Logan. But you also gotta admit, this isn't the best time to talk."

He nods, readily. "Of course. Maybe just a little off-the-record chat, then?"

I rub my eyes, my hip pulsing again. "I suppose. Five minutes, max."

"It's a deal. Five minutes." He takes out his notebook. "Let's start with this. Any idea why she did it?"

"Who?" I ask, unwilling to give him any more than he knows.

"Aubrey Kane."

So he does know. "No idea."

"No motive yet."

"That's right."

"Does the detective think they're close to an answer?" Logan asks.

"You'd have to ask the detective."

He bites his lip with a determined nod, which tells me he hasn't gotten very far in talking to the detective. "Could she have been working for someone? Like some agent that wanted to do you harm?"

I notice a sky-blue thread poking out from under his sweater again. When I look closer, though, it looks as if the thread is braided. "Anything's possible," I say, sorry I made this deal already. I'm grumpy and hungry, and my stomach wound is flaring with pain.

"Like a professor, maybe?"

My breath catches, and I stare at him a moment. "What did you say?"

"A professor." He looks at me with a wicked glint in his forest-green eyes. "Did you like her new tattoo? I certainly did."

I am speechless.

Logan stands up now, towering over me in the bed. "I told you I volunteer there, right? That's what I do. I teach them creative writing. To *expand* themselves." He draws out the word with sarcasm. "I teach, out of the goodness of my heart, but I also have other motives. Less altruistic motives, shall we say." His smile is vicious. "The prison girls like me, you know. Especially Aubrey. She's one of my very best students."

My mind is spinning. Logan is the professor. And I realize suddenly what that thread is on his wrist.

A friendship bracelet.

I reach over for the nurse's button.

"Looking for something?" he asks, then reveals the call button in his palm. "How about I'll get the nurse for you, if you need anything?" Then he puts his hand on my stomach, putting pressure on the wound. My breath sucks in.

"You make one sound, and I will kill you and that fucking baby. Got it?"

I nod, not saying a word.

He stands over me then, gloating, obviously relishing this moment. "Did you get all of your texts, then?" I don't answer, and he laughs, darkly. His boyish grin has vanished. "You're not very good at riddles. Too bad Detective Adams couldn't track down the phone for you. Save the day."

I swallow. "I'm sorry. For whatever I did, Logan."

"Shhh…" He pushes down harder on my wound, and I can feel my eyes fill up. "Remember our deal?"

I nod again.

He releases his hand just a bit, and I gasp at the swell of pain. "I'm so sorry. Does that hurt, Zoe? I'm sure it does. But that's nothing compared to what you did to me."

I try to question him with my eyes, afraid to speak.

"You remember I told you that I had a brother in prison once?"

I am thinking back. Vaguely, I remember that conversation.

"Dennis was his name. Dennis Johnson. Remember him?"

The name pummels me. Dennis Johnson. My first, unalterable mistake. The eighteen-year-old I declared competent to stand trial, who scored the lowest rating on the suicide risk assessment scale. And since it was the first week of the fellowship, I tried to reach Dr. Novaire. I called him three times, had him paged overhead. He finally got back to me, distracted, and said that sounded fine, and I could sign the paperwork.

But five hours later, Dennis was found hanging in his cell.

Dennis Johnson. Logan Johnson's brother. So the chickens have come home to roost.

"I can see by that loathsome look on your face that you do."

"Logan," I say, reaching out for his arm, "I'm sorry."

"Don't you fucking touch me," he hisses, flinging me away. "You *disgust* me. Get that? Disgust me. Everything about you. Especially that monster inside you." As he leans over me, I see spittle on his bottom lip. "You think you'll have a nice little baby with a sister like Sofia? I meant what I said, you sick fucking bitch. That baby is tainted." His face looms over mine, his face red with hatred, his eyes vitriolic. Like one of Andre's devils. "I tried to get done with this at your house, but your big hero of a boyfriend was there."

"Logan—"

"And if Aubrey hadn't been such a pussy, I wouldn't have to waste one more second with you." He lifts his hand from the wound then and whips his tie off his neck in one slick motion. "But you did give me five minutes. And I'm afraid I'll have to spare another thirty seconds or so."

Now the tie is looped around my neck and pulled tight. My throat goes into immediate spasm as I pull at the tie, trying to fit a finger under it. The room tilts. Seconds pass, minutes maybe. I don't know how long. Time has slowed, and I'm trying to suck in air, and the room is dimming, a gray shade lowering. Darker, darker. I reach out but can't get to Logan. No air. Lungs burning. I feel myself falling into a cold place. An ocean. Frigid water surrounds me as the sunlight above me turns watery, then disappears. My mother's face coalesces in front of me then, smiling. My young mom, before her dementia, is there. Stroking my hair.

"Zoe," she says, whispering in my ear. I can barely hear her. She says something, and I am straining to hear, my vision turning a dark, bloody red. The ocean is red, too, now, and I am sinking. The water has turned warm. Finally I can see her lips, my mother's beautiful lips, forming the words.

Kick him.

Her words give me the strength I need for one last chance. I know that's all I have. One chance. And with the last muscle fibers burning out, the final second of my life fading, my mom gives me just an aliquot of energy. Just enough to kick my leg out. One time. One shot.

And I connect.

⟲

"Jesus!" Logan bellows, bending over with hands on his groin.

I rip the tie off my neck, taking in a lung-bursting breath as the black-red ocean opens above me. Colors surge back into the room, and my mother's kindly face fades into pinpricks. Yanking the IV out of my hand, I jump off the bed, fighting through the searing pain. Logan lunges at me again, and I stumble backward to avoid him. Jumping at me again, he grabs my shirt by the neck and slams me against the wall.

I hear my skull crack, and pain washes through my head. My vision divides into two. He is grabbing me by my shoulders, and his knee comes up to my abdomen. Bile rises in my throat as I fall to my knees, a grinding pain in my gut. I am backing away from him, crawling awkwardly like a crab, when the door whips open, and we both look over to see a person standing there with a cup of coffee in each hand.

The coffee hits the tile, splashing in a thousand directions as Mike leaps onto Logan. Mike doesn't size him up or take a stance, he just pounces. Punches are landing, thudding, over and over, his arm arching again and again. Ugly thumps, the sound of bone cracking, his arms a blur, pounding. Logan slumps over. His face is grotesque, eyes swollen up, his nose pushed over an inch to the side.

"Mike!" I am yelling. "Stop!" But he doesn't hear me, can't hear me. Muffled punches to his abdomen. Grunts. Logan has stopped moving. Mike's arm lifts up again. "Mike!"

I scream out as loudly as I can with my sore, hoarse voice. "Please! You're going to kill him."

And he turns to me in a daze, his arm still lifted, then drops it suddenly, breathing heavily in the silence. Mike looks at his hands, his knuckles already pink and swollen, with bits of skin torn off. "Are you okay?" His voice is ragged.

I nod, though my knees are wobbly, and I can barely hold myself up against the wall. I touch my neck, which is tender and bruised. As he comes over and grabs me in a hug, I can smell the sweat on him. I realize he is crying, and I hug him back, my arms so tired I can barely lift them. My abdomen aches where Logan kneed me, and I'm just praying that the lemon is okay. Mike wipes his eyes with a shaky hand, streaking blood onto his cheek.

Detective Adams bursts into the room then with a bulky policeman by his side. "I was coming to warn you." He stops short, though, taking in the scene—the angry purple ring around my neck, Mike's scraped-up fists, the spilled coffee, and Logan's beaten, motionless body. "About the reporter..." His voice trails off.

Dizzy and sick, I slump back onto the bed. "I think you might be a little late."

Chapter Forty-Four

Three weeks later I'm sitting on the couch again.

"I wish you had told me," Sam says.

"I'm sorry." I look down at the oatmeal-colored carpet in shame. "I just couldn't." I move against the couch, frowning at the pain. "I wasn't even sure I was going to keep it."

Sam smiles as he gazes out the window at the gray February day. "It does explain a lot, though."

"You mean why my medicine wasn't working very well?"

"Exactly," he says, laughing now.

I laugh, too, tugging my Steri-Strips. Mike took my stitches out last week. They had shoved me out of the hospital after only one day of observation. (It turns out that patients are expensive.) I feel like a doll that's been ripped apart, then sewn back together wrong.

"So have they figured it all out, then," he asks, "the texts and everything?"

"Logan Johnson. He had poor Aubrey wrapped around his

finger. She was feeding him information on all my patients."

He squints in thought. "How did she know who your patients were in the first place?"

"She got into my computer."

"She knew your password?"

"Rule of thumb," I say, tipping the liquid toy. "Don't use your pet's name as a password. Especially if said pet adorns your mug."

"Ah." Sam scratches his incipient beard. "Lesson learned."

"Logan got other prisoners to manipulate my patients. And they were all vulnerable to begin with. Doesn't take much to push them over the edge."

"To convince a depressed patient to take a bottle full of pills," he says.

"Exactly." I find my foot tapping and stop it, as it's stretching my hip wound. "They're reinvestigating the prisoner who jumped, too. Janaya Jones. Looks like she might have had some help on the way down."

He grimaces. "That's too bad."

"Yeah." I glance at my watch, making sure I won't be late for my meeting with the detective, and find I have plenty of time. "And the most amazing part of it all is that Sofia had absolutely nothing to do with it."

He uncaps his fake Montblanc. "What are you going to do about her?"

"I don't know." A hawk swoops onto a branch outside, then flies away just as quickly. "I don't see us becoming best friends. But I think she's earned some type of relationship, at least."

Sam doesn't agree or disagree. "Be careful."

"My middle name, right?"

Sam doesn't bother to answer that one. "Okay." He places the pen down on his glossy desk with some finality. "No meds?"

"No meds."

"Fine for the moment. We may want to reexamine that later in the pregnancy."

"Uh-huh," I say, which is code for *no way*.

"You're off for one month, then I'm putting you on part-time."

"Wait. I don't think I need a whole month to—"

"Not up for debate." He uncaps and recaps his pen again with an annoying clicking sound. "Meanwhile, get some rest. I know doing nothing isn't exactly your style."

This makes me laugh out loud.

"But you need it." His voice is serious now. "Take some time to heal, Zoe. For you, and the baby."

Andre is sitting up, tearing through his third chocolate pudding.

"Easy there, champ," Detective Adams says. "You don't want to make yourself sick."

Andre shrugs. "I'm hungry, man. And the nurse said I could have whatever I want."

The nurses have all taken a shine to the smiling, soft-spoken young man who, like Lazarus, rose up from the dead and nicely asked for pudding.

"You're looking so great," I say. I still can't believe my eyes. Not only is he not hooked up to any machines, it's as if he's a completely different person. No longer paranoid and deranged, swatting at hallucinations. Now he's lucid, but even more, smart and funny. A solid addition to my win column.

Andre taps his spoon on his plate in a rhythm. "I know I was saying some crazy stuff."

"Don't worry about it," I say. "You were in a crazy situation."

"That's true." He has a faraway look.

"Anyway." I whip the big reveal out of my bag.

His eyes light up. "Really?"

"Really," I say, handing him the latest Avengers comics.

He shoves his empty plate to the side and digs right in, his eyes as voracious as his stomach. "Thanks," he says, looking up just for a second so as not to lose his place.

"Enjoy," I say. We sit for a moment as Andre enters another world. The detective watches him with an almost paternal pride. "So," I say, "how is Newsboy doing?"

Detective Adams shrugs. "He's fine. Broken nose, couple of ribs, nothing that won't heal in time for his trial."

"And he's on the Medical floor?"

"For now," he says. "Handcuffed to the bed with a guard babysitting him. He's not going anywhere."

I nod, relieved at the news. "They managed to save Timothy Gordon," I say. The man looked happier than ever when I visited him. *It's such a relief*, he said, *to finally get that thing off*. That thing being his arm.

"But not Aubrey," the detective says.

"No," I say with a sigh. "Not Aubrey." Who died, literally, of a broken heart. Or a shank to the heart anyway. "I was wondering about something," I add.

"Yeah?" He takes out a piece of mint gum and offers me one.

And I take a piece and unwrap it. "How did he know I was pregnant?"

"From Aubrey. She had quite an extensive diary about him. Was pretty obsessed."

"Right, but how did *she* know?"

"She wrote something about you throwing up once. And seeing some prenatal vitamins."

I think back to our visits and hazily recall both instances, though they seemed trivial at the time. And I didn't notice because I was too busy patting myself on the back over how much I was helping her. Funny to think that she was the one playing me all along, not Sofia. "Maybe she told Sofia?"

"Maybe," he says with a shrug.

But I know the best way to find out. "Well, I better be going," I say, standing up gingerly.

"Yeah, me too." He stands up, too, and stretches with a yawn, his potbelly hanging over his belt. "See you later, Andre."

"Oh yeah. See you." Andre looks up, still smiling from something on the page, and I am reminded again of the

Facebook photo of the little boy with a million-watt grin, holding his prized comic book in front of the Christmas tree.

⌒

"I never thought I'd say this," I admit, as we walk around the worn path in the rec yard. She slows down to my hobbling pace. It's a warmish day for the month, and the leaves are damp at our feet. "But I feel I owe you an apology. And maybe even a thank-you. For saving my life."

God bless her, Sofia does her best not to gloat. She just keeps walking. "Given our history, I'd say you were entitled to your doubts. But you're welcome." A bird alights on a tree. "So I guess we're even, then?"

"I don't know about that," I say with a heavy dose of skepticism. "Considering you tried to kill me twice, and only saved me once."

"True. But I saved two of you this time."

We walk a few more paces. "I suppose there's a certain logic to that."

"And you did say," she adds, pressing her advantage, "in the heat of the moment, that you forgave me."

"Yes." I kick up some leaves, feeling my Steri-Strips strain again. "And I won't retract it."

Sofia snickers at this. "Don't be too enthusiastic now."

"Hey, 'given our history,'" I snipe, "how about we be happy with this for now. Okay?"

"Okay, okay." Sofia puts up her hands in surrender. "I'm happy."

"Fine," I say, sounding like a grumpy little sister after a squabble. "How did you know, by the way?"

"Know what?"

"About...the baby."

She turns to me with her little smile. "A magician can't reveal her secrets, you know."

I shake my head at this one, and we keep walking. "So, are you still going to convert?" I ask. "Now that I've sort of forgiven you. Or does that all go by the wayside?"

"Of course not," she says. "That was for me, not just you." Sun pokes through a cloud, and Sofia tilts her head back to soak it in. "Like that," she says.

"Like what?" I ask.

"That. Can you feel it?" Sofia gazes up, squinting in the light.

I look up. "The sun?"

"Yes, the sun." She looks up to the sky with a smile. "God's countenance, shining upon us."

Her facile reference to the blessing disturbs me, and I don't answer her. I'm not sure whether she's playing me or not but give her the benefit of the doubt and stay quiet. We walk on in silence, and after some time we are back at the start of the loop.

"I guess this is where I get off," I say. "Good luck, Sofia."

"You as well," she says. "And Tanya."

"Yes?" I say, chewing back my annoyance at her little nickname for me.

Her mysterious smile creeps back onto her face. "Take care of that baby."

I run into Jason in the clinic hallway, just as I'm about to leave. "You back already?"

"No, taking the month off," I say. "Doctor's orders."

Wincing, he points to my neck, to the faded, yellow bruises that make a nice addition to my slash scar. "That looks painful."

"Looks worse than it feels," I say, playing it down.

Jason pours some sanitizer on his hands. "Did you hear anything more about psycho Newsboy?"

"Locked up," I answer, accepting a dab on my palm as well.

"Good." He gives a definite nod. "Turns out he probably wasn't even gay. My friend said it was somebody else at Fugazi." Jason drops his hand sanitizer back in his pocket. "I *thought* he was too boring to be gay."

"Interesting worldview," I return.

"Anyway," Jason says, leaning against the wall, "should be quite the month with Novaire gone, too."

"Why, where's he going?" I ask.

He cocks his head toward me. "You didn't you hear?"

"No, I didn't hear." I grab his arm. "What happened?"

"He got axed."

"Really?" I ask. "Why? Just for being incompetent?"

"Nope." A wicked smile sneaks onto his face. "Something even spicier than that." But then his eyes turn nervous, and he doesn't say anything more.

"Come on, then," I goad him. "Don't hold back."

He pauses. "I probably shouldn't have said anything."

I give him a look. "Come on, Jason. Out with it."

"Okay, fine." He leans in to me and lowers his voice. "Novaire was writing love letters." He pauses, reading my expression. "To Sofia."

"He was...what?" I grab a chair to sit down.

"That's what I meant." Jason takes a seat next to me. "I shouldn't have said anything."

"No. That's okay. It would have come out anyway. I'd rather it be you who told me." I think back to Dr. Novaire, how his face lit up while he was talking about Sofia. "That's just so sad."

"Sad?" He scoffs. "How about revolting?"

"Were they actually..." I can't bring myself to say it.

"Who knows? Not something I want to visualize, ever." He flicks his hand, as if waving off a flea. "He denies it, but either way, the warden found the letters. And coincidentally Nowhere finally decided to take a not-so-early retirement."

"Yeah," I mutter. "Definitely not early enough." Destiny walks by, and I give her a wave. She does a quick survey of my appearance but is polite enough not to ask me anything. "It makes sense, though," I say, half to myself. "Why he was so intent on me making up with her. And that stupid project."

"That was a stupid project," Jason agrees.

"Maybe he really thought she had changed." As did I. And she did change, at least a little. Didn't she?

After my time at the prison, I decide that I deserve a reward. So I stop by the Coffee Spot for an extra-large decaf soy chai tea. It sounds complicated but it tastes delightful, and I'm quite addicted to the stuff.

Scotty sits down with me for a quick visit. "So you're still going through with the fellowship, then?"

"Absolutely. Why wouldn't I?"

He scratches his hair, which I just noticed might be thinning the teeniest bit at the top. "I don't know. Um, let's see. A patient tried to stab your baby, and then her crazy boyfriend tried to strangle you?"

"Third time's the charm," I say. I take a soothing sip of tea, enjoying the warmth of the fireplace. "Anything new with Kristy, by the way?"

"No." He looks glumly into the fire, the flames throwing shadows off his face. "I think it's really over."

I take another sip. "Sorry, Scotty."

He sighs. "I guess it's for the best in the end. As she said, we wanted different things."

"Yeah, I guess." I feel bad for my brother—the kind, sweet womanizer with James Dean eyebrows—who now understands how all those other women felt. Romeo finally met his Juliet, and she didn't take poison or stab herself. She just said they had different long-range plans. "So, did you return the ring?"

"Nah," he says, biting at his lip, his eyes downcast. "Not yet." He picks at a hangnail. "I thought I should tell you. I'm thinking about moving out of Buffalo."

"What?" I nearly choke on my chai.

"Think about it, Zoe. Nothing's keeping me here. Mom's gone. Kristy's gone." He throws his hands up, looking about the room. "I can't stay at the Coffee Spot forever. She was right about that, at least."

"I suppose."

"I don't know," he says. "We'll see. I have plenty of time to figure it out." We sit for a bit longer, and his gaze drops to my stomach. "You know if it's a boy or girl yet?"

I rub my belly, which is not really rub-worthy just yet. "No. They did an ultrasound in the hospital just to make sure everything was okay, but I was pretty out of it. We're having an official one tomorrow." I rub the lemon again, which is now, per pregnantbabes.com, the size of a large navel orange. In response to which Mike asked me, *What's with all the fruit?*

"So are you gonna find out?" Scotty asks.

"Mike wants it to be a surprise." I put down my tea again. "But I think there are enough surprises in life. So maybe."

Scotty looks away from the fire. "Any names?"

"If it's a girl, yes," I say. "We would call her Sarah." Sarah was our mother's name.

Scotty nods, a sad smile on his face. "She would have loved being a grandma," he says.

And I realize my kid brother is growing up.

Chapter Forty-Five

Y ou almost ready to go?" I ask. "I really have to pee."

Mike tilts his head toward the clock. "The ultrasound's not for another hour."

I squirm, feeling a special kind of miserable. My bladder is full, I'm craving coffee, and my Steri-Strips are itchy as hell. "I think I mistimed the whole water thing."

"Why don't you sit down?" he asks, fumbling around in his pocket for something. "Maybe that will help."

"Maybe." I sit down at our kitchen table. Arthur thinks this might mean food and comes over to sniff my hand. "Let's talk about something to take my mind off peeing."

"Niagara Falls?" he jokes.

"Shut up." I pet Arthur's puffy back.

"Actually, I do have something that might take your mind off of things." He pulls something from his pocket, and, as quick as lightning, Arthur snatches it.

"No! Jesus, no!" Mike leaps after him. "Get him," he yelps.

339

"What does he have?" I make a halfhearted reach toward him. "Come on, Mike. I'm about to have an accident over here."

"Something very important," he says, lurching after Arthur's collar and just missing.

Arthur runs by me again. "Don't worry. He ate an entire bag of plastic dreidels last week and he was fine. I kept meaning to put it away." Arthur is now playing a fun new game of Deke with Mike. "Come on, seriously, just let him have it. I don't want to be late."

"No, Zoe, give me one minute." He finally gets a hold of Arthur and starts sticking his hand in his throat, gagging him.

I stare at him in disbelief. "What on earth are you doing?"

From elbow deep in the dog's gullet Mike plucks something out, with a look of complete victory. Then he drops down on one knee as Arthur goes in for one more steal and is unceremoniously shoved away.

My body goes loose then, when I see what he's holding.

"Zoe Goldman. Will you do me the honor of becoming my wife?"

Taking the slimy ring out of his hand, I realize it looks familiar. "Was this Scotty's ring?"

Mike turns a shade of red. "I only bought it from him because you said you liked it so much. But we can get a different one if you want. I just didn't have a lot of time here, so..."

"I can't believe he didn't say anything." I recall his uncomfortable look when I asked about returning the ring, and understand it now. "That sly devil."

"We could get a different one," Mike offers.

"No," I say.

"No?"

"No, don't get a different one. I love it. Absolutely and completely love it." And I lean over and kiss him, right by his ear. The way that drives him crazy, good crazy. "And I love you, too, Mike."

He clears his throat. "So, is that a—"

"Yes," I answer. "It's a yes."

READING GROUP GUIDE

Dear Reader,

Have you ever asked yourself: Who am I?

Some people spend years trying to find themselves, through meditation, pilgrimages, or, like Zoe Goldman, therapy.

The question of self isn't a simple one for Zoe. As Sofia loves to remind her, Zoe Goldman isn't even her original name. Her "real" name is Tanya Vallano, which was changed (unbeknownst to her) after she was adopted. And Zoe can be different versions of herself, on and off medication. When she's off medication, her ADHD and anxiety throw her into self-doubt and disconnected thinking. But she also becomes a more keen observer of life, with an unfiltered view. Which one is the "real" Zoe?

As for her patient Andre, he has multiple selves as well. His diagnosis of schizophrenia literally means "split personality." Before his mother dies, he is a straight-A chess champion and comics-loving student. With his apparent psychosis, he turns into a delusional, violent prisoner who tries to kill his father and won't take off his red gloves. His father Abraham also looms large in the book. He may be a congenial, widowed accountant or the devil that Andre sees, full of dangerous lies.

In truth, none of us are who we seem to be. We all wear masks at times, to protect ourselves or to hide our lesser selves. The woman in the secret room feels like her true self only with her beloved Professor. But her true self may just be someone he has manipulated and molded.

Of all the characters, Sofia seems the most straightforward: an obvious psychopath. But as the story develops, even this isn't clear. She claims to be reformed now, to have found God. In fact, she is asking Zoe—her former nemesis—for forgiveness. Her brother Jack doubts her, but Zoe isn't so sure. After all, the psychiatric profession *exists* to help people change. Maybe she should trust Sofia now. Maybe a psychopath really can change.

Who is the real Zoe? Who is the real Andre? Who is the real Sofia?

Who is the real you?

Hopefully, after reading *The Secret Room*, you will have all the answers...

Happy reading, everyone!

SANDRA BLOCK

READER QUESTIONS

1. Did you guess the identity of the woman in the secret room? Did you feel sorry for her?
2. The woman in the secret room has an unhealthy obsession with her teacher, "the Professor." Have you ever felt that way about someone? Could you understand how she felt?
3. The concept of a room holds many meanings. There is the physical room, but also rooms within our psyches. Freud might say we have hidden rooms inside our minds that emerge in dreams or unconscious actions. Discuss.
4. Do you have a physical room that you love, where you feel most yourself?
5. Aubrey carries physical and emotional scars from her guilt and pain. Do you feel sorry for Aubrey? Do you understand her motivation?
6. Do you know anyone with ADHD or anxiety? Do Zoe's struggles seem realistic? Do you think reading fictional

accounts can help you understand someone's real-life struggles?

7. Do you think someone with Zoe's mental issues should be practicing psychiatry? Could it make her a more empathetic—and better—psychiatrist?

8. Andre fights delusions and hallucinations for most of the book. Did you guess that the source of his problems could be physical rather than mental?

9. Andre talks about "doubles," and there are multiple characters with dual identities. His father himself has a double. Can you describe some others?

10. Did you guess who was texting and tormenting Zoe throughout the book? Do you think this character had a valid reason for this?

11. Zoe feels guilty and incompetent when her patients keep dying. Have you ever felt this way during your work?

12. Zoe has a certain "lemon" that she keeps secret during the book. Should she have told Mike about it earlier?

13. Sofia claims she has changed, that she is trying to follow God and become a better person. Do you believe her? Should Zoe have forgiven her?

14. Zoe's brother Scotty has his share of troubles during the book, and in the end considers moving away from Buffalo. Did your siblings ever go through hard times while growing up? Were you able to help them?

Dr. Zoe Goldman is stumped when a young African American girl is found wandering the streets of Buffalo in a catatonic state. And Zoe must take matters into her own hands to track down Jane Doe's family and solve the mystery before it is too late. Because someone wants to make sure this young girl never remembers.

Please turn the page for an excerpt from
The Girl Without a Name.

Chapter One

We call her Jane, because she can't tell us her name.
Can't or won't, I'm not sure. She lies in a hospital
bed, a strangely old expression upon her teenaged face. We
don't know her age either. Twelve, fourteen maybe. A navy-
blue hospital blanket sits across her knees in a neat square
like a picnic blanket. A picnic in a hospital room, with a
stained white ceiling for a sky and faded blue tiles for grass.

Dr. Berringer lifts the patient's arm, and it stays up, like a
human puppet. "What do you think?" he asks.

"Catatonia," I answer. "Waxy catatonia."

"Bingo, Dr. Goldman," he says, his voice encouraging,
with just a hint of New Orleans, where he's from. His voice
doesn't match his face. He looks like a Kennedy, with sandy,
wind-blown hair as if he just walked off a sailboat and blue
eyes with lashes so long he could be wearing mascara. He is,
in a word, handsome. He is also, in a word, married, much
to the disappointment of the entire female staff at the Chil-

dren's Hospital of Buffalo. Let's just say the nurses perk up when Dr. Tad Berringer hits the floor.

Jane's arm drifts back down, her eyes still focused on the wall.

"But *why* is she catatonic?" I ask.

"That's the million-dollar question, isn't it?"

Jane Doe is our mystery. A police officer brought her to our doorstep this morning like a stork dropping off a baby. A few days ago, she was found wandering the streets of Buffalo, dazed and filthy, clothes torn, but apparently unharmed. No signs of bruising or rape. But she wouldn't speak. They coddled her, gave her hot chocolate (which grew cold in the mug), brought in a soft-speaking social worker, and Jane sat and stared. So the police canvassed the neighborhood, fingerprinted her, ran her image through Interpol, put up missing posters adorned with her unsmiling, staring face.

NAME: UNKNOWN. RACE: AFRICAN AMERICAN. DOB: UNKNOWN.

No one claimed her. They brought her to Children's and ran some tests. The ER said there was nothing wrong with her physically. So they sent her up to the psych floor. So we can figure out who she is and what's wrong with her.

"Schizophrenia maybe?" I ask.

"Could be." His eyes crinkle in thought. "But we also have to rule out other, less obvious causes." He leans over the bed and shines a penlight into her eyes. Her pupils contract, then bloom. "You ever hear of the hammer syndrome, Zoe?"

"No," I say, jotting this onto the back of my sheet.

"It goes like this: When all you have is a hammer, every-thing looks like a nail."

I stop writing, and he drops the penlight into his black doctor bag, smiling at me. "What can we establish here?" he asks, more a statement than a question. "Our patient has catatonia; that's all we know. So let's start with that. What's the differential for catatonia?"

"Schizophrenia."

"Okay, that's one."

"Right." I wait for the list to scramble into my head. That's the one good thing about ADHD. Alongside the scat-tered, ridiculous thoughts that pop up relentlessly (and which you have to keep banging down like a never-ending game of whack-a-mole) sprout elegant, detailed lists. Such as differ-ential diagnoses. Lately that hasn't been happening for me, though. I don't know if my Adderall is working too well or not well enough. My dopamine isn't cooperating in any case, which is inconvenient, seeing as I'm on probation. My brain grinds on in slow motion with no list anywhere in sight, so I plow through the old standby mnemonic for the differential diagnosis of any disease. Something medical students learn the first day they step on the wards: VITAMIN D. Vascu-lar, infectious, traumatic, autoimmune, metabolic, iatrogenic, neoplastic, degenerative.

"Status epilepticus," I say.

"Excellent thought. Did we order an EEG?"

"I will," I say, writing it in her chart.

"What else?"

A list crawls into my brain by inches. "Encephalitis?"

"Okay. Does she have a fever?"

I pull off the vital sheet hooked on the bed frame, scanning the blue, scribbled numbers from this morning. Vitals normal. "No fever, but it's still possible. Her labs are pending."

"Get neurology to see her. They can decide on a lumbar puncture. She'll probably need it, though, if the EEG is negative."

"They said she didn't need an LP in the ER."

He doesn't look impressed. "Just means the on-call didn't feel like it."

"We could get an MRI," I suggest.

"Fine. What are you looking for there?"

"Less common causes for catatonia...stroke, lupus, Hallervorden-Spatz," I say, cheered as the differential diagnosis list starts to soar in. "That could show up on MRI. PET scan, too."

"Let's start with an MRI," he says, tamping down my overenthusiasm. "Let Neurology decide on the PET." Jane blinks, grimaces, then stares again. I hand Dr. Berringer her chart, which he balances in his palm, adding a couple of lines under my note then signing it with a flourish. He hands it back to me. "Onward and upward?"

We exit the quiet oasis of Jane's room, emerging into the hallway awash with hospital noises: the overhead speaker calling out, food carts rattling by with the malodorous smell of breakfast that no one will eat, medical students scampering around the floor like lost bunnies. Dr. Berringer's phone rings, to the tune of "When the Saints Go Marching In," and he picks it up as we head down the hall.

"Hello?" There is squawking on the other end. "She just showed up today." He listens a minute while we walk. "I'm sorry. I don't know any more than y'all." This is met with more squawking on the other end. "Right. Listen, I'll tell you as soon as I know something. I promise." He hangs up with an eye roll, smiling at me. "Admissions wants her demographic info. Jane Doe, folks. That's all I got." He strides in front of me into the nurses' station. Dr. Berringer has a jogger's body, long and lean, verging on skinny. He is tall, taller than me even, and I'm over six feet. As he leans in the door frame, a nurse, roundish in her lavender scrubs, openly gapes at him. "Any other consults come in overnight?" he asks Jason, who is sitting at the little brown Formica table, poring through a chart.

Jason adjusts his bow tie. He must have a hundred bow ties with matching shirts. I've never seen him repeat a color. "Three," he says. "I have two, and Zoe's got the new girl."

"And one more I haven't seen yet," I add. "Just came in this morning."

"So let's round later. Around two?" Dr. Berringer asks.

"That's good for me," Jason answers. Jason is chief resident, so he's in charge of rounding. I was all but promised the job when Dr. A (the smartest in our threesome and also the one who saved my life) transferred into the neurovascular fellowship. But then I was put on probation, so that was the end of that. Jason calls me Probation Girl.

"All right. See y'all later," Dr. Berringer says with a wave. His teeth are white-bright, bleached maybe, in perfect rows like pieces of Chiclets gum. My brother Scotty accuses me of having a crush on Dr. Berringer, claiming that "every sentence you say has his name in it," but he's exaggerating. If anything, it's a minor crush. Minimal.

"You want to bed that guy so badly," Jason says as soon as he's out of earshot.

"Please. That is beyond ridiculous."

"Whatever you say," he mutters, leaning over to grab another chart from the rack.

I crack open Jane's chart and finish off the orders. Neurology consult. IV fluids because she's not eating. DVT precautions because she's not moving. "Anyway, you're one to talk."

He pauses to think. "Okay, empirically he's good-looking, I agree with you. But he's just so...white." He pronounces the word with some distaste. Jason, being Chinese American, can say this.

"What about Dominic? Last I looked, he was white, too." Dominic is a nurse at the hospital and Jason's on-again, off-again boyfriend. Mostly off-again.

"Yeah, but he's Italian. He could pass as Hispanic or something. He's not Mr. Ralph Lauren."

"Sure, well, as long as he could *pass* as something ethnic." I shove Jane's chart aside, leaning back in the stiff, metal chair. "So are you back to dating Dominic this week?"

"I don't know. That guy's so hot and cold," he complains. "I see him at the bars and he's all over me. Then we come to work and he flirts with girls. I'm, like, just pick a goddamn team and play for it."

"You should just dump his ass," I say.

"Yeah, probably. Hey, speaking of dumping, whatever

happened with that French dude? You ever hear any more from him?"

"Who, Jean Luc?"

"Yeah. That boy was smoking hot."

Jason is right on that one. Jean Luc *was* smoking hot. Hotter than I am, that's for sure. I've always been a solid six, maybe seven on a good hair day. Jean Luc was more like an eleven, or a twelve. Still is, I imagine. "Not in a while," I answer. "Still with Melanie," I mention, before he can ask. Melanie, the model-beautiful girlfriend he left me for.

"Oh well. All's well that ends well," Jason says, meaning Mike. And he's definitely right about that one.

Jason turns back to his progress note, and I stash Jane's chart back in the rack, ready to see my next patient. On the way down the hall, I pass by Jane's room and see Dr. Berringer standing by the bed, staring at her. He lays his hand on her head, tenderly. Like a father patting his child's head.

Or a priest bestowing a benediction.

Thank you to:

Rachel Ekstrom, my rock star agent, who provides both literary and moral support.

Alex Logan, who helps me see what's broken and how to fix it. (I put a cat in the next book for you. :)

The whole team at Grand Central Publishing for their unwavering support.

Natasha Cervantes, MD, who patiently and painstakingly spelled out the forensic psychiatry fellowship for me. Here's to you, PMG sister...

Daniel Antonius, PhD, who explained the entirety of forensic psychiatry, including all those acronyms, over lunch at Spot Coffee (not the Coffee Spot).

Let it be known: All errors are officially mine, not theirs!

Dennis Delano, detective extraordinaire, who let me spend the day in jail without arresting me. In all sincerity, you are a man of integrity and courage, a credit to your profession and our city, and I am proud to call you a friend.

Thank you to:

Superintendent Thomas Diina, for providing an in-depth, no-holds-barred tour of Erie County Holding Center.

My lovelies at Tall Poppies, who provide virtual hugs and laughter daily.

My PMG sisters: *Aliquot* made it into the final draft!

Jordie and Lexi (and oh yeah, their parents), who try to sell "Aunt Sandra's books" to their teachers, even though they shouldn't even be reading them.

Margaret Long, who is always there to help us out, and who cheerleads my books at the library at Canterbury and beyond.

Mom and Dad, who love and support me no matter what.

Patrick, my forever love and truest partner. I couldn't do it without you.

And finally, Charlotte and Owen, my sun, moon, and stars.